KU-526-891

Harry
and the
Wrinklies

Harry
and the
Wrinklies

Alan
Temperley

SCHOLASTIC
PRESS

Scholastic Children's Books,
Commonwealth House, 1–19 New Oxford Street,
London WC1A 1NU, UK
a division of Scholastic Ltd
London ~ New York ~ Toronto ~ Sydney ~ Auckland
Mexico City ~ New Delhi ~ Hong Kong

First published by Scholastic Ltd, 1997
This edition published by Scholastic Ltd, 1998
Copyright © Alan Temperley, 1997

ISBN 0 590 11349 6

All rights reserved

Typeset by TW Typesetting, Midsomer Norton, Avon
Printed by Cox & Wyman Ltd, Reading, Berks

10 9 8 7 6

The right of Alan Temperley to be identified as the author of this work has
been asserted by him in accordance with the Copyright, Designs and Patents
Act, 1988.

This book is sold subject to the condition that it shall not, by way of trade or
otherwise be lent, resold, hired out, or otherwise circulated without the
publisher's prior consent in any form of binding or cover other than that in
which it is published and without a similar condition, including this
condition, being imposed upon the subsequent purchaser.

Contents

1
Gestapo Lil

The summer holiday, which is the best time of year for most children, was the worst for Harry Barton. Or maybe the second worst: Christmas was *really* gruesome.

The problem was his parents. And Gestapo Lil.

For the Bartons were rich. So rich that instead of staying at home like most parents, working and looking after their son, the Honourable Augustus and Lady Barton spent their lives travelling. They much preferred voyaging on ocean liners and staying in smart hotels, to living in London.

Harry did not go with them, he cramped their style. So while they sunbathed on yachts in Jamaica, skied at Klosters and travelled to far Shanghai, he remained at home in their big house in Hampstead, which is a very expensive part of London. Every so often, to ease their consciences, they sent him a postcard or an extravagant present. Sometimes Harry received two in a week, other times he did not hear for months.

Twice a year or so his parents turned up in London. Then they hugged him and spoiled him and took him to theatres and fashionable restaurants. For two weeks the house was full of parties and friends and laughter. Then, with kisses and expressions of love, they were off once more and the big house fell empty and silent.

To look after Harry his parents had engaged a nurse, companion and housekeeper named Lavinia McScrew. She had come with the most excellent references – which was not surprising since she had written them herself. She spoke well and was immaculate in her appearance, both facts which recommended her to her employers. Her hair was golden and coiled in braids at the back of her head, her make-up was perfect, her clothes were elegant, her nails were long and enamelled, her jewellery came from the best shops. She expected a high salary, which Harry's parents paid.

What they never asked was how Miss McScrew, a house-keeper, could afford such clothes and jewellery – which year by year grew more beautiful and costly. They did not know that money which was to be spent on Harry went straight into her pocket. They did not know that valuable ornaments and nick-nacks from cupboards found their way into auctioneers and salerooms up and down the country.

Nor did they know, for Harry was too terrified to tell them, that she was a bully who ruled him with a rod of iron and kept a gold-mounted riding-crop called *Stinger* locked in her room.

At the age of eight, to his delight, Harry was packed off to boarding school. He was happy there. He made friends, he played games, the work was not hard, he enjoyed the rough and tumble. The first day of every term was the happiest day of his life. Why other boys cried he could not imagine.

Yet always, always, looming on the horizon like fog or a desolate island, were the dreaded holidays and the return to Hampstead. Often he dreamed about it in the dormitory and was woken by a friend or the kindly matron.

"Are you all right?" they would ask him. "You were crying and shouting out."

"Yes, it's OK." He managed a smile. "I was having a night-mare."

Lavinia McScrew had looked after Harry for as long as he could remember.

He called her Gestapo Lil.

Anyway, late one morning at the start of the summer holiday Harry was summoned from his room by a noisy bell.

To save herself the trouble of climbing the stairs when he was wanted, or even going into the hall and shouting, Gestapo Lil had adopted an ancient system. One of those boxes with tiny windows and discs and jangly bells which used to hang in the servants' pantry had been moved to Harry's bedroom. Whenever she wanted him she just pressed a button. To Harry's parents the idea was presented as a game. Hanging an affectionate arm round his shoulders, Gestapo Lil laughed as she described it. Harry did not argue because she had five million ways of paying him back. But the minute his parents had gone, a code was pinned to the wall beneath the bells. Long rings and short rings:

wash up

set and light the fire

scrub the floor

dust and polish

hang out the washing

fetch in coal

lay the table

hoover the stairs

make tea for Miss McScrew

clean the windows

and several more. This way she did not even need to speak to him. But she was always round afterwards, running her handkerchief along a ledge, examining the silver, hunting the hearth for traces of coal-dust.

Tring-tring-trrringgg!

Harry sighed. He did not need to consult the code, it meant *Come Immediately*. Rising from his computer, he performed a ritual of rude signs towards the bell, then checked his appearance in the mirror. Although he longed to dress like other boys in jeans and T-shirt, Gestapo Lil insisted on a white shirt, tie and grey school trousers. Briskly he tidied himself up, ran a comb through his cropped fair hair and started down the stairs.

A stranger sat in the sun-lounge. His hair was greying and he wore a striped suit. An open briefcase stood by his feet. Harry thought he looked like a lawyer.

Gestapo Lil stood by the window, perfectly groomed as always. She wore knee-length boots and a beautiful dress of green silk. From her belt hung a large bunch of keys and a silver knuckle-duster. Between her fingers was a black cigarette in a long jade holder. In each ear was a single emerald. About her throat hung a necklace of shark's teeth set in gold.

"This is Mr Rook, the solicitor." She smiled. "He has some news for you."

Harry switched his attention.

"Ah-hum. Er … yes." The man set down his sherry glass. "You are – er – " he shuffled some papers, "Eugene Augustus Montgomery Harold Barton?"

Harry glowered with embarrassment. "Yes."

"Well, the fact is, er, young man, I've, er … got some … er … I've got some rather … how shall I put it to a boy … er … to a boy … your age? You see…"

"Your parents are dead!" Gestapo Lil said plainly. "Both at once. Your father and your mother. Dead as doorknobs. And he's come to tell you."

"Er … yes. I suppose that's the … er … the gist of it." Mr Rook took a fortifying sip of sherry. "The precise circumstances aren't … er … aren't fully available to us yet. But as far as we know at present … er…"

Harry never heard what they knew at present. His parents were dead!

It was an odd feeling. He should have felt a terrible sense of loss, he realized that, but he didn't. He hardly knew them, when it came down to it. They were strangers, people who had simply popped into his life, hugged him like a puppy, given him presents, and then popped off again.

What had happened to them, details of the accident, Harry did not discover for many years.

Of more immediate importance, *what*, he wondered as he stood looking out at the sunlit garden, was to become of *him*?

"One suitcase, that's all," said Gestapo Lil. "You heard the solicitor, it's all got to be sold. And that means your toys and clothes as well as the house and furniture."

It was a week later. She stood by the window in Harry's bedroom. This day she wore a white leather suit and smoked her black cigarette from a long ivory holder. *Stinger* was tucked beneath her arm.

"No, you can't take your skates – nor your computer. Have some sense, how could you put a computer in your suitcase. No, nor your football signed by that team of yours, somebody'll pay money for that. Let go of it! Let go! By heaven, boy, you're asking for a smacking. Come back here! Do you want me to… That's more like it. Put it down there with the rest."

Harry flung down his treasured football and glared at her.

"And you can take that look off your face. Don't blame me. It's not my fault you had two spendthrift, improvident parents who wasted a fortune on high living. I'm the one should be crying. Ten years of my life I've wasted on you and what have I got to show for it? Nothing! Your father promised me I'd be taken care of. 'Leave it to me, Lavinia,' he says. 'We know the boy is safe with you. We know he's in good hands. I'll see you're properly rewarded.' And what happens – he ups and dies bankrupt. Bankrupt! Him and your mother both. Dead as coffin nails, dead as hedgehogs, and not a button between them. Nothing but debts. And don't tell me the pittance he paid me was reward enough for all I did for you. The cooking and cleaning and washing and nursing! Now I look back on it I must have been mad. To give up a good career for that."

Harry stared white-faced as the torrent of words washed over him.

"And how often were they here? How often did they come back to see their darling boy? Twice a year. That's how much they cared for you. That's all the break I got. Twice a year while they filled the house with parties and dirty dishes and champagne all over the carpets. Swish friends from Scotland and Newmarket, the smart set from Chelsea. Then off again and I'm left to clean up the mess. No, I am not exaggerating, sir, not one bit. It wasn't you had to put the house to rights after they'd gone. Like a midden it was."

It was too much to bear. Harry ran at her, slapping and punching.

"Ow, Master Spitfire! Fly at me, would you! We'll soon put a stop to that little display of temper." She snatched *Stinger* from beneath her arm. Stronger than Harry and fifteen centimetres taller, she grasped him by the arm. The leather riding-crop smacked against his leg and the seat of his trousers. "There! How do you like a taste of your own medicine. It'll be the day when you get the better of me, little savage!"

Furious, his bottom stinging, Harry retreated to the side of the bed. Gestapo Lil hooked the gold-knobbed riding-crop on her belt beside the knuckle-duster and big bunch of keys.

"Yes, I've done my duty, but no more, never again. Once I've packed you off to those ancient aunts at – what do you call the place, Lagg Hall – that's it. I've left a suitcase on the landing, you can do your own packing."

Harry looked through the door.

"No, not one of the new ones. That battered old thing's good enough for a penniless orphan brat like you. And no putting your best clothes and toys in the bottom, I'll be checking before you leave. And your pockets. You're in my charge until you get on that train. Then let your decrepit relatives in the country look after you. I just hope you show them more appreciation than you've ever shown me."

She adjusted the zip on a white crocodile boot.

"But don't think this is the last you'll hear of Lavinia McScrew. Oh no! Those precious great-aunts of yours. I reckon they've got money. Lagg Hall – sounds like a big place. I want what's rightfully mine and when the time's right I'm coming to get it, you can count on that."

She inserted a fresh cigarette into the ivory holder and struck a heavy gold lighter. Harry recognized it as one of his mother's.

"And see how you like having nothing, not a penny of your own, dependent for everything on the generosity of other people: the bed you sleep in, every shoelace, every bite of toast. And you'd better watch your ps and qs, because those antique aunts are all you've got. If it wasn't for them you'd be in a home."

Harry stared at her.

She blew a cloud of smoke and walked to the door. "Now start packing."

2
Two Aunts and a Mercedes

"That's not them, is it?" Harry pleaded with himself. "It can't be! *Please* let it not be them!"

It was a country railway station with flowerbeds and a long platform. Harry stood at one end where he had dismounted, a fair boy in a worn anorak, trousers several sizes too small for him, a shabby suitcase by his side – all he possessed in the world.

Carriage doors slammed. The guard waved his flag. Slowly gathering speed, the train slid past him and was gone.

Harry watched as the passengers who had left the train made their way to the entrance. Soon the platform was empty, empty except for two elderly and very odd-looking women who stood at the far end.

One was tall and thin, and from the angle Harry saw her much resembled the front view of a camel – though when she put on a large straw hat she at once turned into a standard lamp. The other, shorter and plumper, reminded him of a cheerful piece of confectionery, a pink meringue topped by a swirl of butter icing.

Harry looked all round, hopefully, but there was no one else. Then his fears were confirmed. The meringue waved a little handkerchief and began a wobbling run up the platform.

"I don't believe it," Harry whispered to himself. "This is not happening to me." Briefly he contemplated flight.

The fluttering old lady drew closer, all the time crying "Oh! Oh!" and pressing the handkerchief to her face. Though she could not have been less than sixty or seventy years old, her hair was dyed a vivid butter yellow and bounced in curls about her face. She had large baby-blue eyes, badly made-up, and a slash of vermilion lipstick for a mouth. Her nails and toenails were varnished to match. "Coo-eee!" A little pink hat fell over one ear as she ran. A profusion of floating, filmy garments billowed about her like a cloud in disarray.

"Harry!" she gasped as she came close, catching him by the hands and holding him at arms' length. "Harry Barton! Oh, my darling! I'm your great-aunt Florrie!" And right there on the platform she planted a big lipsticky kiss on his cheek, and enveloped him in a cloud of expensive perfume.

Harry was still reeling from the shock-horror of this welcome as his second aunt arrived beside them.

In every way she seemed a contrast to her sister. Not only was she taller and thin as a toasting-fork, her iron-grey hair was cropped short and round granny-glasses sat on the bridge of a nose that was hooked like the beak of an eagle. Behind those bright spectacles the eyes were blue and sharp and clever. The long brown face, devoid of make-up, was clever also. So was the thin, humorous mouth. She wore a grey, figure-fitting costume with a rather long skirt, and a white blouse with a cameo of a very startling gentleman at the throat.

Firmly she shook Harry by the hand. "And I'm your great-aunt Bridget." Her voice did nothing to dispel Harry's impression of a Victorian governess or strict headmistress. "I suggest you call me Aunt, or Aunt Bridget. None of this great-aunt nonsense, makes me sound as old as Methuselah – which contrary to all appearances and however it may seem to you, I am *not*."

"And you'll call me Auntie Florrie, dear, won't you? Mmm-mmm!" She hugged him afresh, like a pink koala bear, and smeared his other cheek with lipstick.

"Leave the boy alone, Florrie, for goodness' sake." Aunt Bridget expressed herself with vigour. "A couple of prehistoric old wrinklies like us – it's a wonder he hasn't run a mile. The very sight of us must give him the heebie-jeebies without you mothering and smothering him every second."

In some embarrassment Harry looked away but Auntie Florrie laughed merrily. As he looked back, his eyes were caught by the cameo at Aunt Bridget's neck.

She glanced down. "Ah! Do you know who that is?"

It was the portrait of a ruffian with a ferocious and blood-thirsty expression. He had a heavy beard, one cheek was slashed, and about his brow was a tangle of scarves topped by a ragged hat.

Harry shook his head.

"That, dear nephew, is Captain Henry Morgan the buccaneer. Isn't he splendid!" She touched it with a long brown hand. "A notorious pirate chief who roamed the Spanish Main. A freebooting and I have to say thoroughly wicked man. One of my particular heroes. I'll tell you all about him some day." She looked down at Harry's suitcase. "But not right now. Is that all your luggage?"

"Yes."

"You can manage it yourself, can't you. Don't expect a dry old stick like me or a silly pink blancmange like her to carry it for you, do you?"

"Ooh, Bridget, don't say such things. You're as strong as a horse, you know you are." Auntie Florrie took the battered suitcase from Harry's protesting grasp. "No, no, duck, give it to me."

Carrying the suitcase as if it were filled with feathers, Auntie

Florrie set off after the swinging figure of her sister.

Clearly, Harry thought, there was more to these eccentric old aunts than met the eye. Vigorously he scrubbed the lipstick from his cheeks with a handkerchief and ran to catch up.

It was nearly midday. As they left the station and crossed the car park, bonnets shimmered in the heat. Leaves hung limply. Above the walls of the small town the hills were green and dotted with cattle.

Long before they approached it, Harry knew which would be his aunts' car. His heart sank. It was ancient. A Mercedes – dull bluey-green in colour, sun-faded and dusty. The bodywork was scratched and there was a bash in one wing. It was, he calculated from the number-plate, seventeen years old.

Auntie Florrie threw his suitcase into the boot and settled herself in the driving seat.

"You sit beside me, dear." She patted the worn leather upholstery. "Bridget will ride in the back."

As she turned the key the engine wheezed and choked, coughed and shook and clanked, and finally settled to an irregular rattle.

They left the car park and soon were on the edge of town.

"Let's take him by the aerodrome," said Aunt Bridget suddenly.

"What a good idea." Auntie Florrie smiled across. "Would you like that?"

"Yes." Harry nodded. "What kind of aircraft use it? Is it very big?"

"Oh, there aren't any *aircraft*, dear," said Auntie Florrie.

"That's not the idea at all," said Aunt Bridget.

"But what's the use of an aerodrome with no planes?" Harry was puzzled.

"You'll see." The two old ladies laughed conspiratorially.

They rattled along leafy lanes, by fields and woods and rivers.

Suddenly, around a blind corner, a giant car came hurtling towards them. It was a dazzling Rolls-Royce, yellow as butter-cups, and doing at least sixty miles an hour. The horn blared, gravel spat from the wheels. Harry had a split-second glimpse of a thick-set man in tweeds, with ginger hair, ginger moustache and a red face. A fat cigar was clamped between his teeth. Angrily he shook a fist at them.

Auntie Florrie swerved across the verge, missing the other car by inches. Harry's head hit the roof as the old Mercedes leaped like a bucking bronco across the grass.

The Rolls-Royce roared on up the middle of the road. *Tootle-tootle-tootle-tootle-tee!* The horn blasted mockingly into the distance.

The Mercedes bounced off a boulder, demolished a clump of yellow gorse, and came to a halt in the hedge. Hawthorn branches pressed against the windows.

Harry's heart thudded with shock.

"That man!" Auntie Florrie tidied her curls and took out a little mirror to check her make-up. "That's the other wing bashed in now. One day he'll go too far!"

"He already has, many times." Heedless of their near miss, Aunt Bridget was hunting in a box of chocolates. She popped a violet cream into her mouth and passed the box forward. "Maybe we'll have to do something about *dear* Colonel Priestly sooner than planned." She pursed her lips. "We simply cannot have him living round here, spying on us, behaving as if he owns the place. And driving like that – one day there's going to be an accident! Lucky you were at the wheel today, anyone else would have hit him."

"We'll have a meeting," Auntie Florrie said.

"Yes, but not for a week or two. We've got other things on our plate before that." Aunt Bridget nodded towards Harry. *"Pas devant le garçon.* We'll talk about it later."

With a screechy scrape the old Mercedes backed out of the thorny branches and returned to the road. But something was wrong: the car bumped awkwardly, the driving wheel twisted in Auntie Florrie's plump hands.

"Oh, drat!" she cried. "Now we've got a puncture. Bother the man!"

They got out. The tyre which had been in the hedge was studded with thorns like a porcupine.

"Ah well! Soon fix that." Auntie Florrie bustled to the boot and pulled out the spare wheel.

"Can I help?" Harry said.

"No, leave her to it. This is Florrie's sort of thing."

In a minute the car was jacked high and the wheel was being changed.

"Who's Colonel Priestly?" asked Harry.

Auntie Florrie looked up. "If we had two or three days, dear, and I wasn't a lady, I could tell you *what* he is." She spun the wheel spanner briskly.

"Colonel Priestly," said Aunt Bridget, hunting the hedgerow for wild raspberries, "Colonel Percival Bonaparte Priestly, DSO, to give him his full name – if he *is* a colonel or a DSO, which I doubt – is the new owner of Felon Grange, a big estate quite close to us at Lagg Hall. Some people, as you'll discover, call him Beastly Priestly, Percy Pig, Bony the Stony, and various less polite names. By profession he's a high-court judge. Also a magistrate and chairman of several local committees. Quite a big cheese. But as you saw, he is not a nice man – *not* a nice man at all!"

She tipped a dozen raspberries into Harry's palm.

"He's power-crazy," she continued. "Sees himself as lord of the manor. Shooting parties, cocktails, banquets! Fills the house with important people: politicians, millionaires, famous actors, that sort of thing. Gets into the gossip columns." She turned sharp eyes on Harry. "Ah, you ask, but where does a mere judge get the money to buy a place like Felon Grange? How can he afford that sort of lifestyle? To which I reply: precisely, where *does* he get the money?"

She returned to her raspberry picking.

"He's so rude," said Auntie Florrie, "that's what I can't stand. And such a bully!"

"Exactly," said Aunt Bridget. "Like a cross between ... between a cow's bottom and a mad Rottweiler."

"A shark and a mouldy tomato pizza."

They both collapsed.

"Oh, very good, Florrie. That's exactly what he looks like."

Harry had never heard grown-ups talk like this. "Why's he spying on you?" he asked.

"Ah, the million-dollar question." Aunt Bridget dribbled a handful of raspberries into her mouth. "Why indeed? There's a mystery for you to unravel."

"Harry, be a dear," said Auntie Florrie. "While I tighten the nuts, pull out those thorns in the back tyre. I don't think any are too deep."

By the time he had finished she was lowering the Mercedes on the jack, and a minute later they were on their way.

"You're a jolly good driver," Harry said. "And wheel-changer."

The big baby-blue eyes smiled. Affectionately she patted his arm and did not answer.

A mile further on, the rattling car turned from the road on to an overgrown track. Swishing grass and thistles grew radiator-high. Beyond the bumper all was hidden. It was like driving through a car-wash of twigs.

At length they emerged into a vast open space. Ruined

hangars and control towers rose against the blue sky. Long grass and bushes grew between the runways – dazzling concrete strips that vanished towards the horizon.

"Built during World War II." Aunt Bridget peered over her granny glasses. "Hasn't been a plane here for twenty years."

"Can we get out and explore?" Harry reached for the door handle.

"No time for that today," said Auntie Florrie. "Got to get you to Lagg Hall in time for lunch."

"But," Harry paused politely, "what did we come for? It's very interesting but – "

"You'll see."

"Seat belt fastened safely?"

"Yes."

"Then off we go." Auntie Florrie stopped the engine and looked under the dashboard. Click – click – click! She snapped three switches then sat back and arranged the floating sleeves of her dress. "Now, all ready?" She turned the key.

With a smooth, powerful roar the engine throbbed into life. She touched the accelerator. *Vroom! Vrooooom!* This was a different motor-car.

Harry sat up, electrified.

"Hold on to your hats then, girls – and boys!" cried Auntie Florrie gaily. "Away we go!" She thrust the car into gear and let out the clutch.

Harry felt himself forced back into the upholstery as the Mercedes surged forward, gathering speed along the disused taxiway that circled the airfield. Forty – fifty – sixty. Still the car was accelerating. Auntie Florrie moved expertly through the gears. Seventy – eighty. The shrubs and yellowing grasses flashed past.

"This is great!" Harry's eyes sparkled.

Ninety – ninety-five – ninety-eight.

Like a doll with her blue eyes and ringlets, Auntie Florrie glanced sideways and smiled. "Are you ready, dear?"

"Yes!" Harry cried.

"Good boy. Then up and over! Here we go!"

Again Harry felt the leather press against his back as the car accelerated. The ton was gone in an instant. A hundred and ten – a hundred and twenty – a hundred and thirty...

The dazzling concrete was a blur. A long way ahead a hare lolloped to the edge of the track. In an instant it was behind them.

Harry began to feel frightened. If they skidded...

Auntie Florrie wound down a window. Air blasted through the car.

"Oh, that's better!" cried Aunt Bridget, not in the least like a schoolmistress. "Lovely! Blow the cobwebs away!"

Auntie Florrie's scarves flew around the car, her yellow curls tossed wildly. For a minute she held the car steady at one hundred and forty miles an hour, briefly took it up to one hundred and fifty – "Just for the fun of it, dear," – then eased her toes on the accelerator.

"I enjoyed that, Florrie," said Aunt Bridget as the car slowed to a more sedate ninety.

"Well, it's hot today," said her sister. "Nutty just fitted a new turbo and did a re-bore. Don't want to push her too hard until the pistons have bedded in." She changed down to fourth. "A lot of work he's done the last couple of weeks: new high-lift camshaft and valve springs, Weber twin-barrel carb. Should give us an extra twelve or fifteen miles an hour. Hope so, anyway."

Comfortably they completed a third circuit of the airfield and drew to a halt by the gaping hangars.

"There, dear, did you enjoy that?" said Auntie Florrie.

"It was fantastic!" said Harry. "But I don't understand.

When we left the station it sounded like a heap of old junk. Now it's like a Ferrari. What did you do to the engine?"

"Not engine, dear, engines. It's got two engines."

"What for?" Harry was puzzled.

"Well – sometimes we like to go fast."

"Florrie!" said her sister in a warning voice.

Harry ignored her. "Yes, but why two engines?"

"Well, for fun, dear." Auntie Florrie reached beneath the dashboard. Click – click – click! "Them as asks no questions…"

Reluctantly the old engine popped and clanked and rattled into life.

"Come on," said Aunt Bridget. "One more chocolate, then back to Lagg Hall."

"Just in time for a nice sherry." Auntie Florrie smiled brightly. "Or do you prefer a gin and tonic?"

"I don't drink sherry *or* gin," Harry said politely.

"Don't you, dear? Well, how about a vodka and orange with lots of ice? What is your tipple? You must try one of my Bosun Blinders, they're delicious."

"I don't drink at all," said Harry.

"Of course you don't," Aunt Bridget cried. "Don't be a fool, Florrie. He'll get a glass of Goody's home-made squash with lots of fruit in it. That do you, Harry? Then lunch."

Harry turned in his seat. "Yes, please."

Happily he crunched a hazelnut cluster. Already he had had more excitement and fun than in eleven years at Hampstead.

3
The Tower

L agg Hall was a stately building of yellow sandstone with a red roof and an ancient square tower at one corner. Near the top of this tower, thirty feet from the ground, Harry was given his room.

"I hope you'll like it up here," said Mrs Good, the house-keeper. "It's nice and dry and there's a wonderful view. A real boy's room, we thought. I'm sure you won't mind the stairs with your young legs."

"No, it's fabulous!" said Harry.

"I'm afraid you'll be alone up here; with these thick walls there's no door through to the house – not yet, anyway. But it was either that or a room at the back and this is much nicer. And there is the intercom, of course. You're sure you won't be frightened?"

"No, I'm too old for that," Harry lied. "And I'm used to being alone. Anyway, I've got Tangle."

He buried his face in the shaggy coat of a mongrel that had attached itself to him the moment he stepped out of the Mercedes. At once Aunt Bridget had said that Tangle could be *his* dog.

"If there are any robbers or anything, Tangle will see them off, won't you, boy."

Mrs Good smiled. "Yes, I'm sure he will," she said.

"I've never had a dog before," said Harry.

As if to show him what a good thing dogs were, Tangle jumped up, eyes like diamonds behind a black and tan fringe, and licked his mouth and eyes with a wet tongue.

"Get off! Groo! Stop it!" Harry wrestled him to the floor.

"If you continue up the staircase," said Mrs Good, "there's a trapdoor so you can get out on the roof. Like a church tower, only not so high, of course. But you've got to promise me you'll take care up there, no silly games."

"Cross my heart and hope to die!" Harry spat on a finger and drew a big cross where he imagined his heart to be.

"I'm serious!" Mrs Good insisted. "No nonsense, no daring. You could hurt yourself."

Harry pushed Tangle away. "All right, I promise."

The housekeeper smiled. "Everyone's been looking forward so much to you coming. It'll be nice to have some young blood around the place."

"But not all squashed up and yukky at the bottom of the tower," said Harry.

"Exactly." She laughed. "Anyway, lunch in twenty minutes. Your aunties have had to go into town again, we'll have it in the kitchen. Come down when you're ready."

Her footsteps faded down the spiral stairs.

Sounds of summer came from the open window. Harry looked round the large chamber. He loved it. His room, *his* room, and no Gestapo Lil. Crooked beams crossed the ceiling. Big posters of Goofy, Aslan, the league champions, and a boy on a motorbike decorated the white uneven walls. For furniture there was a giant wardrobe, a huge chest of drawers, a set of shelves for books and souvenirs, and at one window an old table and chair. Beneath the other window stood a comfortable-looking bed with a Disney duvet. Tangle had settled himself on the foot and lay cleaning his paw with a red tongue.

Harry flung himself alongside and leaned across the broad window-sill. Swallows swooped for flies in the sunshine. He loosened the ancient catch and pushed the window wide. Below him lay the lawns and flowerbeds of Lagg Hall, and to one side the red roof and chimneys of the house. Beyond the lawns lay many acres of woods, a rolling sea of green. A marble folly stood buried among the trees. A white horse grazed in a paddock. Further off Harry saw a tempting flash of water, the end of a reedy lake with a small jetty and a rowing boat pulled up alongside.

"Great!" He jumped down and threw open the lid of his suitcase, rummaging among the old clothes which were all he had been allowed to bring.

Disturbed by the activity, Tangle too sprang down and scratched vigorously on the rug, then stood expectantly, waiting to see what would happen next.

It did not take Harry long to throw aside his grey trousers and pull on a faded red T-shirt, battered jeans given to him by a friend at school – on the small side now with a faulty zip and torn back pocket – and trainers through which his big toes winked at every step. Briskly he ran a comb through his cropped hair. Then, feeling every inch king of the castle and monarch of all he surveyed, he called Tangle and ran from the room.

In the middle of the afternoon Harry sat in a long stone shed with Nutty Slack, gardener and handyman at Lagg Hall. The air was sweet with resin from a stack of newly-split logs. Through the sunlit door he could see a kitchen garden and greenhouses strung with tomatoes.

Nutty was very tall and thin and wore blue overalls. His head was bald, his shoulders stooped, and he had a long humorous face. The shed was his workshop. As they talked he sat on an upturned box and sharpened a scythe with smooth strokes of a whetstone.

"Aye, I'm amazed they never told ye aboot the ghost." He had a broad Geordie accent. "Famous hereaboots. Ol' Goggly, they call it. Don't mention it outside the grounds, mind, but I thought yer aunties would've warned ye."

"What's it like?" Harry enjoyed a ghost story.

"I'm not sure I should tell ye. It's a terrible sight, they say. A big beast, a sort o' cross atween a dog the size o' that door, a dragon, an' a shaggy man. Seems to shift a bit in shape, like. Different people see different things. But they aal agree on one thing, it's got long claws an' teeth, an' big glarin' eyes. An' it scares ye witless."

"That's four things." Harry hugged his knees and gave a shiver. "Where does he walk, Ol' Goggly? Have you seen him?"

"That's the funny thing. Ye'd think it would haunt the tower, up where your room is, that's the oldest part o' the house. But it never does. For some reason that's the safest place of aal – that's partly why they put ye there. Usually folk see it just outside, in them bushes – black at night, mind – an' crossin' the gravel to peer in the windows o' the house, an' mebbe catch somebody wi' them long claws."

"*Have* you ever seen it, Mr Slack?"

"Mr Slack – who's he when he's at home? I'm Nutty to me friends – an' I reckon you an' me's goin' to be friends. Call us Nutty, hinny."

He laid aside the whetstone and took out a battered tobacco tin. With gnarled fingers he smoothed out a cigarette paper and shredded golden tobacco into it.

"Hev I seen it? Well no, not mesel', I hev to admit. But that's cos I've stayed well out the road around the time it walks. Aye." He put the crumpled cigarette to his lips and flicked an ancient lighter. Wreaths of blue smoke clouded his head. "But I've spoken to them as says they've seen it, an' I'm tellin' you – I count mesel' lucky."

Harry scratched Tangle's back. "If I look out of my window tonight, do you think I'll see it?"

"Nah, nah. Ye canna see it just like that. Mebbe ye'll never see it. Or mebbe ye don't believe it exists. Then one night, just when yer least expectin' it – bang! There y' are! There it is! Big glarin' eyes an' claws outstretched! Enough to make yer blood freeze!"

"So if you were me," said Harry, "you wouldn't go wandering around at night."

"Right in one." Nutty shot a glance from beneath shaggy brows. "Not unless ye fancy comin' face to face wi' Ol' Goggly! I wouldn't chance it mesel'."

"Mrs Good said nothing about it," Harry said.

"No? Well, she wouldn't. Doesn't hold wi' ghosts an' such-like. Wouldn't want to frighten ye, not yer first night in the tower."

Harry remembered the lunch he'd just eaten. "She's a good cook, isn't she."

"She is that." Nutty nodded. "A real top-notcher."

"Why, do you like her?" Harry grinned.

"How d'ye mean?" Nutty's face turned pink.

"Just the way you said it."

"Aye, well. Mebbes I do an' mebbes I don't." He rubbed his nose with a big hand. "None o' your business, anyroad."

"I'm sorry, I didn't mean to be nosy." Harry hesitated. "But she said she likes you too."

"Did she?"

"She said to me: You go round and see Mr Slack, you'll not find a kinder, cleverer man ten miles round."

"Did she?" Nutty's ears glowed scarlet. He rummaged in a sack at his feet to cover his confusion.

Harry was not accustomed to shy grown-ups. It seemed best to change the conversation. "Have you been here long, Nutty?"

Still Nutty rummaged. "Aye. Must be close on seven year now. I used to work in the pits, up Newcastle way." His face appeared, pink to the top of his bald head. Vigorously he blew his nose. "Then yer Auntie Florrie took us on to look after her cars, gee them up a bit. I've always been a bit of a dab hand wi' the engines."

"Do you look after the old Merc?" Harry said eagerly.

"Aye. I believe they took ye for a bit of a spin round the aerodrome this mornin'."

"It was great!" Harry leaned forward. "Can you tell me about the two engines?"

"I should be able to. I designed them an' fitted them mesel'. But I wouldn't go talkin' aboot it roun' the countryside. Some folk might not understand. Let's keep it our little secret, shall we?"

Harry longed to ask why. "Will you show me?" he said.

"Certainly, if yer interested. Come round this evenin' after yer dinner. I'll be in the garage." Nutty smiled. "Not too late, mind. Remember Ol' Goggly." He pulled an ancient watch from his overalls. "Time I was on me way. Mrs Good told us to come for me three'ses in a few minutes."

As they left the shed the sun struck hot through Harry's T-shirt. He screwed up his eyes against the glare.

Nutty hitched the scythe comfortable on his shoulder. "Got half an acre o' grass to cut for Chalky an' Socrates. Ye'll meet them later." He nodded across the forecourt and lawns. "If ye head on over there, through the trees a bit, ye'll come to the lake. Ye can swim, I take it."

Harry nodded.

"How well?"

"I've got medals."

"Medals, no less! Aye, well, take care. Don't want ye drownded yer first day. I've fixed the rotten planks on the jetty for ye. Rigged up a bit of a ladder. It'll make a nice divin' platform."

Nipping the stub of his cigarette, he strolled off past the greenhouses.

Harry and Tangle set off in the other direction, heading for the lake in the woods.

4
Into the Woods

It was a wonderful wood, Sherwood Forest run wild. After a hundred metres Harry could no longer see the house. In two hundred he was lost. Clutching a stick he picked his way through the undergrowth. Thorns tugged at his jeans and seeds lodged everywhere; birds flitted from stem to branch; sunlight streamed through the canopy of leaves. Harry loved it.

For Tangle the wood was heaven.

After a while they reached a clearing. Harry clambered on to the trunk of a great tree blown down in the gales of winter. Eight feet from the ground he sat astride, as if it were a giant horse, and gazed across a sea of bracken.

A thicket of yew trees, darker than the rest of the sunlit greenery, reminded him of the ghost. Was it here, he wondered, here in the tangled wood that Ol' Goggly went to ground during the hours of daylight? And at night did he go floating through the trees, shuffling across the lawns to terrorize the inhabitants of Lagg Hall? Harry did not believe a *word* of it.

Lying back on the trunk, he clasped his hands behind his head and gazed at the branches all around. The sun dazzled and he closed his eyes.

"A goggly would a-wooing go..."

He began to sing in a harsh, unbroken voice:

"Hey-ho says woggly,
A goggly would a-wooing go
Whether his wiggle would let him or no
With a boggly-woggly-wiggely-wicket
Hey-ho says goggly-woggly."

Harry sat up again. The bark he was sitting on was rough. Patches were loose. He picked at a flake between his knees and pulled it back with grubby fingers. A slab half the length of his arm levered up – and suddenly broke off. A colony of ants swarmed out. Harry jumped back. Then he saw that he was already covered. Dozens of ants were crawling about his T-shirt and the blue denim of his jeans. Worse still, he saw that his faulty zip had come down and they were scuttling through the gap towards his underpants. With a shout he sprang to his feet, balancing on the trunk, and brushed the hard little insects from him with frantic hands. He yanked at his belt, fumbled with the stud and pushed the jeans to his ankles. The ants were on his bare legs. Careless how many he killed, he slapped them away. He tried to tug the jeans over his trainers but they were too tight. For a moment he staggered and nearly fell. Awkwardly he hopped to an ant-free section of trunk. Perhaps the beasts had got *inside* his underpants! He pulled out the elastic and checked.

"Hee-hee-hee-hee-hee!"

Harry froze, tingling to the roots of his hair. Where had the noise come from?

"Hoo-hoo-hoo-hoo-hoo!"

He looked up. The sun was dazzling. He shaded his eyes.

On a branch high above his head a tiny old lady was kicking her legs and laughing down at him.

"Have they all gone?" she called chirpily. "No ants in your pants!"

Harry blushed scarlet. Bending, he struggled with his jeans. Had it not been for a branch he would have fallen. At length they were pulled up and his belt was fastened. Roughly he rubbed his ankles and legs lest any of the ants were still inside, then holding on to the branch looked up again.

"No need to be embarrassed," came the shrill, budgerigar-like voice. "Seven nephews I've got. You're not the first boy I've seen in his underpants."

She was an extraordinary figure in shiny red tights and a green tunic that might have come from the real Sherwood Forest. But this was no Maid Marion or female Will Scarlet for she had a bush of white hair and was seventy or eighty years old.

"Hang on a minute, I'm coming down."

Nimble as a monkey she swung up on to the branch, ran to the trunk of the tree and swarmed down, knees out like a frog. For a moment she vanished beneath the forest of bracken, the green heads tossed violently, then like an orange pip or a jack-in-the-box she popped out again and stood on the fallen trunk beside Harry and Tangle.

"Hello," she said, bird-bright and alert as a squirrel. "You must be Harry Barton. We heard you were coming."

As if she had so much energy she could never stand still, the old lady did a hand-spring.

"I'm Dot. Not dotty!" She cackled at her own joke. "The Human Fly."

An ant nipped Harry's leg and he slapped it sharply. "Dotty!" he thought. "More like stark raving bonkers!"

"Do you like climbing trees?"

"Yes," said Harry.

"This wood's terrific for it," said the old lady. "Here, come with me, it's much more fun above the gound."

Fearlessly she jumped down and led the way along a narrow ride.

"Course trees aren't the same as the Grand Canyon or the Empire State Building," said Dot, "not the same class at all. But if you want oaks and beeches, giant redwoods – a really good bit of mixed woodland – there's nowhere better."

She sprang up and caught a branch that trailed overhead. A heave, a swing, and she was sitting on it, dappled with sunlight, for all the world like a pixie in a book of fairy tales. She dropped back to the ground and they continued through the summer-smelling bracken.

"Perhaps your aunties told you about me."

Harry shook his head.

"Oh, I used to be quite famous," said the little woman. "Worked for the Grand State Circus in Paris. Queenie, they called me then. Lots of stunts we had. Have you heard of the Eiffel Spider? The Angel of Niagara?"

"I don't think so," Harry said politely.

"No? Oh dear! In all the papers I was." She was crestfallen. "Queen Quong? The Mad Nun of Notre Dame?"

"I think I've heard of that." Harry lied outrageously. "Yes, definitely. I've heard of the Mad Nun."

"Have you?" The little gnome face lit up with pleasure. "Where?"

"It was in a magazine at school," Harry said. "Quite an important page, actually. About how you dressed up as a mad nun – and went climbing all about the top of Notre Dame Cathedral – in Paris – like Quasimodo – and everybody came to see you."

"That's it," Dot said delightedly. "People still remember," and as they came to a little clearing she turned a dozen cartwheels in the grass, so fast that she was a blur of red and green.

Watching her made Harry feel dizzy.

"See that patch of trees over there," said Dot as she came to a halt.

Harry gazed where she pointed.

"That's where Ol' Goggly hides out." She opened her eyes wide. "Did they tell you about Ol' Goggly? The terrible ghost?"

She knew that he knew, thought Harry. She had been sitting right above him when he sang his silly song.

"A real monster," she said without waiting for a reply. "His grave's somewhere in there. If you look now you'll find nothing but stones. But there used to be a cottage where a bloody *murder* took place."

With her circus background Dot told the story more dramatically than Nutty Slack. Harry shivered but still did not believe a word.

"Is he dangerous – Ol' Goggly?" he asked innocently.

"Not during the day," she said. "He never comes out when the sun's up. But at night…"

"What happens at night?"

"He crawls out of his grave," she said, "all bones and covered with soil, and creeps and shivers through the trees until he comes to the house. Then he peeps through the windows and hides in the bushes waiting for anyone foolish enough to go wandering around in the dark. Then when he catches them with his bony hands…"

"What happens then?" said Harry.

"Ohh, terrible things! Too terrible for your young ears."

"Yes, but what? Tell me."

"It's like the ghost says in *Hamlet*:

I could a tale unfold, whose lightest word
Would harrow up thy soul, freeze thy young blood,
Make thy two eyes, like stars, start from their spheres,
Thy knotted and combinéd locks to part
And each particular hair to stand on end
Like quills upon the fretful porpentine."

Her eyes stared, her hands opened and shut.

Harry was impressed by her acting. "But I haven't got

knotted and combinéd locks," he said. "I've got a crew cut. My hair stands up on end all the time."

Dot laughed.

"Are you telling me," said Harry plainly, "that I shouldn't go wandering around at night? That it might be dangerous?"

"That's right!" She laid a hand on his arm. "There's something out there. You stay in your bed. Nothing will touch you high up in the tower."

Harry longed to know what secret Nutty and Dot were trying to keep from him.

Close at hand a giant tree rose from the woodland floor. "This is the one we're going to climb," said the little old lady. "Easy as pie. A good English oak with lots of handholds and comfy level branches to sit on."

Harry looked up. The tree towered above others nearby. Millions of flies hummed about the summery leaves. A fat caterpillar, all green and humpy with bristles, bounced off his hair and began crawling into the neck of his T-shirt.

"Come on," Dot said. "Follow me."

Soon Harry found himself in a different world. All about him were branches and air and blue sky and bunches of green leaves. Far below, no bigger than a mouse, Tangle looked up with his head on one side.

It was a long way down, a long long way. If he fell from that height... Harry began to feel nervous.

"Do you want to rope up?" Around her waist Dot carried a coil of thin white line.

"No thank you." Harry reached for the next branch.

The tops of the smaller trees were now below them. Like a field of giant cabbages the wood stretched away in all directions. Harry had never *been* so high.

"Look." He pointed. "A nest."

"There's loads of nests."

"But this one's got eggs in it."

Carefully he climbed across and peered into the twiggy, moss-lined cup. There were five eggs. They were quite big, bluey-green and mottled with dark spots. Harry picked one out. It was very cold.

"Rook," said Dot. "Careful you don't break it. I did once – pooh! What a pong!"

Soon they were in the topmost branches. Sitting comfortably and rocking in the wind, Harry gazed across the wood. Far off in one direction he could see a range of blue hills. Far off in the other was a thin glittering line of the sea.

"It's fabulous!" he called. "Fantastic!"

A huge seagull came sailing past. Suddenly it spotted them and squawked with alarm.

Harry laughed.

"Ssshhh!" Dot seized his arm and pointed down. In the clearing far below them was a man. He wore a brown tweed suit. Clearly he did not want to be seen for he was crouching and looking to left and right. In one hand he carried a pair of powerful binoculars and around his neck hung a camera with a telescopic lens.

Harry recognized him at once.

"Beastly Priestly!" hissed Dot.

"We saw him this morning," Harry whispered back. "In a big yellow Rolls-Royce. He nearly ran into us. What's he doing? Bird-watching?"

"Bird-watching? That man couldn't tell an owl from an ostrich. No, he's not bird-watching," Dot said. "He's spying on us at Lagg Hall, that's what he's doing. Spying on us, the no-good sneaky miserable toad!" She made a hideous face at the figure below.

"Why?"

"Reasons," said Dot. "You'd better ask your Aunt Bridget that." She moved down a couple of branches to see more clearly. "This is the third time I've spotted him."

Bending double, Colonel Priestly ran from a berried rowan to a clump of purple foxgloves and crouched low. He was fat and his face shone red with his exertions. His ginger hair gleamed in the sun.

"I've got an idea." Dot beckoned. "Come on. Quickly. Take care."

Trying not to shake the leaves they descended to the abandoned nest.

"Are you a good shot?"

Harry nodded. "Yes, quite."

"All right, three for you and two for me." Dot picked up one of the four-month-old eggs, caught hold of a branch and prepared to throw. "Wait until you have a clear shot. Aim for his bonce."

Delighted by the idea of hurling rotten eggs at a grown-up, Harry reached into the nest.

Colonel Priestly had moved from the foxgloves and was peering round a pile of mossy stones.

"Right – ready, steady, go!" Dot drew back her arm and hurled the first egg. Harry watched it sail through the air in a perfect curve. SPLAT! It landed right by the Colonel's shoe.

Startled, he looked all around.

Then Harry threw his first egg. It was a bad shot and he made the branches shake.

Colonel Priestly stared up and pulled out a pair of spectacles. Beyond the leaves he spotted the two figures.

"Garn, Priestly!" Dot leaned out and shook her tiny fist. "Creeping round like a nasty old stoat. We know about you up there at Felon Grange – with your fox-hunts and your summer balls. You don't fool us! You're rotten to the core – just like this egg!"

She threw again. It was a wonderful shot. The rook's egg flew from the branches, sailed down and landed SPLOSH! right on his shoulder.

Harry shouted with delight.

Colonel Priestly shouted too. "I see you there, Dotty Skylark. Grrr! Pooh! What a stink! I'll get even with you, see if I don't. I'll teach you to meddle with Percy Priestly. And who's that with you?" He shaded his eyes. "A boy? Who are you, boy?"

"Let him have it!" whispered Dot.

Harry drew back his arm.

"Come on down! Sharpish! If you take my advice you'll choose your…"

The egg whizzed down like a cricket ball. If Dot's shot had been wonderful, this was fantastic. Even from where they stood they heard the loud POP! as the rotten egg exploded on his forehead. The stinky yolk splashed far and wide – into his hair, into his ear, down his glasses, over his moustache, on to the camera – everywhere!

"Ahhhh! Grooo! Ugghhh!" Dancing with rage, Colonel Priestly pulled out a big handkerchief and began mopping himself clean. "I'll get you! Whoever you are – I'll get you!" His face was livid. His eyes popped like golf balls.

At this moment Tangle, who had been hunting, appeared through the undergrowth. Realizing at once that Colonel Priestly was not a nice man, he began to growl and show his teeth. Darting forward, he took a nip at the Colonel's ankle.

"That's it! Go on, Tangle!" they cried. "Get him! Bite him! Tear a chunk out of his trousers!"

Urged on by their shouts, Tangle redoubled his attack.

"Get off! Let go! Aahhh, my leg! You brute! Ow!" Colonel Priestly began to stumble away.

"Good boy! That's it! See him off!" they cried.

Harry flung his last egg. Dot pulled off acorns and bits of

rotten branch. Missiles rained down upon the Colonel's head. A shaggy fiend with a hundred teeth was attacking from behind, hanging on to the seat of his trousers, driving him like a sheep. He was completely routed. Stumbling and falling headlong, Colonel Priestly beat an undignified retreat.

"That's it, Priestly! Go on, sling your hook! Get off our land!" The shrill parrot voice rang through the wood. "Next time we'll really give you something to think about!"

High in their tree Harry and Dot watched him go. Grabbing hold of branches, they performed a dance of victory.

"Oh wonderful! Glorious!" Dot sighed with pleasure and laughed afresh. "Wait until I tell the others! Harry Barton, you're a boy after my own heart. You're going to get on famously at Lagg Hall!"

Soon Tangle reappeared, wagging his tail happily, and resumed hunting rabbits instead of colonels.

Dot and Harry returned to their high branches.

A short way off lay the lake, blue and silver, reflecting the tree-tops. Ducks landed with a splash, a deer was drinking. On that hot summer afternoon the water was irresistible.

"When you get down you should go for a swim," Dot said.

"I'm going to," said Harry.

And spread his arms in the breeze as if he was flying.

5
The Lake

Harry stood on the jetty. The water was quite deep, six or seven feet. Thin weed grew on the bottom, green as salad. A shoal of tiny fish glinted in the sunlight.

The sun was hot on his bare, city-white shoulders. His T-shirt and jeans, shaken free of ants, lay on the boards. If anyone came, he hoped his blue underpants would pass for swimming trunks.

He looked round. The lake was ringed with trees. Grass and lichen-yellow rocks ran down to the water. A small rowing-boat was pulled up on the shore.

Gripping the edge of the jetty with his toes, he took a deep breath and launched himself in a dive.

The water felt wonderful, no salt or chlorine, fresh as a drink from the tap.

Harry was an excellent swimmer. One of the medals he had mentioned to Nutty was for 1500 metres, another was the gold for life-saving. Floating on his back, he gazed up at the sky and felt the sun warm on his face. Doubling in a duck-dive, he slid to the bed of the lake. Bubbles streamed from his mouth. Twisting like an otter he looked all round, from the weedy pillars of the jetty to the misty blue distance. Another shoal of minnows angled in the sunlight. He thrust himself from the pebbles and emerged in a fountain of spray.

A few strokes took him to the ladder. Seizing the wooden rungs he pulled himself to the jetty. Water drained on to the hot boards. He made a pattern of footprints. Then hurling himself forward, he leaped out over the lake and curled into a depth-charge.

SPER-LUNK!

The water erupted, spray sparkled in the sunlight. For a moment all was confusion. Then Harry reappeared, swimming breast-stroke like a frog and heading out from the shore.

For ten minutes he played in the water, then spread-eagled himself on the jetty, arms and legs wide. The boards burned his back. His skin tickled as the drops of water ran down and dried.

The sun made colours behind his eyelids. Harry squeezed them tight and watched the pale yellow darken through orange and reds to pansy-purple. For a split-second he peeped at the sun then shut his eyes and saw the splodge dissolve and change against a multi-coloured background.

The lakeside was quiet. He listened and missed the incessant roar of London traffic. The only sounds here were the call of a bird, the distant hum of a microlite, and soft growls from Tangle who lay on the gravel shore and tore a stick to splinters.

The heat was gorgeous. He turned on his stomach. The old boards were black and splintery, the new were smooth and creamy-white. The sun drew resin from golden knots. Harry pushed a drop with his nail then squashed it and smelled the strong scent of pine on his fingertip. When he tried to rub the resin away he couldn't get rid of the stickiness.

He pressed his eye to a gap and peered down at the water. Almost directly beneath him a barred fish hung in the green shadows. A summer fly drifted into sight, struggling in the water. The saucer eyes spotted it. The angle of the fish altered; there was a sudden swirl and splash. When the ripples stilled the fly was gone.

Harry rolled on his back again and closed his eyes. Soporific in the heat, limp as a puppet, he thought of Ol' Goggly. Did he, like the fish, crouch motionless in the shadows then leap out, all hairy claws and bony ribs, and snatch his victim back to devour at leisure?

As he day-dreamed, Harry was dimly aware of little noises in the background. A board creaked. A shadow fell over his face. Vaguely imagining that a cloud had crossed the sun, he half-opened his eyes.

Two figures stood above him, towering against the sky. With a cry Harry jumped to his feet.

"Is all right!" said the larger of the new arrivals, a woman. "All right. Sorry ve give you surprise. Ve thought you hear us approaching."

Harry's eyes were wide.

"Yeah! Nasty shock that could be," said her male companion. "Open 'is eyes sudden an' find a mountain like you standin' above 'im! Cor, turn yer tripes to water, that would." He turned to Harry. "Nothin' to be frightened of, son. Just 'Uggy an' ol' Fingers. 'Eard you was down at the lake. Come across to make yer acquaintance, like."

Now that Harry was standing, he saw that far from being a giant, the man was, in fact, unusually short and weedy. The lined face suggested that he was in his sixties. His hair was brown and hung limply across his forehead. A wispy moustache hung raggedly over his mouth. His chin was non-existent, and non-existent shoulders sloped steeply to a thin chest upon which a cheap brown suit hung in empty folds.

"'Ere, you bin swimmin'? Wouldn't mind a bit o' that." He turned to his companion. "What about it, 'Uggy? Fancy strippin' off a bit an' takin' the plunge?" He sniggered inoffensively. "Still, maybe better not, eh! Want to leave a bit o' water in the lake."

As he spoke, Harry was startled to see that various fingers were missing from each hand. He stared. Good manners were overcome by curiosity. "What happened to them?" he asked bluntly.

"What 'appened to what?"

"Your hands." He pointed. "What happened to your fingers?"

"Me fingers?" The man spread his hands as if he had never really noticed that a scatter of fingers was missing. "Oh, I, er," the suddenness of the question caught him unawares. "I, er, 'ad an accident, like."

"*An* accident?" cried his huge friend. "Von accident? Fifty accident, more like."

"Yeah, that's it. I was a little bit careless once or twice. At me work." He pushed the hands into flapping pockets. "That's why they call me Fingers. Fingers Peterman. Pleased ta meetcha."

Harry looked from the hidden hands to his scrawny neck and Adam's apple, then across to his companion.

"Since we're on names," said Fingers, "go on, tell 'im why you're called 'Uggy." He looked at Harry. "She's Russian, you know."

"Half Russian – half German," said the woman. "Oh, this heat! I function better in the cold." Leaning on the rail she fanned her face with a hand like a joint of lamb.

Unlike Fingers, who was smaller than he had first appeared, this woman was larger. She was, indeed, the biggest woman that Harry had ever seen. Standing side by side, she and Fingers looked more like two ill-assorted dogs than two senior citizens: an unkempt Yorkshire terrier beside an unusually large bulldog. For 'Uggy, as Fingers called her, was no beauty. Above the acreage of a good-humoured but alarming face with splayed tombstone teeth, sat a brown rug of hair that scarcely covered the battered ears which stood out at each side like handles. Harry's glance flitted down to her vast jumper full of tractor inner-tubes and party balloons, her straining tweed skirt, and the bulging muscles of her legs above a pair of size twelve shoes.

"Oh, Harry, you're so lucky," said 'Uggy in her guttural voice. "So young and thin! You look so cool in all this heeeeeat!"

"It's lovely in the water," Harry said. "Nutty rigged up a ladder for me."

"Yeah. If yer so 'ot, why don'cha go in like the kid?"

"It all right for him. He vear his pants. Vhat you think it look like if I go in in my undervear?" She laughed like a jelly. "It vould frighten the fishes. They vould be floating belly-up all over the lake! Dead from shock!"

They joined in her laughter.

"Don't you believe a word of it," said Fingers. "Spent 'alf 'er life in 'er underwear, she 'as. Or stripped down to a bavin' suit wiv a strap over one shoulder, which is a'most the same fing."

"Pay no attention to him," the woman said. "It vas long time ago."

"Yeah, a famous lady wrestler she used to be," Fingers said proudly. "'Uggy Bear, she was called. The Strangler! The Bonecrusher!"

"Oh, shut up, Fingers," said Huggy, as Harry now realized she was called. "Or I tell him vhat vas your job. It too hot to go into that ancient history."

Harry stared. "Were you really?" he said. "A lady wrestler? Like they have on the telly?"

"No!" She frowned. "*Not* like they haf on the television. That is rubbish – most, anyvay. I vas qvality. A real wrestler. Top of the bill."

"Will you teach me?" Harry said. "Now I'm staying here."

She shook with laughter. "All right. But not today. Vhen it cooler. Under the trees."

"Thanks!" Harry was delighted.

"You really vant?"

He nodded.

"Then come here a minute." Flatfooted, she moved to the middle of the jetty. "Something I vant show you. Give me your hand."

Grinning, Harry did so. He braced himself in case of a trick.

Huggy smiled back. "Now vhatever happens, you must never…"

What happened next was so fast that Harry was taken completely by surprise. The huge woman scarcely seemed to move, but in an instant he was flying high out over the lake, arms and legs flailing. With a tremendous splash he hit the water, metres from the jetty. A minute later he reappeared up the ladder, streaming and grinning from ear to ear.

"…let anyvon do that to you," Huggy concluded. She clapped him on the wet back. "Oh, your skin is so lofely and cold."

"Do it again!" Harry said.

"No, not now," said Huggy. "It too hot! Maybe later vhen…"

And before he could move, Harry was flying through the air in the other direction. In a fountain he disappeared.

Laughing, Huggy turned to Fingers. "Oh, the vater look so good!" she said. "So cool! I t'ink I join him. You too?"

"Yeah, all right. If you're game, I am. Anyfing for a larf."

"I go this vay. You go that."

Tangle stood wagging his tail. Huggy patted his wet and gravelly shoulder. "Good boy! You svim as vell?"

The huge ex-wrestler made her way to a clump of willow trees to strip to her formidable underwear. Half-hidden behind a rocky outcrop, Fingers Peterman took off his suit and emerged in a pair of baggy undershorts from which his legs stuck out like peeled twigs.

Minutes later four heads were splashing and bobbing in the lake beneath the blue summer sky.

6
Ol' Goggly

"And you called her Gestapo Lil!" Aunt Bridget was still laughing. "Oh, my dear Harry!"

"She sounds an absolute horror," said Auntie Florrie. "Never mind, you forget all about her. You're in Lagg Hall now." She waggled dimpled fingers. "Good night, dear. It's lovely to have you here. And remember, if there's anything you need, just pick up the intercom."

It was ten o'clock. Harry lay in bed. A Donald Duck lamp filled his room with a golden glow.

"And if you don't want your bed full of sand," said Aunt Bridget, "you'll make Tangle sleep in his box where he belongs."

Harry did not mind the idea of a bed full of sand. He looked down at Tangle who stood waiting for his aunts to go.

"Good night," he said.

"Night-night, dear. Happy dreams."

"Sleep well." Aunt Bridget grasped the iron handrail of the spiral stairs and the two figures descended from sight.

The staircase light was extinguished. The tower door closed. Harry was alone.

Hands behind his head, he stared up at the crooked beams.

The bed shook as Tangle sprang to the foot, sniffed

fastidiously and trampled round and round, dragging the duvet comfortable.

"Don't get too settled," Harry told him. "We're going out again soon. I want to know about Ol' Goggly. I want to know what they're all trying to hide."

Tangle paused and regarded him, then resumed his preparations.

In case he fell asleep, Harry set the alarm on the tick-tocking old clock by his bed and lay back again.

A pile of books lay on the window-ledge beside him. Some were old with hard covers, others were bright new paperbacks. He picked through them and chose an adventure called *The Snow Treasure*. Harry enjoyed reading but tonight his mind was not on it. Before he was halfway down the first page the book fell to the bedclothes.

On the wall opposite hung the dark green intercom. It gave him an idea. Perhaps he could overhear their conversation down in the house. Slipping from bed he ran across. The vinyl was cool beneath his bare feet. Like most of the clothes he had brought from Hampstead, his blue-striped pyjamas were too small.

The intercom had a handpiece like a telephone. Carefully he lifted it from the rest. Except for a faint electronic buzzing all was silent. He examined the instrument. The only control was a button on the wall which presumably sounded a bell or bleeper at the far end. Clearly he must not touch that. He listened again. Still nothing. He was just replacing the handpiece when the intercom crackled loudly into life.

"Hello!" exploded a distorted, parrot-like voice.

Harry got such a fright that he dropped the receiver, which went crashing against the wall, bouncing and rattling on the end of its coiled wire.

"Harry?" shouted the dangling receiver. "Is everything all right? Something you want?"

With shaking hands he grabbed it up. "Is that you, Aunt Bridget?"

"No, this is Auntie Florrie. No problems, I hope, dear."

"No." Desperately he tried to think of something to say. "I was just wondering how it worked, that's all."

Behind his aunt he could hear the murmur of voices.

"That's all right then, dear. Aren't these machines awful. You sound like a crow with laryngitis. Anyway, off to bed now. Sweet dreams."

"Night, Auntie Florrie." For a moment longer Harry listened but the receiver at the other end was not replaced. Carefully he hung up.

"That was awful!" he said to Tangle. "Just as if they *knew* I was spying on them."

Tangle raised a whiskery eyebrow.

Harry looked at the clock. Half an hour to go.

He climbed back into bed and a few minutes later took up *The Snow Treasure* again. Tucking the duvet round his chest, he settled to read.

So engrossed did Harry become in the adventure that he failed, some time later, to hear the tower door opening. Footsteps mounted the spiral staircase. Suddenly he heard them: tap–tap–tap on the stone steps. He was so startled that for a moment he panicked. It was Ol' Goggly, come to get him! It was his aunts, furious to discover that he planned to go creeping around in the dark, spying on them! It was... The footsteps were almost to his door. There was no time to think. In a turmoil he shut his eyes and let his book drop to the bedclothes.

Somebody entered the room, breathing heavily from the steep stairs. Soft footsteps crossed the floor. Sleepily he turned and peeped through closed lashes.

Aunt Bridget stood by his bed. He saw the gold and scarlet kaftan she had worn all evening. A long hand picked up his book. For a full minute pages were turned then the book was set back on the window-shelf. A soft voice spoke to Tangle: "What do you think you're doing there, you rascal? You should be in your box, that's where you should be!" A hand tucked the duvet around Harry's shoulder. There was a whiff of springlike perfume as she leaned forward to kiss him on the brow.

Click! The room was plunged into darkness. Cautious foot-steps felt their way to the door. The staircase light came on. Aunt Bridget descended. The light was extinguished. The tower door closed.

Once more Harry was alone.

For two minutes he waited, giving his aunt time to get clear, then leaned across the window-sill and peeped through the curtains.

It was a magical night. Beyond the lopsided panes of his window a full moon sailed among clouds. The lawns were silver. On all sides leafy trees cast patches of shadow. Five legions of Roman soldiers could have been lurking out there let alone a solitary ghost.

Harry eased the window open. A night breeze billowed the curtains. He drew them back. The breeze was warm, bringing with it the scents of stock and honeysuckle, far-off hayfields and the sweet earth. Somewhere a cow lowed, a dog barked, a car accelerated into silence.

It was time to go. Softly he shut the window, leaving the curtains open to admit the moonlight. It did not take long to throw off his pyjamas and pull on jeans, a black sweater and black school gymshoes. He had no torch, he had no weapon – somewhere he would find a length of branch for a club. Briskly he crawled across his bed and closed the curtains, and as an afterthought pushed his suitcase and pillow beneath the duvet to look as if he was sleeping. Then nervously, with Tangle at his heels, he felt his way across the room.

He had just reached the stairs when with a hideous and deafening noise of bells the alarm clock went off. His heart leaped. Fast as he could move he rushed across the room, tripped on a rug, fell against the bed, and seized the clock. Desperately he fumbled. The bell stopped ringing.

Harry listened. No noise disturbed the silence. He waited. No one came. Slowly his heart stopped thudding.

A second time he crept across the floor. The doorway gaped before him. A smell of soap came from his little bathroom on the landing.

The darkness was total, though further down the spiral staircase small windows let in the moonlight. There were, he had counted, forty-seven steps to the tower door. One hand grasping the rail, the other touching the rough stone opposite, he began to descend.

"One," he counted beneath his breath, "two – three – four – five – six…"

"Now you stay by me!" Harry had fastened a length of string to Tangle's collar. "And don't go pulling. Are you listening? If we bump into Ol' Goggly, bite him! And if we see Aunt Bridget or anyone, sssshhh!"

Tangle stood obediently, ignoring Harry and staring round into the darkness.

They stood beneath trees a short distance from the tower. Lagg Hall was steeped in moonlight. A stretch of open lawn separated them from the gable wall. Harry's eyes were wide. He listened intently. The coast was clear.

"Come on, quick." He tugged Tangle's string.

Boy and dog scampered across the dewed grass and vanished into the black spear of shadow at the end of the house.

Harry's cropped head emerged into the moonlight as he peered round the corner. Before him lay the gravelled forecourt.

Above him, rising from a wide border of flowers, was the grand front of the house. All the windows save one were unlit. Thirty metres ahead, the French window of the drawing-room cast a golden glow across the pebbles.

Harry took a deep breath, grasped Tangle's string firmly and stepped out into the glare of the full moon. The forecourt pebbles scrunched under his feet. He stepped on to the border but his gymshoes left deep prints in the earth, wallflowers and lupins smashed around him. He returned to the gravel.

All about him was the night life of the garden: bats hunted for moths; a prowling cat, carrying something in its mouth, slid into the shrubbery; an owl flapped from the roof on silent wings.

Harry came to the broad step of the French window. Heavy curtains, cream and green and orange, hid the grand drawing-room. He peered round the edges. Nothing was to be seen but a strip of elegant wallpaper.

He pressed his ear to the glass. Someone was speaking, a woman. He blocked his other ear. It sounded like Aunt Bridget. He shut his eyes, concentrating. Still he could not make out what she was saying. Another voice, a man's, interrupted. Then he thought Aunt Bridget said, "Yes, Florrie will take the car and..." But that was all – and he wasn't sure.

He rubbed off the smudge his ear had left on the glass.

"Well, what now?" He looked down at Tangle.

The dog was sitting bolt upright and staring back the way they had come.

"What is it, boy?" His scalp prickled.

For a moment he saw nothing. Then he spotted it, a dark shape crossing the lawn. A hedgehog!

Harry relaxed, grinning, and patted Tangle's side.

But his relief was short-lived, for as he watched the humpy hedgehog, a light flickered in the trees beyond. His heart stopped.

The light disappeared. He waited and a moment later it came again, suddenly seemed to flare up – and was gone.

What was it? Who was there? One thing was certain, Harry needed to get out of the moonlight, back into the shadows where he could not be seen. Or was Ol' Goggly waiting in that leafy darkness behind the tower? At least Tangle seemed unalarmed. Feeling very exposed, Harry flitted back across the gravel and vanished into the shadows beneath the gable wall.

For a moment he stood panting, then stopped breathing to listen intently. Little rustles and whispery noises came from all over the garden. An owl screeched and his head jerked round. From the patch of woodland came a low moaning sound.

"There's no such *thing* as ghosts!" Harry told himself.

Then again came that faint ripple and flare of light, like hidden lightning beyond the trees.

Harry shivered. He should have done what everyone told him, he thought, and stayed in bed. But now he had seen the light and heard the moaning he wanted to know more. Keeping to the moon-shadow as far as possible, he circled the lawns and came to the wood from behind the tower. Their feet, boy and dog, left tracks in the cold dew. Harry's gymshoes were saturated. He hardly felt it.

It would be difficult to lead Tangle through the trees. He untied the string. "Now be a good boy," he whispered earnestly. "Stay by me. You hear! No wandering off. And no barking!"

Cautiously Harry advanced. Twigs brushed his face. Icy cascades of dew fell on his head and shoulders. His ankle struck a fallen branch. Picking up a bleached fragment the length of his arm, he continued.

Dead twigs snapped beneath his feet. Frightened birds flew off through the branches calling loudly. Tangle spotted a rabbit and shot off in pursuit, crashing through the undergrowth like a team of runaway horses.

Harry froze. But the disturbance had not distracted whatever was lurking a short way off through the trees. The unearthly moaning was louder now. He heard tramping. The flicker and flare of light was brighter.

At length he came to a small opening in the trees and halted. The night breeze had freshened. Overhead dark branches swayed and rustled against the moon. All about him shadows were moving.

A minute passed. And then another minute. His stomach rumbled loudly. He grimaced and sucked it in behind his belt. Still he waited, motionless as the tree-trunks which surrounded him.

Suddenly, at the far side of the clearing, there was a tiny *snap* like the breaking of a twig.

Harry's head jerked towards it.

"Aaahooohhh!"

There was a low moan. A ghostly ripple of light floated just above the ground. It began to spread. Giant feet rose from the woodland floor.

"What *is* it?" Harry was terrified.

"Aaaahoooohhh!" The cry was louder, longer, all about him.

In the same instant the light flared up into the trees, four metres from the ground, and he was staring at a hideous, ghostly apparition. From the waist down it had long robes like a monk, but the head and torso were those of a beast with shining eyes, terrible fangs, and claws outstretched as if to rush across the small clearing and seize him. The creature moved, billowed strangely and was gone.

Though the nightmare was visible for no more than a second it was enough for Harry. Uttering shouts of terror he fled. Branches and thorns scratched his face as he fought through trees and thickets. Something caught him round the ankle and he fell full-length. Desperately he tugged his foot free and ran on.

At his back there were sounds of pursuit, heavy footsteps and something crashing through the undergrowth. While all the time the cries of Ol' Goggly rang after him from the wood.

"Aaahooohhh! Aaaahhoooohhhh!"

The tower gave him protection.

Harry sat at the foot of the spiral staircase and licked blood from a scratch on the back of his hand. His cheek was scratched too, and his leg. Both ankles were stinging. He did not mind, they would soon heal.

The panic had passed and he was thoughtful.

At his feet Tangle, who had joined him in the wild dash from the wood, was also licking himself. Their wet footmarks covered the entrance. Harry had bolted the studded door securely against the night and switched on the staircase lights.

There was something fishy about Ol' Goggly, he told himself, something very fishy, several things in fact. For a start, despite all the people who had warned him – which was suspicious in itself – there were no such things as ghosts. No matter what he had felt, no matter how he had fled screaming, they simply did *not* exist. Then the light had appeared so regularly, once every three minutes or so. And it was always accompanied by the moaning. He had never heard the moaning without the light, or seen the light without the moaning. Then there had been that little *snap* just before it started – it could have been the click of a switch. And to support that, the first time he fell his ankle had been tangled in plastic cable, not brambles or thorny briar – he had felt it with his fingers as he tugged it off, smooth and slippery. Finally, what harm had Ol' Goggly actually done him – none! All the terrible ghost had done was to appear and groan and billow strangely.

Tiny beads of blood had welled up again. He licked them off

and reached down to pat Tangle. *He* had not been frightened and dogs were supposed to be sensitive to anything supernatural.

Harry decided to investigate. Quickly he ran up the forty-seven steps and collected the old clock from his bedside table. He ran back down, tugged open the bolts of the ancient door, switched off the lights, and a moment later boy and dog were back in the moonlit garden.

Harry needed one hand free and left his club against the wall by the tower door. If the worst came to the worst, the two-belled alarm clock could be a formidable weapon. He balanced it in his hand. That was heavy enough to give anyone, ghost or man, a nasty headache.

The wind blew in his face and whispered about the tower. Quickly he ran to the edge of the wood and vanished into the shadows.

Softly Harry advanced through the trees – and stopped. He advanced again. Suddenly he saw the first low, flickering light and heard the ghostly groan. He waited and a moment later saw the flare. There was a sound of crashing footsteps. The groaning ceased.

He consulted the luminous clock in his hand. Fourteen and a half minutes past eleven. Briefly he searched for a comfortable patch and sat down with his back to a tree.

"Come here, Tangle."

One arm around his shaggy companion, he watched the minute hand creep round the face of the clock.

The low light came again; he heard the moans; the light flared and faded. Harry consulted his clock. Eighteen and a half minutes past eleven.

He waited. It was very eerie. Anything, madmen and tigers, could have been lurking in the rustling black shadows which surrounded him.

The light flared again. Twenty-two and a half minutes past eleven.

Precisely four minute intervals.

Harry rose.

It was easy to get lost in the moonlit wood. For a while he floundered about, uncertain of the way. The light guided him – from an unexpected direction – and at length he found himself back at the edge of the clearing.

No sooner had he arrived than the faint *snap* made Tangle prick up his ears. Immediately the first lines of light shimmered above the woodland floor. A blood-chilling moan rose through the trees. The light grew and flared up, revealing the nightmare figure of Ol' Goggly. The moans grew louder with a noise like heartbeats and the smashing of branches.

It ceased.

The performance was over.

Harry advanced through the dew-laden ferns. His jeans were soaked, his jersey wet to the chest. Before him, where the apparition had manifested itself, a black rectangle was silhouetted against the trees. He stepped forward to examine it. "Ow!" His shin struck something sharp. It sounded hollow. He kicked it. It was a box. Harry bent to investigate. Exploring hands felt wood and cloth and wires. It was an old loudspeaker. He straightened and continued to the black shape. It was material, black canvas, tied with ropes between tree-trunks and bellying like a sail in the breeze. The moonlight revealed faint lines. He traced them with his fingertips. It was the outline of Ol' Goggly.

Harry was still standing there when at his feet came the *snap* of a switch. At once the bottom lines of the drawing were illuminated. He leaned forward to examine them. It appeared to be some kind of conductive, luminous paint. The loudspeaker began its moaning, so loud and eerie close at hand that Tangle threw back his head and began to howl in unison.

"Aaahooohh!"

"Yoo–ooo–ooo!"

"Aaaahoooohhh!"

"Yi–ooo–ooo! Yi–ooo–ooo–ooo!"

"Oh shut up, Tangle!" Harry said.

As he spoke the whole canvas was illuminated. High overhead the monk's robes merged into a shaggy breast. The terrible eyes stared, claws and fangs seemed ready to tear an intruder to shreds. Although it was only a luminous cartoon, a kind of hoarding, in that place at the dead of night, accompanied by the groans and crashing footsteps, it was terrifying.

The light was extinguished, the loudspeaker fell silent. Harry retreated into the trees.

"Well, Tangle." He crouched and took a wet forepaw. "What a trick *that* was! What a lot of *trouble* somebody went to. The question is – *why*?" He glanced over his shoulder just in case. "Why do they want me to stay in the *tower*? What are they trying to *hide*? Do *you* know?"

Tangle did not reply.

Harry rubbed the rough head and rose. "Well I don't either. So let's go and find out."

The wet jeans clung to his legs. He pulled them straight and wriggled icy toes. The discomfort did not bother him at all.

"Isn't this great!" He looked up at the moon. "Out in the wood and nearly midnight. A real adventure!"

7
The Listener

At the far end of Lagg Hall, balancing it with the tower, stood an enormous white wrought-iron conservatory.

Harry stood at the door. He was alone. Much to Tangle's disgust Harry had shut him in the tower, for he planned to go into the house and Tangle would have made discovery more likely.

He squashed his nose against a pane and peered into the interior. Potted palms and other large-leafed plants rose all around. Vines with clusters of unripened grapes coiled about the pillars and roof. The mingling of Victorian design, strange shapes and moonlight made it the landscape of a dream. From what Harry could see, however, it was unoccupied. He twisted the iron handle. The mechanism squeaked rustily and the door cracked open.

Great!

He was just about to step over the threshold when an inner voice cautioned – feet! His sodden gymshoes would leave prints for the next hour. Quickly he pulled them off, tucked his socks inside and hid them behind a tussock of grass. The dew was icy. He scrubbed the soles of his feet against his jeans, stepped into the conservatory and pulled the door shut behind him.

The air was warm and fragrant. The lunar foliage writhed

above him. Comfortable cane furniture and occasional tables stood about the patterned tiles.

"Ow!" Harry winced as he trod on a sharp piece of gravel. Briefly he rubbed his foot then continued towards the inner door of the conservatory which led into the house.

It, too, was unlocked and a minute later Harry found himself in an unlit passage. Wellingtons and walking sticks stood against the walls, waterproofs hung from pegs. The floor was covered with vinyl. Walking on the sides of his feet he passed the laundry room, Mrs Good's kitchen and the breakfast room. The air smelled of polish, fresh ironing and the thick bacon sandwich he had eaten for supper. A sound of distant voices rose on the silence.

As he reached the grand hall the mosaic floor struck cold. A sweeping staircase with carved banisters rose to the bedrooms above. Gorgeous pictures – not stern old ancestors but land-scapes, still lifes, foreign scenes – hung on the panelled walls. From a high cupola a shaft of moonlight struck the landing.

More like a burglar-boy than a nephew, in his black jersey and torn jeans, Harry tiptoed to the door of the drawing-room where his aunts and their friends were congregated. Crouching, he put his eye to the keyhole.

The drawing-room was the finest room of the house. After the shadows of the garden and hall the light was startling. He saw the patterned cream carpet, lamps with cream and golden shades, polished tables with coffee pots and liqueur glasses. A scatter of stylish oldies – wrinklies his aunt had called them – sat back in comfortable armchairs. He saw Auntie Florrie, Huggy and Fingers, and a man called Max whom he had met at dinner. In the middle of the room Aunt Bridget, statuesque in her rich kaftan, half sat on the arm of a settee. Her granny glasses winked in the lamplight. A large sheet of paper was in her hand and she was talking.

Harry pressed his ear to a panel of the door.

"…as I said before," Aunt Bridget was saying, "Florrie will park in the next side-street, that's Market Row, opposite the little paper-shop. And remember, Nutty's replacing the wings and spraying the Mercedes red. And we're using the Manchester number-plates, so there should be no mistake."

"Small correction, dear." Auntie Florrie interrupted. "It won't be the Manchester plates 'cause people keep forgetting. Nutty's knocked up a personalized one that's easier to remember: TBJ 123. It's our tenth bank job, so TBJ for that – and 123."

"Yes, that seems a good idea," said Aunt Bridget. "Will you all amend your sheets: TBJ 123."

Pencils moved across sheets of paper in their laps.

"Yeah, that's better." Fingers was speaking. "Manage that all right. All them other numbers, kept gettin' 'em mixed up, like."

"And you von't," Huggy laughed, "you von't try getting into a police car this time, vill you, Fingers!"

"Yeah, yeah! Keep draggin' that up again. I was confused an' all them mad jewellers was after me, wasn't they!"

"I'm sorry," she said. "You made it, anyvay."

"Yeah, fanks to Florrie, there. Cor, some chase that was!"

"Well we don't want that to happen this time, do we," said Aunt Bridget firmly. "Let's get back to the job in hand. As I was saying, Florrie will be waiting in Market Row, so when we come round the corner from Gas Lane – "

"Which is mostly old terrace houses waiting for demolition," chirped Dot.

"As you say, which is almost deserted, then anyone who sees us will assume we've come from the pub in the next side-street – "

"*The Bull an' Feather*," came a voice.

"*The Lamb and Mallet*," Aunt Bridget corrected.

"It was the right idea."

"I suppose so. Anyway, try to look as if you've had a few – not enough to draw attention, just a couple of laughs and a bit of nonsense."

"Then into the car with the loot and back by Greenharbour and Hayford," said Auntie Florrie. "Good open roads and close to the motorway in case we have to make a run for it."

"Good," said Aunt Bridget. "And that about covers everything, I think. Any questions?... No?... Well, we'll go over it once more, just to be sure. Will you check your plans, please."

Harry was aghast. He drew back from the door. No wonder they wanted him to stay in his room! No wonder they didn't want him to go wandering round the grounds at night! They were a bunch of bank robbers! His only relatives in the world, the people he had come to live with – and they were criminals! He could not believe it. Everyone was so nice. Aunt Bridget – the leader of a gang of thieves – all senior citizens! It was ridiculous! And yet it was true. From what he had heard there was no doubt about it. Fingers, the fast car, Ol' Goggly, the cameo of a pirate – it all made sense now. And Colonel Priestly was a judge! Harry's hand flew to his mouth – he had thrown rotten eggs at him! From Gestapo Lil to a nest of bank robbers! Out of the frying pan and really into the fire! What was he to do?

He returned to the door and pressed his ear to the panel.

"...sorry to keep you so late," Aunt Bridget was saying. "But with Harry arriving today and everything, the time just seemed to slip by."

"Such a nice boy!" said Dot. "So brave! I think I'll take him climbing in the Alps."

"Von of the best!" said Huggy. "Already I love him as my own. I vish I get my hands on that bitch of a housekeeper you tell us about. I teach her a thing or two!"

"Great kid," said Fingers. "Yeah."

"Oh, you're all such loves!" Auntie Florrie started to cry. "He is a dear, isn't he! I'm so happy you all like him."

"Come on, Florrie, pull yourself together!" said Aunt Bridget sharply. "It's nearly midnight. We've still got work to do."

"Yes, Bridget." She dabbed her mascara. "You're quite right. I'm sorry. But he's had such a rotten time with those parents and everything that – " She collapsed afresh.

"Oh dear!" said Aunt Bridget. "Well, we'll continue and you join us as soon as you can, Florrie, dear. Now, where were we?"

"We were just going to start," said someone.

"Before you do," came the cracked, budgie voice of Dot, "what date is all this going to take place? I know you told us but I've forgotten."

"Mem'ry like a sieve," came another voice, Fingers. "She's told yer an' told yer. Nex' Sat'day, nine o'clock. Come on, Dot, pull yersel' togevver."

"No it's not!" Aunt Bridget sighed. "Next Saturday's the special tea for Harry – and it's at *six* o'clock. The job's the following Friday and we leave here at eight."

"Oh, yeah! Sorry, Bridget. What's at nine o'clock then?"

"That was *Crimebusters* – on TV tonight."

Somebody giggled loudly.

"How we're not all back behind bars again I'll never know," said Aunt Bridget. "Right, now we'll go through the whole thing one last time, and for goodness sake pay attention. Huggy – wake up! That's better! Now. Only five of us are needed for this job: that's Dot, Huggy, Fingers, Florrie and me. Max and Angel, you've got the night off. I know you've got schemes of your own on the go, we'll hear about those in your own good time.

"Now the five of us leave here at eight. We drive into Oakborough to arrive about nine and Florrie drops us opposite the *Lamb and Mallet*. Then she takes the car off to the multi-storey and doesn't come back until eleven."

"And wait for you all in Market Row," said Auntie Florrie.

"That's right. Now after Florrie's gone," Aunt Bridget continued, "the rest of us stay chatting outside the pub while Fingers goes ahead into Gas Lane – remember it's not very well lit – and opens the door of number fifty-seven. It's marked on your plans. We'll give you exactly one minute, Fingers."

"Don't need no minute. Blimey, started openin' locks like that wiv a dummy-tit in me chops."

"Nevertheless, after one minute we'll decide *not* to go to the *Lamb and Mallet* and start drifting along Gas Lane. When we reach number fifty-seven we'll go straight in and shut the door behind us. This is probably the most dangerous part of the job. If we see anyone hanging about or looking from a window across the road, we'll go straight past and wait round the corner by the paper-shop, then try again fifteen minutes later.

"As soon as we're inside we're safe for a while. Once business is finished for the day everyone goes home. Nobody lives in any of the premises overlooking the back gardens."

"No vorkers, no residents. So ve vill not be seen."

"Very good, Huggy! We go straight across the gardens – they're full of long nettles and weeds so be careful – and over the wall to the back of the bank."

"How do you know they're all nettles and rubbish?"

"I looked from the window of the Ladies in the tea-shop two doors along." Aunt Bridget paused for a sip of coffee. "Now to get into the bank we have to go through an upstairs window and they are probably alarmed."

"No problem," said Fingers.

"Excellent! But we have to get you there first. The nearest drainpipe is about ten metres away. That's where you come in, Dot. We can't carry a wooden ladder, it would be too obvious.

So you take that nylon climbing ladder you use in the Rockies and the Himalayas."

"The one we used on that diamond store last Christmas?" said Dot.

Harry gasped. The noise startled him and he prepared for flight. No one appeared, however, and when he peeped through the keyhole the scene was unchanged.

"Oh! And Fingers," Aunt Bridget was saying, "I hardly need to say this, but you'll remember your wire and TNT and whatever, won't you. Or is it nitro-glycerine this time?"

"Gelignite," said Fingers. "Not usin' nitro no more – not after that job at the fag ware'ouse. Blew open the safe all right, but couldn't get the cash cos 'alf the flippin' building come down an' all, didn't it! Buried us under a mountain o' fags. Nearly croaked, didn't I. Nearly suffocated. Talk about a gasper!" There was laughter. "No, 'ave to be careful wi' nitro, see. Can't 'old it properly wi' these 'ands. Nearly took 'alf me toes off an' all, last time."

"Well gelignite then. But you will be careful, won't you, Fingers, darling. I mean, we all love your big explosions, but we're worried for you. Lose any more of those precious digits and you'll not be able to open the marmalade, never mind pick locks and feel the combinations of safes."

"No worry, love. I'm the best, I am."

"Yes, we know you are, sweet, and we all adore you. But you are running a bit short, aren't you?"

Harry was so engrossed by the scene within the drawing-room that he failed to spot a figure on the moonlit landing. The figure saw him, however, his ear glued to the door. For a minute the figure watched, then came creeping down the broad staircase at Harry's back.

"Originally I thought we might break through from the boutique next door," Aunt Bridget was saying, "but the walls are too thick. It has to be the window. So the next thing is to get Fingers up there to do his stuff. The roof guttering has just been renewed, it looks good and strong and should take his weight easily. So Dot, if you shin up that drainpipe with your ladder and a couple of hooks, it will be – "

"Hello there, Harry lad!" A hand fell on his shoulder.

If an electric wire had suddenly been applied to his bottom Harry could not have jumped more violently.

"Havin' a bit listen, then?"

It was Nutty Slack. Harry froze, then ducked and took to his heels like a whippet. Nutty's big hand grabbed him by the back of the jersey.

"Oh no ye don't, young fella-me-lad. You stay here wi' me."

Fighting and struggling, Harry was dragged back to the door. His foot struck it with a bang.

"Let go!" he shouted. "Let go! Let go of me!"

Squirming like an eel he slithered from his jersey and half fell to the floor. In a flash Nutty caught him by the back of his jeans.

Turning wildly, Harry pummelled at his chest and shoulders.

"There, there! Ow, ye little tyke!" Nutty pinioned him in strong arms.

Harry kicked out. Again his bare feet struck the door. Crash! Wallop! Bang!

In the midst of this turmoil the door of the drawing-room was suddenly flung wide. Light streamed into the hall.

"What on earth's happening here?" Aunt Bridget stood silhouetted in the entrance.

Still struggling, Harry was carried past her into the middle of the room and dumped unceremoniously on the carpet.

"By, the lad's some fighter!" said Nutty.

Scratched across the face and wearing nothing but a pair of wet and ragged jeans, Harry stared round the circle of elderly crooks who regarded him with astonishment.

8
Biscuits at Midnight

Wrapped in a blanket and smelling of antiseptic, Harry sat on the big settee. A mug of steaming Ovaltine was in his hand, a plate of biscuits by his side. Tangle had been fetched from the tower and lay snoozing by the French window. All the clothes Harry had been wearing, including his socks and gymshoes, hung drying in the kitchen.

"Well you had to find out some time, of course," Aunt Bridget was saying, "but I didn't imagine it would be so soon, not on your very first night. You've only been here twelve hours."

Harry held his Ovaltine in both hands and took a sip.

"But weren't you frightened, dear?" said Auntie Florrie, cheerful in pink chiffon and somewhat haphazard make-up. "The idea of a terrible ghost wandering the grounds? Didn't it make you want to lock the door and leave the lights on all night?"

"Not really," Harry said.

"Ooh, it would have terrified me when I was a girl," said his auntie.

"Me an' all," said Fingers, "when I was a boy, like. Saw a film once – *The Beast from the Pit*. Wouldn't go out after sunset for the next six months. Scared out me wits."

"I also," said Huggy. "In Petropavlovsk everybody believe in ghosts. No von go out after dark. But Harry, he different. That still not explain vhy he go exploring in the middle of the night."

"But don't you see!" Aunt Bridget was exasperated. "That's exactly it. Harry's not like we were. He's a modern boy: he asks questions, he watches TV, he studies science. He knows about computers! You all go rabbiting on about this fantastic beast, this ghost in the garden. What do you expect him to do – hide under the bedclothes? Of course not, he wants to know what it's all about. He goes exploring. I told you and told you! But no, you wouldn't listen. And there you all are, while he's safely in the kitchen having his supper, helping Angel to rig up that contraption in the trees. Really!"

Munching on a chocolate digestive, Harry turned to look at the man she had called Angel. He was short and fat with wild hair and a wild grey beard. Thick pebble-lensed spectacles made his eyes look enormous. His hands, Harry saw, were streaked with paint and black beneath the nails. He wore a baggy tweed suit and lopsided orange tie. Finding himself observed, the man gave a thick-lipped smile that revealed broken teeth.

"I don't think you've met Angel yet," said Aunt Bridget. "We have many talents in our little community – remarkable talents, I may say – but Angel is our one true genius." She smiled proudly. "Angus McGregor from the Isle of Skye."

"But we call him Mike McAngelo," piped Dot.

"And Vince McGoch."

"Or Mr Pic."

"They're our little jokes," explained Aunt Bridget. "He's an artist."

"Ach, haud yer wheesht, the lot o' ye!" cried Angel, who had an unusually high-pitched voice. "Ma ghost, son. Did ye see ma ghost?"

"Yes."

"What d'ye think of it?"

"It's good," Harry said. "Really spooky!"

Angel shrugged. "It's all right – especially when ye think they gave me only two hours to make the whole thing!" He glared round the room.

"Those are some of Angel's pictures on the stairs," said Aunt Bridget soothingly. "And on the walls here."

Harry looked round the gorgeous oil paintings. One of a vase of sunflowers and another of a little bridge over a lake of water-lilies he thought he recognized.

"Beautiful, aren't they," said his aunt.

"And they ask me to paint monsters that light up in the dark – like some ghost-train in a fairground," said Angel crossly. "They forget I have a reputation to keep up!" His eyes fell on the plate of biscuits at Harry's side and he brightened. "D' ye think I could maybe have one o' your custard creams? I'm very partial to a custard cream – or a lemon puff."

"Of course." Harry passed the plate across.

"Thank ye kindly." The black nails scraped all the biscuits into his lap. Then, thinking this might appear rather greedy, he replaced a broken rich-tea and passed the plate back.

Harry was astonished.

"Oh, you pig, Angel!" Aunt Bridget laughed. "It's all right, Harry, we'll get you some more."

"I'll do it!" said Dot eagerly. Jumping to her feet, the old lady tucked her skirt into her knickers and did a couple of hand-springs. Then walking on her hands she picked up the biscuit plate in her feet, made her way to the door, opened it and disappeared down the hall.

"Such energy!" said Aunt Bridget. "And after you have eaten them and finished your drink, Harry – bed. I know you have a thousand questions, I know you think you've landed in the middle of a nest of robbers, but it's too late to go into all that now. I promise we'll explain everything tomorrow. So no setting your alarm clock for three and running off in the middle of the night." She smiled approvingly. "We're finding out a lot about you, Harry Barton. You've got guts and you're resourceful. Pretending to be asleep when I went upstairs! You had it all planned out, didn't you. So I want your promise: no vanishing act, all right? When Goody goes up to call you in the morning, you're still in bed."

Harry mumbled.

"Promise!"

"I promise."

"While we're waiting for Dot," Auntie Florrie mixed herself another Bosun-Blinder, "why don't we tell him a bit about ourselves? Take the edge off his curiosity."

"Ja, good idea."

"Sooner the better," said Fingers. "Kid keeps lookin' at me as if I'm flippin' Jack the Ripper."

"Well, who shall we start with?" Aunt Bridget looked around the room. "Angel – you know something about him already. What do you think *he* does for a living?"

"He's a crook!" Harry said bluntly.

"Oh, my dear Harry!" Aunt Bridget kissed the top of his head. "It is lovely to have you here. So refreshing! Yes, of course he's a crook – and a dustbin for sweeties and cakes – but what sort of crook?"

Harry hesitated. "Is he a forger?"

"Right in one!" Aunt Bridget gestured towards the sun-flowers and water-lilies. "I saw you looking at our Van Gogh and Monet. And that one over there's a Constable, and that's a Cézanne. And if you go into the hall you'll find Rembrandt and Turner and Picasso. All quite quite beautiful, all by Angel and absolutely indistinguishable from the real thing."

Harry gazed about the walls. "But can't the experts tell? I mean, if a painting's old?"

"Aye, ye hit the nail on the head, laddie." Angel popped up in a storm of biscuit crumbs. "But ye see, I'm more expert than the experts. I use the old pigments and linseed and varnish, an' bake them in a wee oven that Nutty made for me. Naebody can tell the difference."

"You'll find his work in galleries all round the world," said Aunt Bridget. "Of course, they don't know they're by Angel, they think they're by Toulouse-Lautrec and David Hockney and all these people we've been talking about. They sell for a *lot* of money."

"What if they found out?" said Harry.

"They'd be mad!"

"But they're no' goin' to find out." Angel scratched his whiskers complacently. "I'm the best forger in the world." Greedily his eyes turned to the door. "I wonder what's keepin' that wee wifie wi' the biscuits."

As if on cue the door of the drawing-room swung open and a huge tray appeared, laden with mugs of hot chocolate, a big pot of tea and plates piled high with cake and biscuits. Invisible behind it, staggering under the weight, came the tiny figure of Dot.

"Ah! Delicious! A midnight feast!" Huggy took the tray from her. "No, Angel! Put back the plate! I varn you! Two biscuit, von slice of cake, that your share. Right, now sit down. Sit. Sit! That better. These for the rest of us."

Harry took his chocolate and a thick slice of fruit cake.

"Well, dear." Cup in hand, Auntie Florrie looked round the big room. "Who next? What do you make of Dot?"

"Oh, he knows about me, Florrie. We've already bin climbing together, haven't we, love?"

"Ah yes, the Human Fly. But does he know that you were a cat-burglar – the best in Europe?"

"And the States, love! And the States! Said so at me trial, they did, ever so often. Especially after that job up the Statue of Liberty. Never 'eard of nothing like it, they said. I've shown you me cuttin's."

"Yes, all right, Dot, sorry. *And* the States. Anyway, Harry gets the picture, don't you, dear." Auntie Florrie's eyes moved on. "Who next? Fingers?"

"Prob'ly 'eard ye talkin' about me froo the door." Fingers sucked chocolate from his wispy moustache. "Knows I'm a cracksman a'ready."

"Is that somebody who breaks into safes?" asked Harry.

"Yeah, safes – an' offices, bank vaults, post offices, casinos, bettin' shops, that sort o' fing. Anywhere there's a lock, it's my job to open it."

"And like Dot and Angel," Aunt Bridget looked round the room, "like everyone here, he's the best there is."

"That's right, Harry, dear," said Auntie Florrie. "You probably don't realize it but you're in very distinguished company."

Harry looked at the little safe-breaker. "How d' you do it?" he said.

"Years o' trainin'," said Fingers. "Touch mos'ly, a good set o' tools, an' explosives."

"About vhich the less said the better!" said Huggy pointedly.

"All right, all right! No need keep goin' on about it. 'Ad a couple of accidents, that's all."

"A couple of accidents!" Huggy laughed. "You know what they call him also? Blaster! And H-Bomb! My heavens, the explosions! Vhen he blow open a safe it is like the Third Vorld Var broke out!"

"Say what ye like," said Fingers, "but 'oo dressed up for 'Allowe'en an' did the Bank of England job, eh? 'Oo borrowed the Queen's tiara for 'is daughter when 'e took 'er to the gala ballet? 'Oo nicked the coppers' pay packets from the strong room at Scotland Yard? 'Oo sprung 'is mates out o' Dartmoor when that lying git Judge Priestly put 'em away for ten years? Fingers Peterman, that's 'oo." He turned to Harry. "'Uggy's goin' to show yer a bit o' wrestlin' – that right? Well, when ye got a bit o' spare time on yer 'ands, I'll teach yer a fing or two an' all."

A burglar teaching him to pick locks! Harry was taken aback.

"It's all right, dear." Auntie Florrie smiled. "No harm in knowing a bit of lock-picking. You don't have to start breaking into people's houses."

Harry's attention was divided between listening, eating cake and rolling bits of grit from between his toes. "What do you do, Auntie Florrie?" he said.

"I should have thought you could work that one out for yourself, dear."

Harry furrowed his brow. "Do you drive the getaway car?"

"Of course," she answered cheerily. "We went for a little spin this morning, didn't we?"

"Never heard of Florrie Fox?" said Max. His voice was smooth and educated. "The first woman to win a Formula 1 at Brands Hatch."

"The only woman, dear," said Auntie Florrie placidly. She tapped a cigarette on a case of gold and crimson enamel. "And at Monaco and Le Mans."

"And then she went in for motorbikes and won the Isle of Man TT."

"Yes, I preferred the bikes," said Auntie Florrie. "Being out in the wind, leaning into the corners, accelerating up the straight. A hundred and fifty feels like something on a bike. Still," she lit her cigarette and was clouded in blue smoke, "the doctor said I had to give it up. Never understood why – spoilsport! So now it's only cars. But I've still got an old Norton *Commando* out in the sheds somewhere. Lovely bike.

Better than all these Harleys and Hondas everyone talks about nowadays. It has style! Ask Nutty, he'll show it to you."

"All greased up and ready to go," said the tall handyman.

"Really? After all this time? Oh, Nutty, you are sweet!" She blew him a kiss. "No racing, though. Maybe take Harry a little run through the lanes one day. We'll see." She settled herself comfortably in the big chair and reached for a chocolate.

"Then there's Max." Aunt Bridget sat with a straight back. "The man of a thousand faces."

Harry looked across. Max was a striking figure, slim and flashily handsome. Sleek hair, black as a rook's wing, was brushed straight back from his brow. When he smiled, as now, his teeth were dazzling – with one gold filling. On his upper lip was a thin spiv moustache. He wore an immaculate blue suit with a pin-stripe. A red handkerchief peeped from the breast pocket. On his wrist was a large gold watch and on his fingers were large gold rings.

"A consummate actor," Aunt Bridget continued. "Today you see him as he really is – or rather, as he likes to be seen. Tomorrow – a bishop? an airline pilot? a managing director? a rambling old professor in tweeds?"

"If my memory serves me correctly, Miss Barton," said Max, his voice and expression changed so totally that Harry was startled, "it's a policeman you want next time, isn't it?"

"For the Heathrow job, yes," said Aunt Bridget. "But we'll talk about that later."

"Could have made his fortune on the stage," said Angel, eyes enormous behind his thick spectacles. "What a performer! When I was an art student he was playing at the Old Vic. Wonderful he was – Hamlet and Othello. I made a set of drawings of it. With Sir Laurence Olivier was it, Max?"

"That's right." Max crossed his legs and brushed a fleck of cigarette ash from an elegant knee. "Back in my old theatrical days. One night Larry played Othello and I played Iago, the next night we changed round."

"The most promising actor of his generation, they called him. Then one day he just gave it all up." Angel raked among his whiskers for a lost piece of biscuit. "A terrible waste, Max. A terrible waste!"

"I grew tired of the theatre," came the beautiful voice. "You say I gave it all up. I prefer to say that I took my talents out through the proscenium arch into the real world."

"Ach, you make it sound very fancy and fine, Max," said Huggy. "A con man, that's vhat you are, a con man! Say it out straight."

Max smiled without rancour. "Very vell, my darlink Huggy," he said in a perfect imitation of her voice. "A con man, if that's the vay you are likink to put it. I should myself prefer to say 'an artist of the streets'. But say it how you vill." He gestured with a languid hand. "It is only vords."

Huggy laughed.

"And what about yourself, my cuddly but formidable Russian brown bear?" Max continued in his own voice. "If I am a con man, what are you? Once a lady wrestler, now – ?"

"*The* lady wrestler, if you don't mind!" said Huggy haughtily. "Fingers told Harry all about me this afternoon, down by the lake."

"All right," said Max, "*the* lady wrestler."

"Famous throughout the whole wrestling vorld, I vas," said Huggy.

"I'm sure you were, my adorable *Bonecrusher*, my enchanting *Strangler*, ma chérie *Casse-Noisette*, ma *Bête Humaine*. You see, I know all your professional names. But did Fingers tell our young friend how you became a machine-gun-toting heavy for the Chicago Mob?"

"She never did tote no machine-gun!" said Fingers indignantly.

"Well, whether or not, she *was* a heavy for them, you can't deny that. *And* Black Morrie's Bunch, *and* the Limehouse Gang. She went around with Screaming Mad Sam for a while, as well."

Huggy rose and stood above the slim, moustached Max. Though her face wore a pleasant smile her muscles bulged ominously. "That vas long time ago. Vhen I been in trouble recently? Vhen I go vith you on your jobs to protect you – vhen I hurt anybodies?" She gestured towards the settee. "You ask that boy. I teach him to wrestle, ja? I gentle vith him. Ve have good time."

All eyes followed her arm. On the big settee Harry's hand lay limply on the blanket, still holding a biscuit. His head had fallen to one side. He was sound asleep.

9
Norton and Sapphire

It was gorgeous! Midnight blue with silver trimmings. A Norton *Commando*! 750cc!

Harry hugged the back of Auntie Florrie's studded leather jacket and peered past her shoulder. He wore goggles and a black helmet with a golden wing stencilled above each ear. The wind buffeted his face, the hedgerows rushed past, the powerful engine roared and throbbed beneath him.

"Now, lean!" cried Auntie Florrie.

The great motorcycle heeled over and swept them round the corner.

Auntie Florrie straightened up and changed gear.

RRRAAAHHHH!

With a wonderful surge they accelerated away up the road ahead.

"Over there!" His auntie shouted above the noise of wind and engine.

Harry looked where she pointed. A huge white mansion, surrounded by parkland, stood on the hillside.

"Felon Grange!" she shouted. "Colonel Priestly's place!"

Harry saw the long avenue of beech trees, the magnificent pillars, the white broad-horned cattle in the meadows.

He leaned towards Auntie Florrie's ear. "It's a big place!"

"Yes! And all bought with rotten money!"

A series of S-bends rushed towards them.

"Are you ready? Right – lean! And lean!"

Left and right and left and right they swung in a thrilling series of manoeuvres.

"Great!" Behind the goggles Harry's eyes were shining. "Fantastic!"

Flies hit his cheeks like bullets. Beneath his legs he felt the buck of the road and throb of the engine.

They rode for an hour through woods and hills and farmland, and at eleven o'clock arrived back at Lagg Hall. Gravel scrunched beneath the wheels as Auntie Florrie swung across the forecourt and drew to a halt. With a final VROOM – VROOM she switched off the engine, swung her leg over and flipped down the stand.

"Well, that was fun!" Happily she pulled off her helmet and shook her yellow curls free. Even on that hot summer morning she wore her colourful make-up. "Did you enjoy it, dear?"

Harry struggled with the buckle beneath his ear. An intoxicating smell of hot metal and oil drifted to his nostrils. "Can we go out again this afternoon?"

Auntie Florrie was pleased. "I don't see why not. Let's go to Fairhaven. A breath of sea air. Get Goody to make up a picnic and we'll have it on the cliff-tops." She loosened his chin-strap and tugged off the helmet. "In the meantime how about an ice-cream. I'll get out of these leathers and make us each one of my special whoppers: raspberries, best ice-cream, triple flake, butterscotch topping and roast almonds. Give it a try?"

"Mmm! Please."

"We'll have it on the lawn." She flapped away towards the house.

Harry dropped his jacket on the ground and examined the *Commando* controls. Then, swinging his helmet, he crossed the grass and flopped at the picnic table beneath an ancient chestnut tree. Tangle joined him, panting in the heat, and ten minutes later Auntie Florrie emerged from the French windows. She wore a floral swimming costume and a straw hat. In her hands were two long glasses heaped above the rim.

"This is terrific!" Harry crunched a creamy almond and probed for a raspberry with a spoon a foot long.

"It's my favourite. With a dash of Cointreau. I'm afraid you didn't get any, dear. Goody's such a Puritan about these things." Her eyes wandered across to the shining motorbike. "Fancy Nutty keeping the Norton greased up all these years. Looks good, doesn't she."

Happily they talked about motorbikes and racing. Steadily the ice-cream sank down their glasses.

"You know what we were talking about last night," said Harry, a smear of butterscotch on his cheek. "Well, is *everybody* at Lagg Hall a crook? I mean, there's you driving the getaway car, and Fingers and Dot and Huggy," he counted them on his fingers, "and Max … and Angel…"

"And there's Mr Tolly, dear, he completes our little band. But he's not with us at the moment. Having a bit of a rest."

Harry understood at once. He was startled. "You mean he's…?"

"That's right, dear. Eighteen months. Wormwood Scrubs. Silly man! He's a magician, see, a stage magician. You know – card tricks and vanishing horses, women floating in mid-air, nicking people's braces in front of an audience. Well, if you can do that sort of thing you can nick wallets in the street, can't you?" She sighed. "Been ever so good, he had. Not lifted as much as a Mars Bar for years. Then once, just once, he slipped back to his old ways – just to see if he could, he said – and they had him. Turned out it was one of the Royal Family, see, opening a new building. Well, Mr Tolly didn't know, did he? All he sees is this smart geezer walking towards him and he thinks: hello, I bet you got a bob or two, nice suit like that. So he goes into his routine and the next thing's a hand on his shoulder. Hullo, hullo, hullo! Well, that was it, wasn't it! There's Mr Tolly surrounded by thirty-five million detectives and Prince Whatsisname's wallet right there in his pocket. A bit hard to talk your way out of that sort of thing. And the really sickening part, they never carry any money anyway, do they, the Royals, so there was nothing in it." She scooped up a big blob of ice-cream on a chocolate flake and bit it off. "Still, he's done his stretch and he'll be out in three months – three months and four days. You'll meet him then." She smiled affectionately. "It'll be nice to have him back, silly old sausage."

"Everyone has such funny names," said Harry. "Huggy, Fingers, Angel. Mr Tolly – is that his real name?"

"Oh no, that's his stage name, dear. *Autolycus* – somebody who makes things disappear. Very old that name is – in mythology."

Harry made a note to look it up. "I think I understand about the rest," he said, "except Max. If he keeps changing his voice and what he looks like, does he change his name as well?"

"Oh, yes. A dozen names he's got, a new one for every scam – that means a swindle, dear, a con-job. Rosco Burbage he called himself on the stage – after two very famous old actors, that was. Now he calls himself Maxim Beauguss – or sometimes Maximilian Doppelganger. *Très* snob and fancy I call it. His real name – you'll not believe it – his real name's Fred Smith. Makes me laugh!"

Harry rescued a raspberry that had fallen on the table. "What about Nutty Slack?" he said.

"Well, Nutty's not exactly one of us," said Auntie Florrie. "He comes from Newcastle. Nutty Slack – it's a name up there, I believe. He looks after the garden and the cars, any odd jobs that need doing about the place. I don't know what we'd do without him."

"And Mrs Good," said Harry. "Is she not one of *you* either?"

"Goody? Oh no, she's just the sweetest, kindest person who ever walked the earth," said Auntie Florrie. "And it's her own name too, isn't it funny. She looks after us all. If we didn't have her we'd all just die, I think."

"Not like Gestapo Lil," said Harry. "She was paid loads to look after me and she was horrible. If Ol' Goggly pounced on *her* in the garden he wouldn't stand a chance, she'd eat him alive."

Their ice-creams were finished. Auntie Florrie raked noisily in the bottom of her glass.

Harry licked as far down as his tongue would reach then pushed it away. "That was good," he said.

Auntie Florrie looked at her watch. "An hour till lunch. I'm going to have a deck chair and read the papers." She collected the glasses and rose. "Just look at that."

Harry followed her gaze.

Far across the lawn, where the grass gave way to flowerbeds and woodland, Nutty was crouching on his heels and holding out a hand. A pair of red squirrels, quite unafraid, seized something from his fingers and sat back to pull it apart with busy paws.

"Peanuts," said Auntie Florrie. "He's got such a way with animals. You'd not believe the poor creatures he's found injured and nursed back to health in that shed of his: foxes, badgers, hawks, you name it." She shook her head wonderingly. "It's a gift."

When she had gone and all was quiet, Harry started across the lawn. Even though he moved softly, foot at a time, the squirrels spotted him at once. One gave a little chirrup of alarm and a moment later they bounded back to the safety of the trees.

"Sorry," he called out.

"No worry, son, they'll be back." Nutty stood up. "Fond o' their grub, see." With a horny nail he cracked a shell and threw the peanuts into his mouth. "So yer auntie had ye out on the bike, eh? How d'ye get on?"

They never got to Fairhaven, that day at least, for in the afternoon dark blue clouds shaped like cauliflowers heaped above the woods and it began to rain. Rumbles of thunder rolled about the sky and the leaded windows ran with raindrops.

Harry made his way to the kitchen.

"Hello, love." Mrs Good looked up from the big scrubbed table where she was baking. Pounds of butter and bags of flour and packets of dried fruit stood all around. "Help yourself to some juice or milk, they're in the fridge."

Harry poured a glass of apricot crush and stood watching.

"Pity it's raining – so soon after you've arrived, too. Still, I daresay it won't last long." Mrs Good smiled. "What do you say to a nice hot scone?"

"Mmm. Yes please."

"Do you want to lend a hand?"

"I don't know what to do." He was embarrassed. "Gestapo Lil never let me in the kitchen – except to do the washing up."

"Never let you – !" Mrs Good was shocked. "Well, I can't say anything about that lady, but you're welcome in the kitchen here *any* time."

She gave him a big motherly hug, which Harry quite liked.

"Oh, dear!" She laughed. "Now I've gone and got you all floury. Stand still a minute." With dishcloth and towel she dusted him down. "A bit streaky but it'll come out in the wash."

They moved to the table.

"Let me see your hands."

Harry held them out.

"Tap!" She pushed him towards the sink. "And a good scrub under those nails, you've got half the wood in there."

When he returned, rubbing his hands on his jeans, Mrs Good said, "I've had an idea. Why don't you make the scones – give everyone a surprise? And I'll get on with the evening meal."

Harry stared at her.

"Oh, I'll show you what to do. There's nothing to it. Here – " She pulled forward a mixing bowl.

So while Mrs Good chopped meat and made pastry for a steak pie, scrubbed potatoes and carrots, topped strawberries, and started a cake for Fingers' birthday, Harry made scones. Precisely he weighed out the ingredients – though Mrs Good never seemed to bother – and mixed them with a wooden spoon. The result was a sticky and stickier mess.

Mrs Good laughed. "Another handful of flour – and stop picking at those currants!"

Like magic the mixture turned to a dough. Harry rolled it out and cut out the scones with an ancient beer glass. Carefully he arranged them on two greased trays and put them in the oven.

"Probably turn out like rock cakes!" he said.

"Nonsense, they'll be delicious."

Thunder rumbled above the kitchen garden. Tangle wandered in and snapped up the tag-ends of meat that Harry dangled above his nose. Contentedly he settled on a rug near the door, a favourite spot from where he could keep an eye on all that happened in the passage and hall beyond.

Harry turned the pages of a battered cookery book.

"See if the scones are ready, love."

He opened the oven door. A blast of hot air hit him in the face. The currant scones stood golden-brown like kings.

He was astonished. "I think so."

Mrs Good joined him. "Perfect," she said. "You take them

out. Here, use this cloth. Then turn it down to four and I'll pop in the cake."

Five minutes later Harry and Mrs Good were perched on stools at a corner of the table, tucking into big mugs of tea and hot scones filled with melted butter.

"Hey, these are good!" Harry spoke with his mouth full.

"You made them. Maybe you're going to be a chef." Mrs Good smiled. "Have another."

Harry examined the wire cooling tray and chose one like a lopsided top-hat.

"You know last night," he had been putting off asking, "last night I was in the drawing-room, late?"

"Mm-hmm!" Her eyes twinkled.

"Well, they told me about everybody, what they did and everything. But not Aunt Bridget."

"Because you fell asleep and they shot you off to bed. And you'd like to know now."

"Mm." Harry licked the butter from his knife.

"Well, your Aunt Bridget's behind the whole thing, isn't she," said Mrs Good. "She's the brains. Got a mind like a computer. Plans every job down to the last tiny detail. Never forgets a thing. She used to be a lecturer at Oxford, did you know that?"

Harry shook his head.

"I think she might have been a professor. Very high up, anyway." Mrs Good gathered some crumbs and popped them between her lips. "National bridge champion she is now. Oh yes, ever so clever. Well, you just have to look at her to see that."

"But if she was a professor, how did she come to meet all the others? I mean, Dot's a cat-burglar, Fingers is a safe-breaker, Max is a con-man. Was it through Auntie Florrie? She used to drive a getaway car – she still does, she's got one in the garage. Was it through her?"

"Oh no, love. You've got it the wrong way round. It was your

Aunt Bridget was the naughty one. So clever she was, wanted to pit her wits against the detectives. Formed her own little gang in Oxford, all women. *Sapphire,* they called themselves – the *Sapphire Lady Adventurers*. So of course it was handy for Bridget, having her sister the top woman driver in Europe. Very successful they were too. So daring! Got headlines in all the papers – and never anything nasty. Ever so popular they were, made everybody laugh. But in the end they got caught, of course. One trick too many. So they all ended up in Holloway – that's the ladies' prison in London. They were naughty, I know that, but everyone was so sad."

"I like the name," said Harry. "Sapphire."

"Well, there was a reason for that," said Mrs Good. "There were seven of them, see, from all different backgrounds. One girl was a nurse, another was a sweeper-up in a factory, there was a primary school teacher, and a vicar's wife … I can't remember the rest. But by chance they all had one thing in common – as well as being daring and ever so nice. They all had blue eyes, like yourself. So they called themselves Sapphire – the Sapphire Seven."

Harry was eyeing the tray of scones.

"Go on." She pushed them towards him. "Your young appetite! But that's the last, else you'll have no room for your dinner."

"So Aunt Bridget and Auntie Florrie were both in prison?" He dug into the butter.

"Wasn't it *crooks* you called everybody last night?" Mrs Good laughed. "Yes, they were. They'd been naughty and they paid the price."

"It must have been horrid."

"But your Aunt Bridget and Auntie Florrie are very special people," said Mrs Good. "You must realize that already. Your Auntie Florrie organized classes in driving and car maintenance so the women could get jobs as taxi-drivers and van-delivery girls when they got out. And your Aunt Bridget started a school. Never had a chance most of the inmates, poor souls. Put them through all their exams, she did, so they could get jobs as secretaries and office girls when they'd done their stretch. The prison governor said they both should have got the O.B.E. when they got out – for all the good work they did."

Harry was impressed.

"But your Aunt Bridget was the one." Mrs Good laughed. "Have you heard of *Mastermind?*"

"On the TV? The quiz programme?"

"That's it. Well, because of all the work she was doing, the governor let her go to the BBC for trials. Nobody from the nick could have any chance, they thought. Well, didn't she go and win the title outright that year! Mastermind, with everyone shaking her by the hand, and the guards going wild in the audience, and millions of people watching. So exciting it was! Then there was a banquet, with Bridget guest of honour. Then they put the handcuffs back on, loaded her into a Black Maria and took her back to her cell."

Harry was thrilled. His aunt a Mastermind! "What subject did she choose?"

"For the final it was *The Lives and Times of Great British Criminals*. She had a nerve!" Mrs Good laughed again. "And before that it was *Prison Reform* and something like *The Mathematics of Philosophy* – I couldn't understand a word of it." She pointed through the house. "The winner gets a lovely crystal bowl. You'll find it hidden in that corner cupboard in the drawing-room. She doesn't like it on display, thinks it looks showy."

Harry had finished his scone. Elbows on the table, he patted his bristly hair with a palm. "How long were they in for?"

"Well, the *judge* gave them fifteen years! Can you imagine!

Fifteen years! And a recommendation that they should serve every one of them. There was a national outcry. The appeal court cut it down to eight. So with good behaviour they were out after five."

"That was a difference – fifteen years and five!" said Harry. "When you said *the judge* like that, did you mean...?"

"You're quick on the uptake, aren't you. That's right, love, Colonel Priestly. *Beastly* Priestly!" Mrs Good's good-natured face took on a frown. "A right nasty piece of work that man. The things I've heard about him – ! So unfair! And he's bent as a fourpenny piece himself. I tell you, if I had him here for ten minutes I'd not half give him a piece of my mind. I'd like to – Mm!"

The kindly housekeeper took a mouthful of tea to calm herself down.

"Everybody seems to hate him," said Harry. "What else has he done?"

"Don't let me start! Your aunties can tell you all that." She rubbed a rosy cheek with her fingertips. "Where was I? Oh, yes. Well, it was while they were there, in Holloway, that your Aunt Bridget had the idea for this place."

"Lagg Hall?"

"That's right, Lagg Hall. Well, you know what an old lag is, don't you?"

"Is it something to do with water pipes?"

"No, no. That's lagging, love. No, an old lag is a convict, a jailbird, someone who's done time, lived at Her Majesty's expense. That's why they renamed this place Lagg Hall, because they're all old lags."

"What, all of them? *All* jailbirds?"

"Except Nutty and me, yes."

Harry thought about this. "What was it called before?"

"The house? If you look at the old maps you'll see it called *The Hermitage*. That's what drew your Aunt Bridget's attention to it. A nice hideaway for them all to live and be safe when they got out."

"Sapphire?"

"Well, some of them but others too. Fingers and Angel aren't very ladylike, are they?"

Harry smiled. "So was that the idea? A sort of retirement home for prisoners?"

"Not exactly, love. And who said anything about retirement? You heard them last night, didn't you? No, all those that were interested in the *Big Idea* had a bit of money stashed away somewhere – under floorboards, buried in forests, plastered up in walls, sunk in lakes, that sort of thing – and they clubbed together and bought this place. It was all very run down. Seeing it now you can't imagine: wallpaper hanging off, windows boarded up, crows' nests in the chimneys, ivy everywhere, trees growing right up to the front door. A lot of work it was."

Harry gazed around the comfortable kitchen and thought of the beautiful hall and drawing-room along the passage. Beyond the window bright flower-beds and rows of vegetables drank in the summer rain.

"But what was Aunt Bridget's great idea?"

"Let me tell you." A voice at the door made Harry jump out of his skin.

10
The Merry Outlaws

Aunt Bridget stood in the doorway. Lightning flickered at the window and was reflected in her granny glasses.

"Mmm! Scones!" said this Oxford lecturer, head of Sapphire, jailbird and Mastermind. She licked her lips with a pink tongue. "Can I have one, Goody?"

Without waiting for an answer, she pulled a stool to the floury table and reached for the knife and butter.

"Gorgeous!" She took a bite and closed her eyes. "I adore scones."

"It seems to run in the family," Mrs Good said drily and looked at Harry. "Go on, then. You might as well have another one. But don't you dare say you haven't got room for your dinner!"

Harry stretched out a hand and burped.

Aunt Bridget smiled. "Well, young man. Closer and closer to the heart of our little secret. You don't waste any time, do you?" Her clever blue eyes wrinkled but she was serious. "You're resourceful, you have imagination, I like that. But before I tell you *what* we're all doing here at Lagg Hall, the last piece of the jigsaw, I want you to understand one thing. It must be a secret! All of it! Something that ... mad vampires and Chinese torturers couldn't drag out of you. Or much more dangerous than that – friends! You must *never* blab. One word in the wrong place and we're finished here. *Kaput! Finito! Ausgespielt!* The end of Lagg Hall!" The bright spectacles regarded him. "Can you keep a secret like that?"

"I think so."

"*Think* isn't good enough."

"Actually I know I can," Harry said. "I've had practice all my life – with Gestapo Lil."

"Of course, I should have thought of that. Broken rules – it must have been the only way to survive." Aunt Bridget patted his hand and took another bite of scone. "Scrumptious! Really delicious, Goody."

"I'll let you into a little secret," said Mrs Good. "Harry made them."

"What! Never! I don't believe you!"

"I did!" Harry grinned delightedly.

"Right from the flour bag and jug of milk," said Mrs Good.

"Is there no end to my nephew's talents: tree-climber, swimmer, ghost-buster extraordinary?" She sucked buttery fingers. "Incidentally, since you mention her. We had a letter from that lady this morning – your favourite nurse and house-keeper."

"Gestapo Lil?"

"Mm."

"What did she say?"

"Well, more or less what you led us to expect. How she's looked after you all these years; how she gave up a good career for it; what a difficult child you've been; all the promises your father made – according to her; how shattered she's been by their tragic deaths. And what is she going to do now, houses being the price they are?" She shrugged. "Basically she just wants money."

"Oh, the cheeky besom!" Mrs Good pursed her lips.

"How much?"

"Well, she didn't name a precise figure, but reading between the lines – ten to fifteen thousand, maybe twenty?"

"Twenty thousand pounds!" Harry's voice was a shout. "You're not going to give her anything?"

"Of course not." Aunt Bridget smiled. "What do you think! I have replied, though. Nutty posted it this morning."

"What did you say?"

"Oh, I'll leave that to your imagination. But I think it's a fair bet we won't be hearing from Miss Lavinia McScrew any more."

"I wouldn't count on it. You don't know what she's like."

"Well, we'll cross that bridge when we come to it. No need for you to worry, anyway. She's gone out of your life. You don't live in Hampstead any more, you live at Lagg Hall. You've got Goody and Tangle and all the rest of us on your side now. Isn't that right, Goody?"

"It certainly is!" Mrs Good topped up their teacups. "If that woman came through the door this minute – well, I don't know what I'd do. But she wouldn't forget it in a hurry, I can tell you that!"

"Well said! And that goes for the rest of us too." Aunt Bridget turned to Harry. "But what were we talking about? Ah, yes – our little band of soldiers. Did Goody tell you about Sapphire?"

"Yes."

"Happy days! Well, in Sapphire we had a little set of rules. Number one was daring and adventure. Number two was that we wouldn't hurt anybody nice. And number three was that we wouldn't rob anyone who couldn't afford it."

Harry twisted his legs comfortably round the stool and settled his chin in his hands.

"Well, when we were in Holloway Prison," Aunt Bridget continued, "I had plenty of time to think – weeks and months and years. And it came to me that all over the country there are people – and organizations – who have more money than they know what to do with. Rich people, really rich, filthy rich – millions and billions some of them. And all over the country, all over the *world*, there are poor people – nice families, children, pensioners, charities, down-and-outs – who desperately need money. Starving, some of them, homeless, sick – and all for the want of a few pounds. It seemed unfair, very unfair! Something should be done about it.

"Then one night, in a blinding flash, it came to me. Like a vision. All at once I realized that people like us, criminals in jail, had the skills to do something about it. Instead of stealing for ourselves we could steal to help others! Take some of the money from the rich and give it to the poor!

"I was so startled I jumped right out of bed. It was three o'clock in the morning. Beyond the bars on my cell window I could see all the sleeping roofs of London. I'll never forget it."

Like some great bird, Aunt Bridget perched on the edge of her stool.

"Listen: if you want to build a house, what do you need? You need tradesmen, don't you – bricklayers, plumbers, joiners and so on. They make a team. It's the same for any operation – running a school, making a film, winning a war. You need a *team*. And if you want to take money from lots of people it's exactly the same – teamwork! A team of specialists!

"And it came to me that right there in Holloway we had all the specialists, all the skills we needed – every kind of criminal known to man. But that wasn't enough. For the scheme I had in mind I wanted the best. And maybe the best were men. They wouldn't be in Holloway, that's a women's prison, they'd be in Strangeways or Barlinnie or Wormwood Scrubs. Maybe they weren't in prison at all.

"Anyway, I began asking and very slowly, one at a time, the people I was looking for began to pop out of the woodwork.

People who liked the sound of the *Great Idea*. People who took a pride in their work. People who wanted a chance to do something for somebody else for a change, something generous and kind.

"Also I was looking for people of a certain age. Florrie and I weren't as young as we used to be and I had decided to use a retirement home as a cover.

"So, what skills did we need? I made a list." Aunt Bridget counted them off on her fingers.

"First we needed a *planner*, someone to run the whole operation: that would be me.

"A *getaway driver*: Florrie would be with me, of course, and she's the best in the business.

"A *safecracker*, someone to pick locks: Fingers Peterman.

"A *cat-burglar*: Dottie Skylark.

"A *con-man*, an actor who could play parts: Maxim Beauguss.

"A *forger* for documents and signatures: Angus McGregor's in a class of his own.

"A *pickpocket*, to get information and switch things around: dear Autolycus.

"And finally, in case the going got rough, some *muscle*: Huggy Bear.

"And that's our team. Eight specialists, all top of the tree, all dedicated to the perfection of their art. A little community of friends who want to make the world a fairer, happier place. A houseful of antique jailbirds who like to have a bit of fun."

Absently Aunt Bridget licked the tip of a finger and picked some crumbs from the table. "I'm not saying that one or two of us might not be a bit naughty from time to time – like poor Mr Tolly. After all, we're only human."

"Does anybody know you're here," said Harry, "I mean apart from Colonel Priestly? Lagg Hall's so hidden away. You can't see it from anywhere, not for miles."

"Well, one or two people – the postman and tradesmen – but as far as possible it's our little hideaway. They all think it's a retirement home. They see the ancient car, have a cheery word with the old folk, deliver the pension books. But nobody, absolutely nobody, knows who we are and what we do. Nobody knows our secret."

"They'll never find out from me." Harry spat on a forefinger and drew it across his throat.

"Promise promise hope to die,

Chop me up and make a pie."

Aunt Bridget cuffed him affectionately across the side of the head. She rose. "It's stopped raining."

The clouds were opening. Sunlight lit the flowers and vegetable garden, glinting on raindrops.

"Aunt Bridget," Harry said. "You know in Oxford you had a name for your group, the Sapphire…"

"Lady Adventurers," she completed. "Yes?"

"Well, have you got a name like that here?"

"Now we're at Lagg Hall?" Aunt Bridget rinsed her fingers at the sink. "We haven't, actually. We never got round to it somehow."

"It's like Robin Hood, really, isn't it," said Harry. "Robbing the rich to give to the poor."

"Exactly!" Aunt Bridget was delighted. "Just like Robin of Sherwood. But they were all young, weren't they. We're old enough to be their grannies and grandads."

"Not really," Harry said politely.

"Of course we are." As she dried her hands Aunt Bridget examined herself in the kitchen mirror. "A load of old fogies. Should be in a museum along with the fossils and the dodos. Crumblies, isn't that the modern slang? Crumblies and wrinklies?"

"But the people here aren't like that. They don't seem old at all."

"That's nice to hear," she said. "I wonder why? Anyway, can you see any other similarities between Robin Hood and the people here?"

"They were a band of brothers," said Harry. "That's like here."

"Good."

"And they were called Robin Hood and his Merry Men, so they were all happy and having adventures – and doing good."

"We try our best. Any more?"

"They lived in Sherwood Forest," Harry said after a little thought. "They hid away among the trees and Lagg Hall's surrounded by woods."

"Excellent," said his aunt. "And the Sheriff was after them as well – but we won't talk about that." She rescued a butterfly that had blundered through the open window. "And you were asking about a name. Any suggestions?"

"You could call yourselves … *The New Robin Hoods*."

"Not very original."

"The Forest Gang." Harry thought hard. "*Greenwood Eight*."

"That's better. I like that. But these are all Robin Hood ideas. How about something totally different, something that's just us. Like," Aunt Bridget gave a little smile, "*The Wrinklies of Lagg Hall*."

Harry giggled.

"What nonsense, Bridget. The Wrinklies of –" Mrs Good tutted.

"Why? Harry likes it. Don't you think it's got a certain style?"

"I do not."

"You couldn't say Lagg Hall," Harry said, "it would give the game away."

"Just *The Wrinklies* then."

"Hmph!" said Mrs Good.

"It's accurate."

"It's ridiculous, and well you know it!"

"I think it's a hoot." Aunt Bridget laughed. "We could get Angel to design a logo. Leave one every time we do a job."

"You and your imagination! Now stop it, Bridget!"

"It's not really accurate," Harry said.

"In what way?"

"Because there's me now."

"How do you mean?"

"Well, I'm not old, am I? It would have to be *The Wrinklies and Harry.*"

"You? My dear Harry, you don't think you're going to join us in our little escapades, do you?"

He nodded.

"Good gracious!"

"Why not?"

"Why not? Because you're eleven years old, that's why not. Because we care for you. Because it's dangerous, that's why not."

"But Aunt Bridget, I can –"

"I'm sure you can, Harry, you're a capable boy. But there's no discussion about it. You're not coming, ever, and that's final."

"The idea!" said Mrs Good.

11
Raspberry Cart

The fine weather continued. Every evening, high in his stone tower, as Harry lay in bed reading and listening to the sounds of the night, his shoulders tingled from the beating of the sun.

Every morning he woke to blue skies and the twittering of swallows. Day-long the parents swooped back and forth above his window, beaks full of squashy insects to feed their hungry chicks. Briefly he leaned across the broad sill and pushed the window wide, then jumped from bed, tugged on jeans and T-shirt, ignored the washbasin in his little bathroom on the landing, and ran downstairs with Tangle scampering at his heels.

After breakfast his first job was to visit Chalky with a bucketful of cabbage leaves, overgrown lettuces and crusts from the kitchen. Chalky was the white pony Harry could see from his window. He lived in a paddock in the woods a short distance from the house. Overhanging hedges gave shelter from the sun, a trough sparkled with clean water, the door of a stable spread with fresh straw stood permanently open. Chalky was not lonely for a good-natured grey donkey called Socrates kept him company. Day and night all the creatures of the wood paid visits to their green enclosure.

"A cabbage leaf for you," Harry patted Chalky's strong neck. "And a cabbage leaf for you," he pushed the mane from Socrates' dark eyes. "Half a crust for you ... and half a crust for you."

The big animals looked for him coming and cantered across the paddock when they heard his tuneless singing and spotted his red T-shirt among the leaves.

Sometimes Harry climbed on to Chalky's broad back, gripping it tight between his legs and clinging to the mane as Chalky walked and galloped briefly around the enclosure.

A few times he rode Socrates too.

Then Harry called Tangle and they rambled on through the woods or returned to help Nutty about the grounds.

By the time he had been at Lagg Hall for a fortnight it was hard to believe Harry was the same boy his aunts had met off the train, the boy who had spent his life in the grey streets and respectable suburbs of London. His arms and legs were gypsy-brown from long days in the open air. His hair was bleached several shades lighter. Mostly his back was bare and he wore either the ragged jeans or ancient shorts that would scarcely meet round his waist. His days were so full and happy that there was no time to think of the old days in Hampstead with Gestapo Lil.

One afternoon was to change all that.

"Aunt Bridget, I've been thinking," Harry said as they sat at lunch one Thursday. "You know how we have so many raspberries – more than we can eat, Mrs Good says."

"Yes." His aunt sipped grape-juice and spread a corner of toast with pâté.

"And lettuces and cucumbers."

"I really don't know, but if Goody says so."

"Well could I pick some and arrange them on that cart in the shed? Nutty says he'll help me to hitch up Chalky and I can sell them down on the road. To passing motorists."

Aunt Bridget thought. "No. It's too public. Parked down there at the end of the drive – people will want to know where they come from. Sorry."

Harry was crestfallen.

"It don't 'ave to be right at the end o' the drive." Fingers took Harry's side. "'E could take 'em a mile down the road. Set up in that lay-by under the trees."

"I just don't think it's a good idea," said Aunt Bridget.

"Garn, don't be an ol' spoilsport! Ye can see the kid's got 'is 'eart set on it. What 'arm can it do? 'S long as he don't stick up a notice sayin' *Lagg 'All Farm.* I thought you was all in favour of a bit of enterprise. Earn 'is sel' a few quid pocket-money."

"I don't know." Aunt Bridget shook her head. "What do the rest of you think?"

The vote was in Harry's favour.

His aunt gave in gracefully. "All right, on condition you make a good job of it. There's a lot of work, you know. You'll have to scrub the cart and pick the fruit and arrange it nicely, and give Chalky a good brush down."

"I'll do it," Harry said eagerly.

"You look the part, anyway," Aunt Bridget said drily. "Just like a tinker boy except your hair's the wrong colour." She looked him over. "We'll really have to take you into town one day to get some new clothes."

"These are fine," said Harry who liked his old T-shirt and jeans.

"Maybe so, but one day those shorts are going to go POP and give us all a fright."

The table laughed. Harry blushed.

"Ach, do not tease the boy," said Huggy. "You embarrass him. Look."

Aunt Bridget ruffled Harry's hair. "Away you go if you've finished your lunch. Better make a start on that old cart. When you've got it all ship-shape and loaded up with Chalky in the shafts, we'll take a picture of you."

For two days Harry laboured. Rivers of foam flowed from the cart shed. Chalky had never had such a delightful scratching of comb and brush in his life: sackfuls of white hair floated on the wind. At seven o'clock in the morning Harry tumbled out of bed, and at ten in the evening he tumbled back into it. On Friday night, when he took a bath after hours of raspberry picking, the water turned pink.

And then it was Saturday morning. In freshly washed denims and T-shirt and wearing a battered straw hat, he sat on the front of the cart holding the reins. Before him Chalky was resplendent, white as his name. He too wore a straw hat, and bunches of flowers tied to the polished harness. Tangle also, much to his disgust, had been washed and brushed and stood by the shafts with a nosegay tied to his collar.

At Harry's back the cart was laden with raspberries and strawberries, blackcurrants, vegetables and bright flowers from Nutty's garden. Paper bags lay beneath a tin of loose change. Polished brass scales winked in the sunshine.

His friends stood admiring.

"Look this way a minute, laddie." Angel drew lightning lines on a board pressed to his stomach.

"You vork hard," said Huggy. "Your cart look better even than the summer fairs in old Vladivostok."

Dot climbed up the spokes of the big cartwheel to get a better look.

Harry noticed that her hands were unusually red – almost burned-looking. So was her face, right to the roots of her hair. Fingers and Huggy were the same. Perhaps they had sat too long in the sun.

"Smile!" Auntie Florrie pressed a camera to her bright blue eye. "One – two – three –" Click!

"Good luck," said Mrs Good. "You've got your flask and sandwiches now?"

"And we'll look for you at tea-time." Aunt Bridget too was flushed, her forehead was aflame. "Your cart looks wonderful."

"Bye!" Harry flicked the reins and Chalky started forward. Scrunch, scrunch, scrunch, his hooves went on the gravel: pad, pad, pad, on the packed earth of the drive. The harness jingled. The little bell that swung beneath the cart tinkled merrily.

His adventure had begun.

A broad grassy verge separated the lay-by from the road. On the other side of the lay-by, hedges overhung a drystone wall. Half-way along, where Harry planned to set up his stall, a clump of giant beeches spread green shade. It would protect his fruit and flowers from the heat of the sun.

He pulled lightly on the reins. "Whoa, Chalky, whoa."

As the good-natured horse came to a halt, Harry tugged the long lever which operated the wheel brake. Then he jumped to the ground and swung down the props which would hold the cart level.

"Good boy!" He rubbed Chalky's soft muzzle and gave him a handful of breakfast cereal. Then he slipped a long halter over his head, tied it to a branch and turned the horse loose to graze. At once Chalky started to munch the succulent leaves that grew all around. His white tail swished at a few late-morning flies.

"Come here, Tangle." With a length of cord Harry tied him to a cartwheel. Tangle was disgusted but cheered up as his master produced a large hambone with meat attached. Lying belly-flat beneath the cart he held the bone with shaggy paws and began a toothy examination.

From the back of the cart Harry pulled two freshly-painted

placards and ran to set them up at the roadside. They read, in every bright colour he could find in Angel's studio:

HOME FARM PRODUSE
STRAWBERRIES
RASBERRIES
BLACKCURRENTS
VEGTABLES
COUNTRY-FRESH
CHOOSE YOUR OWN

He returned to the cart. Nervously he wondered if anybody would stop.

For fifteen minutes the only passers-by were a curious tractor-driver, two lorries and an escaped cow which wandered across the grass. If Harry had not chased it away it would have made short work of his display.

He began to feel disheartened and pulled out an egg-and-tomato sandwich to keep up his spirits.

It was a pretty part of the country, however, and in the summer there were many tourists.

A large silver car slid by. Faces peered from the open windows. At the far end of the lay-by it stopped. Harry watched hopefully. The car drove on. He felt a lurch of disappointment. The car stopped again. It reversed – and the next moment turned down the lay-by towards him.

Five people jumped out. Immediately a girl with long hair, a year or two older than Harry, crossed to Chalky and began making a fuss of him. A young boy crouched to talk to Tangle. The rest gathered beside his cart.

"Ooh, what lovely rasps!" exclaimed a fat woman in a print dress, the mother of the family. "An' so reasonable! An' look at them delphiniums – look at that blue! Gran would love a bunch o' them. From round 'ere, are you, love?"

"Yes." Harry lied without turning a hair. He pointed away from Lagg Hall. "My dad's got a farm over there."

"Well, good for you, settin' up a nice stall like this at the road-side. I'll 'ave a couple o' punnets o' the rasps, a pound o' goosegogs, two lettuces – them two there – an' a bunch o' the delph's. 'Ow much is that, love?" She turned to her husband. "'Ere, Norman, give us a bit o' cash, me bag's in the car."

Carefully – for nobody at Lagg Hall possessed a calculator – Harry wrote down the figures in pencil and added them up.

"There y' are, dear."

He put the money in his battered tin and gave the woman her change.

"Thank you, love. You made a real nice job of it." She examined the money in her palm and extracted a fifty-pence piece. "'Ere, buy yerself an ice-cream wi' that. An' good luck wi' the sales."

Clutching their purchases they turned away.

"Come on, our Sylvia. Leave that 'orse alone."

The family piled back into the car and drove away. Hands fluttered at the windows, the horn toot-tooted, the noise of the engine faded into the distance.

Harry was delighted. Opening the tin he surveyed his profit, rattled the coins, tilted it this way and that.

Chalky looked round curiously.

"Did you see that!" Harry shook the tin towards him. "Nearly three quid *and* a tip."

Chalky lowered his head and resumed munching.

So did Tangle.

Harry pulled out another sandwich.

The excitement soon faded because he had nearly an hour to wait for the second sale – it was lunchtime – but after that the cars stopped more frequently. At one stage three different groups clustered round his cart, all at the same time.

As the cart grew lighter, his cash tin grew heavier.

By half past two his stock of flowers, fruit and vegetables had more than half gone.

Harry was leading Chalky to a new patch of hedgerow when he heard a powerful engine in the distance. The car was travelling fast. He stared up the road. Far beyond the bend a yellow streak, bright as butter and sunflowers, came flashing past the trees.

"Oh, no!" he breathed.

The huge yellow car screamed round the bend and came hurtling down the straight towards him. Holding Chalky's rope in his hand, Harry stood frozen.

The Rolls-Royce passed his advertisement. The engine howled. It was level with him. The driver stamped on his brakes. With a squeal of tyres on tarmac the car scorched onwards, leaving a trail of rubber a hundred metres long. It came to a halt, white smoke pouring from the bonnet, black smoke pouring from the mudguards; then shot backwards, swung violently, crashed through gears, and accelerated along the lay-by towards him. In a cloud of dust it skidded to a halt.

Chalky was frightened and leaped at the end of his tether. Harry tried to calm him.

"All right, boy! Ssshhh! All right!"

Hastily he tied the rope to a branch and crossed to his cart.

Two figures were in the car but Harry had eyes only for the driver. His face was red, his moustache was ginger. Hot-tempered piggy eyes stared from the window. Quickly they glanced up and down the lay-by and saw that it was empty. His mouth opened in a nasty smile. The yellow door swung open and Colonel Priestly stepped out.

"I think we met before." He had a high nasal voice. "In the woods. You remember?"

The passenger door opened and his companion emerged into the sunshine. It was a woman.

Harry's heart stopped. The blood drained from his face. He clutched the cartwheel for support.

It was Gestapo Lil.

12

The Broken Cucumber

"Well, it didn't take you long to revert to type, did it?"
Gestapo Lil regarded Harry with scorn and distaste, as
if he were some loathsome worm that had crawled out from
beneath a stone. "Look at you: workman's clothes, stained
hands, driving a horse and cart like some urchin from a rag-and-
bone yard. All those years I tried to make something decent of
you – just wasted effort."

She wore a corn-gold safari suit with red accessories – red
earrings, a red silk scarf, red boots to her knees. Her hair, the
same shade as the suit, was immaculately braided and fastened
with a red clasp. With red lips she smiled mockingly. Between
red-nailed fingers she held a long red cigarette holder.

"I told you, Percy, didn't I," she said to Colonel Priestly. "You
can't make a silk purse out of a sow's ear. And this one's a real
little swine."

"Ill-mannered young beast as well." Colonel Priestly wore
tweed trousers with a giant green and orange check, a waistcoat
of the same material crossed by a thick gold chain, and a silk
cravat. His oiled ginger hair and moustache gleamed like metal.
The sunshine winked on his gold tooth and heavy gold rings. "A
real hooligan. Shouting and throwing eggs! I see them in court
every day. They should never have done away with the birch. A

thorough good hiding, that's what he deserves – and I've half a mind to give him one. Might teach him some manners."

"Go on, Percy, why don't you. There's no one about." Gestapo Lil stepped from the side of the Rolls-Royce. "After what he did to you. A few clips round the ears – he deserves it. I should know, I've had a lifetime of the little rat."

Harry's back was against the cart. Apprehensively he looked around and picked up a long cucumber to defend himself.

"Don't think I've forgotten what I said back there in Hampstead," she hissed at him. "Thousands of pounds your family owes me and I'm going to get it, one way or another, you can set your mind on that. I'm not giving up all those years for the pittance your father paid me."

"He paid you loads," Harry muttered under his breath.

"What did you say?" She took a threatening step towards him.

"I said he paid you loads!" Harry shouted. "Whatever you wanted he gave you. Always! And you made me do most of the work, anyway."

"Why, you lying little wretch!"

"It's you that's the liar!" Harry was reckless. "You know I did! And you're a thief as well." Years of frustration came pouring out. "You helped yourself to anything you wanted. After they died – d'you think I didn't notice how things kept disappearing! Those silver candlesticks from the dining-room, and the pictures from the landing, and the ornaments from the display cabinet. And the antiques van at the gate that time you sent me off to the museum. And my mother's jewellery – what she left behind. That's her brooch you're wearing now. You're a common thief! And a bully! And a cheat! And I hate you!"

"Ow! Percy! Did you hear him! The poisonous little reptile!"

Colonel Priestly was regarding her with a smile of admiration.

"Well don't just stand there!" She advanced on Harry. "You've gone too far this time, my boy!"

Desperately Harry looked from one to the other. Colonel Priestly was closing in from the other side.

"Keep back!" He waved the cucumber. "I'll hit you! I will!"

Click, clack, click, clack! Gestapo Lil came on, high heels tapping on the tarmac.

"Don't come any closer!" Harry's back pressed hard against the cart. "I warn you!"

Still she ignored him. Her face was twisted with fury. She pulled up her sleeves and drew back a hand to –

With a great blow Harry struck her across the head with the cucumber. There was a thud and a loud snap as the cucumber broke and went bouncing across the lay-by.

At the same moment Tangle decided that he did not like this woman, especially since she was attacking his master. With a snarl he rushed out from beneath the cart and sank his teeth into the red leather of her ankle.

"Oh! Ow! Help! Get off! Aahhh!" Gestapo Lil staggered backwards. One of her heels broke. The immaculate hair was knocked from its clasp and straggled over her shoulder.

At the sight of the dog Colonel Priestly backed away. He still had memories of Tangle's teeth locked in the seat of his trousers. Hastily he scurried across the lay-by and began tugging at the branches. After a brief but intense struggle he managed to break off a thick stick.

One blow from a club like that would have dashed out Tangle's brains. Harry pulled the string from his collar. Boy and mongrel retreated behind the cart.

Gestapo Lil hobbled after him. "Wait till I get my hands on you!" she screamed.

Colonel Priestly, face scarlet and brandishing the crooked stick above his head, ran the other way to intercept him.

"Go on, Percy! Clout him! Let him have it!"

Clonk! Thud! The colonel's blows missed Harry and hit the side of the cart.

"Tangle! Quick!" Harry darted out of reach.

For twenty metres Gestapo Lil and Colonel Priestly pursued him. Her hair trailed more wildly. The Colonel stumbled and fell, rolling on the tarmac like a ginger pig. Harry was much too fast for them to catch him.

But his precious cart! His fruit and vegetables! The money!

Beyond their backs he saw his cash tin sitting on the end of the cart.

Gestapo Lil saw the direction of his gaze and turned to look. She saw the fruit, she spotted the cash tin. Her fury turned to a smile of triumph.

Harry sprang forward like an Olympic sprinter. He had never run so fast, his feet scarcely touched the ground. Like a rugby player he dodged the clutching fingers of Colonel Priestly.

But Gestapo Lil had a long start. She was running also, hobbling on her broken heel, hair flapping, hands outstretched like talons. It seemed she was bound to get there first – then her red boot skidded in a pile of Chalky's manure. "Uggghhh!" For a second she faltered. It was enough. Harry flew past. His chest crashed into the cart. With both hands he grabbed the precious tin.

Instantly Gestapo Lil was upon him. Her red nails caught the back of his T-shirt. Harry struggled wildly and broke free. Momentarily he stumbled then was on his feet again and running, his T-shirt torn open, the rattling money tin clutched to his chest.

"Aaahhh! Damn you, you weasel! You guttersnipe! Gypsy brat!" Furiously she smashed her fist into a punnet of fat raspberries. Scarlet juice and seeds erupted like a fountain. She struck another, and another. A few boxes of blackcurrants remained. The explosions turned black. Her face and safari suit looked as though she had caught a virulent form of chicken pox or the black death.

Colonel Priestly joined her at the cart. His stick smashed beans and marrows, roses and sweet-peas. Using it as a rake, he swept everything to the ground. Like people on pogo sticks or children having a temper-tantrum, they jumped up and down upon it.

Harry and Tangle watched with astonishment. Chalky, who lived a gentle life at Lagg Hall, was frightened by the violence. Tugging his halter loose, he cantered to the end of the lay-by.

To finish their work of destruction, Colonel Priestly put his shoulder beneath the cart. Gestapo Lil grasped it with manicured hands. Together they heaved. With a great crash it toppled over. Spokes turning slowly, Harry's cart lay amid the ruin of his vegetables.

"I'll tell on you!" he shouted. "I'll tell Aunt Bridget and everybody. They'll have the police on you!"

"That's likely, I don't think!" came the Colonel's high voice. "Bridget Barton! Florrie Fox! Fingers Peterman! A load of old cons like that. I've put half of them away myself. Go to the police! Do you think the fuzz would take the word of a bunch like that against *me* – a high court judge, magistrate, chairman of the school board, a big landowner?"

"Besides, we weren't here, were we, Percy?" Gestapo Lil's cigarette holder lay among the squashed fruit. She rescued it, dripping with seeds. "It must have been that gang of bikers we saw – or that painted van full of travellers."

"That's right." The Colonel nodded.

"We did drive past your vegetable stall," she said.

"Thought it looked very nice."

"Lovely, all that fruit and flowers."

"Didn't stop, though."

"No."

"But there were no bikers," Harry said.

"Ah, but who's to know that?" Colonel Priestly took Gestapo Lil's hand affectionately. "We *saw* them, didn't we, Lavvy-Poo."

"That's right, Percipops." She smiled simperingly. "Such rough people. Not to be trusted at all."

They laughed and craned necks to exchange a kiss.

Harry thought he was going to be sick. "I'll tell, anyway!" he shouted as they turned back to the Rolls. "I'll get my own back on you! You see if I don't!"

Colonel Priestly opened the driver's door. "I warned you about keeping bad company. You might find we've got a few surprises in store for you."

"Bye-bye, tinker-boy." Gestapo Lil waved. "See you again soon."

The engine sprang into life. The jazzy Rolls-Royce set off along the lay-by.

Harry looked round for a missile. All he could see was squashed fruit. Scooping up a handful of raspberries he sprinted after the car and flung it at the rear window. Splat! Rivers of juice ran down the yellow paintwork.

Tootle-tootle! The mocking horn shattered the afternoon.

"Rotten pigs!" Harry shouted.

The car turned away down the road. The sound of the engine faded into silence.

13
Locks, Thieves and Newspapers

A few days after his adventure with the raspberry cart, Harry was lounging in the drawing-room. Brown legs and bare feet dangled over the edge of a giant settee. He wore a new red T-shirt with a swooping eagle on the chest and khaki shorts with a Swiss army knife hanging from the belt.

The previous evening there had been a ceremonial bonfire of all the clothes that came with him from Hampstead – all except the ragged jeans which he liked too much to part with. Now he had new clothes – denims, trainers, tracksuit, anorak – all of his own choosing.

All except the grey trousers, navy jersey and striped tie for school, which day by day drew closer.

In Harry's lap, that sunny afternoon, lay a large lock which had been given to him by Fingers. Using only a thin probe of steel, he was endeavouring to unlock and re-lock it again within thirty seconds. There was no difficulty: Fingers had explained the mechanisms of far more complicated locks than this, shown him the tumblers, taught him where to exert pressure. Harry was trying to develop speed.

Click! The lock opened. Scritch, scratch, scrabble – snap! The lock shut. He consulted the old alarm clock by his side. Thirty-seven seconds. Not bad.

The sound of a distant engine, like a bluebottle, rose above the cries of Dot and some others playing croquet on the lawn. The note grew louder. Harry gazed towards the window. Blue and silver, like some darting bird, Auntie Florrie flashed up the drive on the Norton. Spraying gravel like a snowplough, the big bike swung in a circle and came to a halt.

She switched off. Peace returned to the afternoon.

Harry held the lock ready and waited for the second hand to reach twelve. Before it did, however, feet scrunched on the forecourt and Auntie Florrie came through the French window in her studded leathers.

"Hello there, dear." From inside her jacket she pulled a copy of the *Evening Gazette* and threw it on a coffee table. "Doing your homework, I see. What have you got it down to now?"

"Thirty-seven seconds."

"Very *good*, dear! Oh, you are making progress. Fingers must be quite proud of you." Auntie Florrie flapped on towards the hall. "Well, I must go and change. Bye-bye for now."

"Bye."

Auntie Florrie departed – then popped her head back round the door. "Oh, by the way, dear, you should look in the *Gazette.* There's a photograph there I think might interest you. And I meant to say this morning – have you read the *Telegraph* yet?"

"Just the sports pages."

"Well turn to the Home News. Two little snippets there worth having a look at."

"What about?"

"Ah, you find them for yourself. Most interesting the papers have been today. Pip-pip." The head vanished and a moment later Harry heard the clump of her bike boots on the stairs.

He set the lock and probes aside and collected the newspapers. For no reason, except that his imagination was lively that day, he carried them in his teeth and crossed the room on all fours, growling like a lion.

He did not spot the gangling figure of Nutty Slack in the hall doorway. The kindly handyman, still wearing his blue overalls, was heading for the kitchen. Briefly he watched and went on his way laughing.

It did not take long to find the photograph in the local *Gazette.* There they stood in evening clothes, hand in hand and the centre of attention at some smart society function – Beastly Priestly and Gestapo Lil. They were smiling broadly. So were the other guests who stood round in a semi-circle applauding. Two short paragraphs accompanied the photograph. Harry read them.

Colonel Percival Bonaparte Priestly and Miss Lavinia Lucretia McScrew, who chose the occasion of the Police Charity Ball to announce their engagement.

Colonel Priestly of Felon Grange is an eminent local landowner and circuit judge, chairman of numerous committees and well-known for his charity work. Miss McScrew has recently arrived from London to work in the area.

Harry looked back at the photograph and resisted a temptation to add Dracula fangs to those grinning faces.

He laid the newspaper aside and took up the *Daily Telegraph.* Could that be as interesting? It took several minutes to find the articles Auntie Florrie had referred to. His eyes opened wide. Settling himself comfortably, he read them in order.

Bank Raiders Escape with £70,000
On Friday night thieves broke into the premises of the Norland Bank in Oakborough and got away with £70,000 in gold and used bank notes.

Police, who withheld details until the extent of the robbery had been determined, say that the break-in had the hallmarks of an experienced gang and link it with a spate of recent robberies.

Entry was gained through an upper window at the rear of the premises. The newly-installed alarm system was neutralized. The gang then proceeded to the basement where the bank's main safe was protected by a security device on a time switch. This was overcome by a considerable charge of explosive, which not only blew open the safe door but brought down the ceiling and with it the manager's desk.

Passers-by at once alerted the police but by the time they arrived the raiders had gone. Eye-witnesses spoke of an elderly-seeming quartet who were seen in a back-street adjacent to the explosion and appeared in a dazed condition. Police express uncertainty as to whether this was disguise or the four were innocent revellers who had been drinking in a crowded nearby pub.

They were seen to climb into a smart red Mercedes, registration number TBJ 123, which drew away at a smart pace. One public-minded citizen gave chase in his Lotus Elan but was unable to maintain contact. "They took off like a bat out of hell," he told reporters.

Police are anxious to interview the driver and passengers of the red Mercedes. TBJ 123 is the number plate of Her Majesty's official limousine at Balmoral.

Harry collapsed with laughter. That explained the red faces on Saturday morning. It wasn't sunburn – Fingers had blown them all up! He had done it again! They had been staggering around in the street like drunks, pockets and bags stuffed with gold and banknotes.

At the same time – his laughter faded – they had actually carried out the raid he overheard them planning. They really *were* bank robbers and thieves! The newspaper said so plainly.

He turned to the second article.

Minibus for Orphanage

An anonymous donation of £70,000 has enabled Winkle Manor, a home for handicapped orphans, to purchase a minibus.

The matron of the home, which for some years has been struggling against financial hardship, told our reporter: "It is wonderful, like a gift from heaven. Half of the money has gone on the specially adapted minibus which we desperately need. The rest will be used to provide medical and play equipment for the children. At last we will be able to take them away for a holiday."

In tears she said: "We don't know who our benefactor is, but could you please thank him from all the children, and tell him how very much his kindness is appreciated."

A photograph showed a group of children outside Winkle Manor. Some wore calipers, some sat in wheelchairs. A little girl in the foreground held out a slip of paper which he took to be the cheque for £70,000. All were laughing and cheering, waving their arms in the air.

Puzzled, Harry stared across the room. What his aunts and their friends were doing, was it wrong or was it right? He did not know what to make of it at all.

14
Summer Days

Glorious summer! The first proper summer of Harry's life. The days flew past.

Often, wearing his new swimming trunks, he climbed to the top of the tower and stretched out in the sun. At his side lay a plate of Mrs Good's biscuits and a flask of lemon squash. Overhead, with curved wings and long forked tails, the swallows swooped for insects.

Leaning on the warm stone parapet, he looked down on the garden and shouted to Nutty.

Beyond lay the woods, a dozen shades of green. There, ringed by trees, were the silver lake and Chalky's paddock. Three miles off stood Felon Grange, the stately home of Colonel Priestly. Further away, in other directions, the hills were blue and the summer sea glittered enticingly.

Every morning, on the lawn at the front of the Hall, Huggy gave him a wrestling lesson, while Nutty tended to the flower-beds, Aunt Bridget sat in a deckchair and did *The Times* crossword, and Max, who was a late riser, watched from the window with a cup of coffee in his hands.

Both were barefoot. Harry wore his shorts and T-shirt. Huggy wore a vivid pink body-stocking with her purple wrestling costume on top. On the back, in big blood-red letters, was printed *The Strangler*.

Although Huggy was a formidable figure, she laughed so much and was so good-humoured that Harry was not in the least frightened of her. All the same, he decided, he would not have liked to face that mountain of muscle if she was angry.

First Harry learned how to fall safely on the soft grass. Then, one at a time, Huggy taught him the basic throws and holds – the backheel, cross-buttock, hip lock, flying mare, and various combinations.

Left and right he sailed through the air. Helpless he lay pinned to the grass beneath Huggy's scissors and arm locks.

Until one morning, to her great surprise, Harry caught her off guard and the *Strangler* herself went flying through the air like two hundredweight of potatoes and landed crash at the foot of a huge beech tree. Birds exploded from the branches with whirring wings and cries of alarm. Huggy, equally startled, sat scratching her mat of hair then laughed uproariously and clapped him on the back with a giant hand.

One afternoon he went to Angel's studio.

The wild-bearded Scot stared at him briefly. Eyes like blue fish swam behind his thick spectacle lenses.

"Aye, well, yer welcome to look around," came the high, peppery voice. "Help yersel' to paper and paints if ye want – but dinna make a mess. An' dinna disturb me while I'm workin'. If ye do, I'll cut off yer lugs."

He vanished behind his easel then the whiskery head popped out again.

"Ye wouldna happen to have a sweetie about yer person?"

Harry patted his pockets. "Sorry."

"Ah, well. Mind what I say!"

The studio was riotously untidy. Every ledge and shelf, two

long tables, the broad windowsills and most of the floor were littered with tins and squeezed tubes of paint, palettes, knives, brushes, bottles of turps and linseed oil, lengths of picture frame, sheets of glass, charcoal, pencils, empty coffee mugs, old pipes, broken spectacles, wonderful smudgy sketchbooks – and canvases.

Canvases everywhere. Harry had never seen, never imagined, such an explosion of shapes and colour.

In an old wooden frame, hanging where it caught light from the window, was the oil painting Angel had made of him on the raspberry cart. Beneath the big straw hat his face was a blur yet somehow, magically, it was a perfect likeness of Harry as he had been that morning – old jeans, T-shirt, brown with sunburn. Chalky tossed his white tail and almost smelled of horse. Eyes bright beneath his chopped-off fringe, Tangle looked up expectantly. The flowers, vegetables and punnets of raspberries glowed in the morning sun. It was a wonderful picture.

For half an hour he wandered round the studio, peeping into open drawers, testing brushes, squeezing dots of glorious colour and smearing them with a fingertip.

"Time for ma afternoon snooze." Angel emerged from behind the easel wiping his fingers on a filthy rag. "Then it'll be tea-time, eh! Got to keep ma strength up." He pushed aside some clutter with a foot and to Harry's astonishment lay down on the floor with a paint-stained overall beneath his head.

He headed for the door.

"Afore ye go, laddie." Angel called him back. "I saw ye lookin' at yon picture o' the South Seas. Over there. Wi' a big moon-flower an' some natives. A red signature in the corner."

Harry crossed to the picture – orange and white and greens and gold and dark. With a finger he traced the artist's name. "G-a-u … g-u-i-n. Gauguin?"

"Gauguin." Angel corrected his pronunciation. "Aye, that's the one. D'ye like it?"

"Yes, very much."

"Take it, it's yours," said the artist. "I was plannin' tae send it tae Sotheby's – that's the big art auctioneers. If we'd got away wi' it, it'd have fetched a hundred and fifty thousand pound. Mebbe twice that. But take it if ye like it. It'll look nice on the wall o' yer bedroom."

"A hundred and –" Harry was aghast. "Oh, no, I couldn't."

"Why not?" said the horizontal figure, his eyes now closed. "It's mine to do what I like wi'. D'ye want it or no?"

"Well –" Harry stopped uncertainly.

"Well I'm giein' it to ye. I'd like ye tae have it. So will ye tak' the damned thing awa' an' gie me a bit o' peace."

"Thank you very –" Carefully Harry lifted the canvas from a nail banged roughly into the wall. "I'll take great –"

"Ha'e ye got it?" interrupted Angel.

"Yes."

"Then go on, get *out* o' here. Shoo! Shoo!"

That visit to Angel's studio fired Harry's enthusiasm for art. He had always enjoyed drawing and now, for hours at a time, he sat in his tower room, or on the main staircase, or in some interesting corner and sketched the scene before him. Sometimes he made his way to the kitchen and drew Mrs Good at work.

But his favourite venture was when he loaded Chalky with the stained easel, folding chair and other equipment that Angel had given him, pulled on his battered straw hat, and set off through the woods.

The trees were dense as the Amazon jungle and as they advanced Harry imagined he was an intrepid explorer. Half a mile from the Hall, though seeming much further, they came upon the white marble folly he could see from his bedroom window. Like a temple from some lost civilization it stood among the trees. Nobody had visited it for years. Fir cones and pine needles carpeted the steps. The heavy door creaked open on a musty interior. Plaques to men and women long departed were set into the walls; high white columns were strung with cobwebs. For decades birds had built nests in the roof and the floor crunched with dried droppings and twigs.

It was often here that Harry would set up his easel and draw the folly with the wild trees growing around it.

They were idyllic outings: Chalky munched the fat green leaves; Socrates, who accompanied them, stood in the dappled shade and thought deep donkey thoughts; Tangle hunted in the undergrowth; while Harry worked at his painting, explored, and munched his way through the bags of sandwiches, cakes, biscuits and juice provided by Mrs Good in case of emergencies.

He had never been so busy or so happy.

In the woods with Dot he climbed to the top of the giant redwood, tallest of trees, and sat for an hour swaying in the wind.

Auntie Florrie drove them twelve miles to a cliff above the sea. Roped to Dot for safety and with the blue waves swishing below, he took his first lessons in rock climbing.

In the kitchen with Mrs Good he learned to make toffee and pizza, lemonade, chocolate crispies, bacon sandwiches, fudge, Welsh rarebit, pancakes, sausage rolls, and other favourite snacks.

Almost every day he and Tangle swam in the lake.

He repainted the old rowing boat and Nutty gave him a length of line, some fish hooks and a trowel. It only took a few minutes to dig up some juicy worms. Then, often in his trunks and wet-headed from swimming, he pulled on the oars and went fishing, while Tangle planted his forepaws on the side and stared down into the water.

In the mothy evenings he built a fire in the woods and everyone came to his fish suppers. Sitting round the pine-scented flames they cooked his perch and grayling on sticks, baked potatoes in the embers, ate them with fingers, and washed them down with glasses of cider.

But all good things, sadly, must come to an end. And one Monday morning when Harry woke and stretched and climbed out of bed – the summer holidays were over.

It was time for school.

15
Black Day at Barleymow

Barleymow Junior School stood on the edge of town. It was a fine brick building with a low white extension, a tarmac playground and two playing fields. Most of the children lived in town. A school bus picked up those who lived in the surrounding countryside, and at nine o'clock Harry found himself in a classroom with twenty-seven other children waiting for their teacher.

The air was loud with chatter and laughter. Girls in grey jerseys and boys in navy jerseys sat on desks and ran from group to group swapping gossip and holiday news. Eyes were bright, faces tanned from the long hot summer.

Harry stood alone, ignored except for a few curious stares. Then two boys, one West Indian, the other ginger and heavily freckled, crossed the room and greeted him.

"Your first day? What's your name?"

Harry told them.

"Harry who?"

"Harry Barton."

"I'm Akku – Akku Apiliga. He's Charlie."

"Charlie Donkin – and don't call me Donkey."

"Or Blackie."

Harry shook his head.

"D'you play football?"

"Yes."

"You can play for us at break. Who's your favourite team?"

Harry told them.

"Heyyyy!" Akku punched the air. "Me too."

Charlie made a face. "They're rubbish!"

"He supports Man. United. Uhhhh!"

Harry laughed. He had not expected to make friends so quickly.

"What's the teacher like?"

"Dunno. Last year it was Mr Lewis. He was great. Took us for rugby."

"But he left. This year it's some new guy."

" 'D you see his car, that red Aston Martin? Wow!"

"Fog'll be bringing him along in a minute."

"Who's Fog?"

"Mr Foggarty, the headmaster. Everyone calls him Fog 'cause he's thick and wet."

As Harry laughed a girl who was keeping watch at the door came running into the room. "It's Fog. He's got the new teacher with him."

Children scrambled down from desks. They fell silent. The glass-panelled door swung open and Mr Foggarty entered.

The headmaster was a stout man with a broad kindly face. Short silver hair shone above a pair of gold-rimmed spectacles. He wore a lightly-checked grey summer suit.

At his back followed the new teacher.

Harry froze. He felt the room swim about him and for a moment everything turned black. Then the dizzy turn passed. No one had noticed. All eyes were on the new teacher.

It was Gestapo Lil.

She was smiling amiably, meeting the children's eyes as she entered the room. Several of the girls smiled in return, pleased to have a lady teacher, especially one so blonde and beautifully dressed.

"Good morning, children." Mr Foggarty stood at the front of the class with the new teacher at his elbow.

"Good morning, sir," came the singsong reply.

"Sit down please. Anywhere will do for now."

The children scattered for chairs. Harry grabbed a seat behind Akku and Charlie.

"Have you had a nice summer?" said Mr Foggarty. "I hope so. You all look very healthy and brown, anyway." Benignly he smiled around the class. "Goodness, how fast you're all growing."

His eye fell on Harry. "Ah, a new face, and you're – ?"

"Barton, sir."

"Barton, eh? Is that your first name or your second?"

"My second, sir."

"And what's your first?"

"Harry, sir." He felt everyone staring at him.

"Harry Barton, eh? Yes, I've seen your papers. Well, I hope you'll be happy with us all here at Barleymow. We're not such a bad bunch I think you'll find. Met any of the others yet?"

"Yes, sir."

"Good. Who's that?"

Charlie and Akku put up their hands.

"Excellent. Got you roped into their teams yet, have they?"

"Yes, sir."

Mr Foggarty smiled. "I expect so. Right, you pair, I want you to look after him and show him the ropes. And none of your nonsense. Understand?"

"Yes, sir." They grinned and looked round.

Harry's face was scarlet.

The headmaster's eyes finished roving the class. "Know all the rest of these ugly faces I think, don't I?"

No one disagreed.

"Very good. Well," he turned to the smiling woman at his side. "This is your new teacher for this year – Miss McScrew. In the past, as you know, we've always had a man to teach you in senior year but this year we've been lucky enough to obtain the services of Miss McScrew. She comes from London with the most glowing of references and is, I am sure, going to keep you all very firmly in your places."

He murmured in her ear and she nodded, smiling more broadly.

"I'll let you into a little secret – a little *open* secret. If you read your local paper you may have seen her name linked with that of Colonel Priestly, Chairman of the Board of Governors of this school."

"Whoo–ooo!"

Mr Foggarty laughed. "In fact, if you look very closely you might just catch the glimpse of a new engagement ring."

"Whoooo–ooooo!"

"But that's none of your business. Like young Harry Barton, Miss McScrew is new to the school. I want you all to behave yourselves and give her a true Barleymow welcome."

Somebody blew a raspberry.

The class giggled with shock. Akku collapsed in helpless laughter.

"I shall take that as a joke," said Mr Foggarty. "Akku Apiliga, behave yourself." He turned to Miss McScrew. "The first day of term. You'll find they're a good bunch on the whole. By and large I think we run a happy ship." He looked back at the class. "Right, I'll leave you in the capable hands of Miss McScrew."

The door closed behind him.

"Harry Barton." Her clear voice rang like a bell in the silence. "Was that you made that impertinent noise?"

"No." Harry was startled, his eyes wide with innocence.

"No, what?"

"No, I didn't."

"No, I didn't – what?"

"No, I didn't make any noise."

"No, I didn't make any noise – what?"

At last Harry understood her meaning. "No, miss," he said. "I didn't make any noise."

"I think you did. Not a very good start on your first morning, is it?" Her eyes were like ice. "I think you'd better stay behind and have a word with me at morning break."

Harry looked down, shaking.

"Did you hear what I said?"

"Yes, miss."

The class was shocked. The boy who had blown the raspberry, sitting some distance from Harry, bravely put up his hand.

"Put your hand down, please."

"But –"

She looked at him. The boy put down his hand.

Gestapo Lil smiled again.

She wore an immaculate suit of peacock blue and a dazzling white blouse. All her accessories – boots, brooch, earrings, hair clasp – were matching shades of blue and green. So was her eye-shadow. Not a hair was out of place in the coiled golden braids. Her lipstick and fingernails were perfect.

"Well, you all know a little about me. Let me find out something about you." She sat at her desk and surveyed a typed sheet. "We'll fill in the register. I have here a list. I'll write down your surname and you tell me your full Christian names."

From her bag she took a mottled-blue fountain pen and un-screwed the cap.

"Right. Andrews?" She wrote boldly.

"Polly Jane," said a pretty girl with a white hair ribbon.

"Apiliga?"

"Akku Amos. That's A-k-k-u."

"Thank you, Akku, I think I can spell your name. Bailie?"

"Janet," said a sturdy little girl whose nose was peeling with sunburn.

"Baldwin?"

"Peter."

"Barton?"

"Augustus Harold," said Harry.

"Rather more than that, I think," said Gestapo Lil.

Harry looked down, blushing scarlet. "Eugene Augustus Montgomery Harold," he muttered.

A titter ran through the class.

"I'm not sure I caught all of that." The teacher looked up smiling. "Speak clearly, please. *Eugene* – and did you say *Augustus – Montgomery – Harold*?"

"Yes, miss."

"Goodness, I don't think I have room for all of that," said Gestapo Lil, writing. Thank you, *Eugene-Augustus*. Crabtree?"

"Daisy Rose."

"Donkin?"

"Charles," said Charlie.

"Goodfellow?"

The boy who had blown the raspberry hung his head. "Brian Oliver."

Several of the class giggled. He shot them a look of hatred.

Gestapo Lil looked up.

The boy's face was aflame.

She smiled and returned to the register. "Grant?"

"Cameron Scott," proclaimed a sturdy boy.

"Hastie?"

"Thamantha Luthie," lisped a small girl with a hair ribbon.

The list continued.

Charlie's head was bent as he wrote something. He passed back a note.

> *Harry,*
> *Rotten luck about your name. Dont*
> *worry. Why has she got it in for*
> *you?*

Inch at a time, trying not to be noticed, Harry searched his school bag for his pencil case. Taking out a pen, he turned the note over and wrote:

> *Charlie,*
> *Thanks. Tell you later.*

Then, knowing that he was dicing with death, he added:

> *She worked for my parent's in*
> *London. She was realy horri—*

"Eugene-Augustus!" The clear voice made Harry jump. "What was that piece of paper he passed back?"

"What piece of paper, miss?"

"That piece you're writing on."

"I'm not writing, miss."

"Oh, dear!" She laid down her pen. "I saw you. It's under your hand. Bring it out, please."

"It's nothing, miss."

"Bring – it – out!"

Rising, Harry did as he was told. Akku's hand touched his back as he walked past.

Gestapo Lil took the note in her clean fingers and read it. Slowly she raised her eyes, first to Harry and then to Charlie.

Her basilisk stare – blue as glaciers, hot as blowlamps – bored into him. She drew a deep breath, her nostrils widened.

"Thank you. Sit down now."

In a deathly hush Harry returned to his desk. Gestapo Lil consulted the register and took up her pen.

"Perkins?" came the icy voice.

"Rosemary," whispered a big girl.

"Quince?"

"Daniel John."

"di Stephano?"...

16
A Matter of Survival

"She said what!" Aunt Bridget was white with anger.

"If I wanted to have an easier time in school," said Harry, "I'd tell her what you're all doing up here at Lagg Hall."

"And this was – ?"

"At morning break."

"You were alone."

"Yes, in the classroom. The rest were out playing football."

It was quarter to five. A crowd sat around the kitchen table.

"From the very first she picked on you; blamed you for something you hadn't done; called you Eugene-Augustus; then when she got you by yourself – !"

"And she said I'd better not cause any trouble because if I did she'd – they'd – see I was taken away from here. Because –"

Huggy put an arm around his shoulders.

"Taken away by social workers and put into a children's home, was that it?" said Aunt Bridget. "Because Auntie Florrie and I have got criminal records, we're all ex-cons, and Priestly could rig up a case that we're not fit people to bring you up – not a good moral example."

Harry nodded. "A home for no-good orphan brats like me, she said." He looked down at his plate.

A steaming teapot and wire trays of cakes stood in the middle of the table. Mrs Good pushed a batch of squashy millionaire's shortbread towards him. Harry took a slice.

"My gollies!" said Huggy angrily. "If that voman come vithin my reach! I'm telling you, she no need vorry about teatime no more! No vedding arrangements, neither. No nothing!"

Surrounded by such friends Harry began to cheer up.

"Let me get it right," said Aunt Bridget. "It wasn't you made that rude noise."

"No."

"But she blamed you and used it as an excuse to talk to you at morning break."

"It was just a joke. The boy who did it, Ollie Goodfellow, tried to own up but she wouldn't listen."

"An' after all that she give yer five hundred lines!" exclaimed Fingers.

"Nae need to worry about that, laddie." Angel clawed beneath his whiskers. "If ye write a couple o' dozen I'll print them off so's Scotland Yard couldna tell the difference. Nae bother at a'. Five hundred, five thousand – just say how many ye want."

Several people laughed.

"This is important." Aunt Bridget ticked off the points on her fingers. "She told you that Priestly knows we're up to something here at Lagg Hall –"

"That's why he's sniffing round in the woods like an old stoat!" came Dot's shrill voice.

"– that she expects you to tell her all about us," continued Aunt Bridget; "that if you, or presumably we, cause trouble you'll be taken into care; if you tell the class about Hampstead or the raspberry cart she'll make your life a misery –"

"She called it lies!" said Harry.

Aunt Bridget nodded, "– and she still expects to get what she describes as 'rightfully hers' out of Auntie Florrie and me."

"Yes, she said Colonel Priestly knows there's something

going on up here. And although my father died bankrupt, that makes no difference, the family still owes her thousands."

"What a charming woman!" said Auntie Florrie.

"Like her boyfriend, don't you think," agreed Aunt Bridget. "Beastly Priestly and Gestapo Lil."

"And they send *us* to jail." Auntie Florrie sipped her tea and dabbed her lipstick. "But apart from that horror, dear, what was the rest of school like? All right?"

"It was great," Harry said. "We played football at lunchtime. Charlie reckons I might get in the school team."

"And the work?" said Aunt Bridget.

"It was easy. We had to write an essay: *What I did in the Summer Holidays.* I wrote about these two vandals who messed up my fruit cart."

"Harry, you didn't!" Auntie Florrie was dismayed.

Aunt Bridget repressed a smile.

"Well, I didn't use their right names. But I wasn't going to tell her about all the things I did up here, was I?" He spoke through a doughnut. "And I'm miles ahead of them in maths. Easy-peasy."

"So, you like Barleymow," said Aunt Bridget, "but there's a problem. If we complain about your teacher – and there's no proof about most of what you've told us – then we get investigated by social workers; who knows what the outcome of that would be. And if we don't complain, then she's going to make your school life a misery. So," she regarded him keenly, "what do you say about going to a different school? Forget about Barleymow and we'll send you off to boarding school again."

Harry's mouth fell open. "No! I'm staying here! I want to stay at Lagg Hall. You said this was my home!" He shook his head. "I don't want to go back to boarding school. I want to stay here!"

"But what about Gestapo Lil?"

"I'm not leaving because of *her*!" Harry said contemptuously.

"Whatever she does. I'm not going to change schools or leave Lagg Hall and all of you and Tangle and Chalky and everything just because of – a rotten bully!"

"Of course you're not!" Aunt Bridget was fierce. "You've got too much spirit. I said it the morning you arrived, you're made of the right stuff, Harry Barton. Good for you. You're going to stay at Barleymow and Lagg Hall and we'll beat her – we'll beat them both!" She gripped his hand. "But for the time being keep your head low. No point in looking for trouble. Apart from her it's a good school. You do your work well and enjoy your friends and your football. Don't give her any excuse for picking on you."

"She made me sit at the front," Harry said, "right in the middle, where she said she could keep an eye on me. And she put Akku halfway back at one side and Charlie in the far corner. Three trouble-makers, she called us."

"You can put up with that for a month or two. Think how mad she'll be when you get your work right and do exactly what she tells you."

"We'll fink up somefing for yer to tell her about us," said Fingers.

"And Bridget will work out a plan, won't you, dear," said Auntie Florrie.

Aunt Bridget gave a cat-like smile. "I've been working on something for Colonel Priestly for some time. Ever since he put us into the hedge with that Rolls-Royce. Now he's engaged to Gestapo Lil and she's Harry's teacher – yes, it's all starting to come together. But we need Mr Tolly back first – and I want time to think about it." She gazed thoughtfully at the wall. "Three stages probably: first move about mid-November."

Harry was thrilled.

"I think it has to be the next operation," Aunt Bridget continued. "I won't have Harry messed about like this. And speaking personally, I must say I'll feel happier to know Percy P. isn't snooping around like –"

"A nasty old pole-cat," said Dot.

"Precisely."

"Aunt Bridget," Harry said. "That first morning, on the way to the aerodrome, you said you'd tell me about him – Colonel Priestly. But I hardly know anything yet. Apart from creeping around in the woods and my raspberry cart, what has he done? Why does everybody hate him so much?"

"Not everyone, dear boy, only us. Only the few people who really *know* about him." Max ran elegant fingers through his dyed locks and stroked his pencil moustache. "To the world at large Colonel Priestly is a distinguished judge, a friend of the famous, a big landowner, chairman of this and that, a great philanthropist.

"He owns racehorses: every year you'll find him at Aintree and Ascot in a grey top hat. He has a yacht at Cowes. He regularly attends the Lord Mayor's Banquet in London, Henley Regatta, Wimbledon Finals Day, Glyndebourne, the gaming tables at Monte Carlo, the Queen's Garden Parties, and all the other big social occasions. For his – oh, so public! – charity work he has been awarded the C.B.E. Every week his photograph appears in the society pages of one newspaper or another. He is a widely-admired and respected man."

"But ve know different, don't ve, Max," said Huggy.

"Yeah," said Fingers.

"He's a nasty piece of work, that's what he is," said Mrs Good, quite pink in the cheeks. "The things I've *heard* about him!"

"Go on, Max," said Aunt Bridget. "You tell Harry why we call him *Beastly* Priestly."

"The Beast!" said Auntie Florrie.

"Colonel Stonyheart."

"If you wish." Max examined a polished fingernail. "The underworld, however, has a very different picture of *Colonel* Percival Bonaparte Priestly. To them he's one of the biggest operators in Europe. All those glittering galas and banquets with film stars are just a front. He uses them to hide his real operations. Where do you think he gets the money to run a string of racehorses, take a suite at the Ritz, buy a huge estate like Felon Grange?"

"Give his fiancée that Aston Martin," said Auntie Florrie.

"Exactly," said Max. "Where does a judge get that sort of money? From his work on the bench? Not on your life. Colonel Priestly, your 'Percipops', is Mr Big in the most notorious gang of thieves in Britain. He organizes the jobs, uses his contacts and position to gain inside information, then sends the mob out. He doesn't go himself, of course, he stays safely in the background. If the heist's under way at one o'clock in the morning, you can bet your granny he's having a late drink with some politician or playing poker with the Chief of Police. Then, once the loot's safe and the hue and cry has died down, he disposes of it. Gold and cash and jewels vanish straight into his Swiss bank account. Antiques and paintings and silver go to dealers and private collectors, people who know how to disguise its ancestry. We're not talking about televisions, you realize, cheap ornaments and three-piece suites. These things are worth thousands – tens of thousands. And so," Max gestured, "Percy P. gets richer and richer, and the world thinks what a wonderful man he is."

"Sometimes he stores the loot at Felon Grange," said Aunt Bridget. "I'm sure of it. That's where he keeps it until the outcry has died down. Then he breaks it up into lots for distribution – around the country and overseas."

"Aha!" said Huggy. "Do I detect a glint in your eye, Bridget? Is that vhere you think there might be a little chink in his armour?"

Aunt Bridget shrugged.

"All right. I not going to press you," said Huggy. "Ve know you not like to talk. Not before you vork everything out."

Aunt Bridget smiled.

Harry looked round the table. "But why does he go snooping around in the woods here? Why does everyone hate him so much?"

"That's easy." Fingers sucked tea from the ends of his straggling moustache. "Y' expect a judge to be honest, don't yer? Where can y' expect honesty an' trufe an' justice if not in a court o' law? But not wi' Priestly. Oh, no! Not wiv 'im! Not in 'is courts! Rotten as a mouldy cat, 'e is. I'd rahver trust a mad cobra than 'im. An' 'e's playin' wiv men's lives, in't 'e, not jus' a few sparklers an' ol' candlesticks. Uses 'is position to protect 'is-sel', see. Anyone get in 'is road, 'e puts 'em away for ten year, that's wot 'e does. Wevver they've done anyfing or not. You know somefing an' keep yer mouf shut, 'e'll get yer off – then blackmail yer to do somefing 'orrible for 'im. 'E fink yer a danger, ye'd better watch out. Some o' my mates – innocent as new-born babbies, they was – 'e put 'em away for 'alf a lifetime. It took ol' Fingers, 'ere, to spring 'em free. Still on the run, 'alf the pore souls. That's wot Priestly does for yer. That's why I can't *stand* 'im!"

"That's why they call him Colonel Stonyheart," said Auntie Florrie.

"And vhy he is snooping around in the voods," said Huggy, "like vhen you and Dot bomb him vith rotten eggs? He is frightened of Bridget, that vhy. Vhen he buy that big big house three year ago and set himself up as a country gentleman vith fox hounds and peasant shooting, he not realize he have us for neighbour – Bridget, Florrie, Fingers and the rest of us. He know ve know about him. Ve are a threat. He vant get rid of us. Also he guess ve are up to something – but vhat? Vhy else so many top operators gather in von place? And vhy ve do no big jobs? His ear he has close to the ground. All his contacts in the undervorld – they come up vith nothing. Ve are a mystery. So he snoop around, to try to find out the answer."

"And now he's met up with your Gestapo Lil," said Auntie Florrie, "a woman as nasty and two-faced as he is himself."

"Two peas out of a pod," said Mrs Good.

"A couple of rats," said Dot.

"Rattlesnakes!" said Fingers.

"Him being Chairman of the Board of Governors," Auntie Florrie continued, "he got her that job she wanted as your teacher at Barleymow."

"Old mates, see," said Fingers. "Knew 'im before. Must a done. Prob'ly used 'im to pop that stuff o' yours she nicked from 'Ampstead."

"And now they plan to use you," said Aunt Bridget, "to find out about Lagg Hall and what we're all up to."

"So's they can get rid of us."

"That's the only way he's ever going to feel safe."

"D'ye follow, laddie." Angel's eyes filled his glasses like blue oysters. "We've got no choice in the matter. If we dinna get rid o' him, he's goin' to get rid o' us – one way or another."

"It's a question of survival," piped up Dot.

"In addition to the fact that I simply will *not* have that woman interfering with you and your education," said Aunt Bridget.

"So ye see, son, ye've got aal of us on your side." Nutty squeezed Harry's shoulder with a big hand. "United we stand! An' I'll tell ye one thing, yer Aunt Bridget's a cracker! If she don't win I'll eat me gardenin' boots – an' that's a promise!"

Mrs Good broke up the gathering. "Well, if we're going to have any dinner tonight I want you all out of my kitchen. Come on, shoo! Off the table."

In ones and twos they drifted from the room.

Angel touched Harry's arm. "Do yer lines now, laddie. Blue pen on a sheet o' A4. Rest it on somethin' soft, I'll need tae reproduce the depression." He thought. "Aye, then bring it tae the studio. I'll get the printer ready."

Harry's schoolbag lay against the wall. He slung it over his shoulder and picked up his jacket.

Mrs Good had cleared an end of the table. "If you want to do your homework down here you're welcome," she said. "Or up in your room, whichever you like."

Harry looked around the friendly kitchen. "I think I'll stay down here," he said.

Tangle, who had been exploring and missed Harry's return, danced through the door and jumped up, paws against his school trousers. Harry rubbed the shaggy head. Briefly they wrestled. Then Tangle trotted to the corner where meaty scraps lay in his bowl.

Harry unbuckled his bag and settled himself at the end of the table. Carefully he checked in his new General Book. There, at the top of the first page, lay his punishment in Gestapo Lil's bold handwriting:

Bad manners and impertinence will not be tolerated.
500 times – for Wednesday.

"Twenty-four times!" Harry muttered under his breath. "Rotten old bag!"

Taking up a blue biro, he began to write.

17
Magic

Harry survived the next few days and as the autumn term drew on he settled down in his new school.

Akku, Charlie and he - the *Three Musketeers* as Mr Foggarty called them – became inseparable friends. Every Saturday morning they played football for the Barleymow team. When apple time arrived, Harry took big bagfuls into school to share with his friends. From the Lagg Hall woods he collected conkers that made them champions of the playground.

By working hard and doing exactly what the teacher said, he managed, sometimes for hours at a time, to avoid trouble in the classroom.

Gestapo Lil made life difficult, however, by a series of dirty tricks. His lively essays and drawings got lower marks than they deserved. When all his maths was correct she deducted marks for writing. When he did not know an answer he was always asked, and when he did know his raised hand was ignored.

Worse than this, she discovered a page torn from his new textbook. In another book she found scribbles and a clumsy cartoon. Although Harry was innocent, each of these earned him a harsh lecture in front of the class and another five hundred lines – which Angel ran off on his printer the same evening.

More seriously still, he found objects hidden in his desk and in his jacket pocket in the cloakroom. The first time it was a mouth-organ, pride and joy of one of the other boys. By sheer good luck he spotted a glimpse of silver under his books and pulled it out before it was missed.

"Miss, this was in my desk." He held the mouth-organ aloft. "I didn't put it there."

Gestapo Lil's lips tightened with annoyance.

The next time it was a girl's purse in the inside pocket of his anorak. It was only by luck that Harry found that, too, hunting in his jacket for a square of chocolate as he came in from playing football at lunchtime.

After that he checked his pockets and desk every time he came into school – he did not want to be branded a thief as well as a troublemaker. It was well that he did so, for later he found cigarettes and a dangerous sheath knife. Both were confiscated by the angry teacher.

Finally, at four o'clock one day the jacket of a boy he had quarrelled with – a fat tell-tale known to the others as *Crawler* Lane – was found torn in the cloakroom. His parents complained and the following morning Mr Foggarty carried out an investigation. Luckily it was proved that Harry could not have done it.

Akku told the headmaster all the things that had happened to his friend. Mr Foggarty, who liked Harry, listened carefully and sent the trio on their way.

The weather grew colder. Squirrels and hedgehogs hibernated, Tangle's coat grew thicker. As Harry walked down the drive each morning the spiders' webs were white with dew or frost. A new football scarf kept his neck warm.

Half-term came and went.

Then it was Hallowe'en at Lagg Hall with games and dressing up, ghost stories, turnip lanterns, apple ducking and Ol' Goggly moaning in the middle of the lawn.

Next came Guy Fawkes Day with a huge bonfire and clothes smelling of wood-smoke, baked potatoes, sausages on sticks, and spouting, soaring fireworks.

In mid-November Mr Tolly was released from Wormwood Scrubs.

It was a Saturday. As Harry came in to lunch, his hair still wet from the shower after football, he found two strangers at the dining-room table. One, silver-haired and distinguished, was sipping an aperitif. Auntie Florrie introduced Harry to the other.

"This is Mr Tolly, Harry." She smiled fondly. "You know how thrilled we are to have him back with us."

Shyly Harry shook hands.

"And how did your match go?" beamed the famous magician.

"We won five - three."

"Did you score?"

"Yes, one. And Charlie got two - he's one of my friends."

Mr Tolly was a large pink man with a bald head. He wore a comfortable tweed suit of grey-green check with a red handkerchief tucked into the breast pocket. As Harry regarded him he produced a tiny lacquered box from his waistcoat and took snuff, tapping a quantity on to the back of his hand and sniffing it up his nostrils with great enjoyment.

"Ah!" He rubbed his nose with a forefinger and beamed around the table. "It's so good to be home."

"We know!" Aunt Bridget smiled. "Did you manage to keep in training?"

"So-so." Mr Tolly made a face.

"Do a trick – for Harry."

"What, now?"

"Yes." She looked around the table. "Something with the knives and forks."

"Without a warm-up? Goodness!" Mr Tolly raised his eyebrows mischievously. "Well, see what we can do. No promises, mind."

He took a knife from the table and held it before his face in the fingertips of his left hand. "You see this knife?"

Harry nodded.

"Watch it carefully."

Mr Tolly tweaked back his sleeves and moved his right hand across. The knife had vanished.

Harry could not believe his eyes.

The right hand returned. The knife had become a fork.

A ripple of applause went round the table.

"Not yet," said Mr Tolly. "Give us a chance."

The fork became a spoon. It vanished.

He made some magic passes in the air. Nothing happened. Mr Tolly looked surprised. He repeated the movements – still nothing.

"Adjo fiddly dum-ya kum!" he said in a deep voice.

His fingers remained empty.

The table sat expectantly.

"I don't know what's happened. They've gone." Sternly Mr Tolly glared at Harry. "Have you got them?"

Harry shook his head.

"I don't believe you! Come round here. At once, sir! And mind, I'm watching you!"

Grinning broadly and never taking his eyes from the magician's hands, Harry circled the table.

"Closer," said Mr Tolly. "You're sure you didn't take them?"

"Yes."

"I think you've eaten them! Open your mouth!"

Giggling, Harry did so.

"Wider!"

He strained his mouth to its widest.

Mr Tolly peered inside. "I think I see them. Yes, deep down. Look."

He raised an empty hand, put the pink tips of his fingers into Harry's mouth, and to everyone's amazement drew out a large silver object.

"Oh, dear!" exclaimed Mr Tolly. "It wasn't the knives and forks at all. You'd eaten the pepper pot! Greedy boy! Open again … and the salt cellar!"

He put them on the table and there was another round of applause.

Delighted by the conjuring tricks, Harry returned to his seat.

"Before you sit down," said Mr Tolly. "What's that in your pocket?"

Harry looked down. He wore his favourite old jeans – Mrs Good had fitted a new zip. He patted his tight pockets. They lay flat against his legs – empty!

"Nothing," he said.

"Are you sure?"

"Yes."

"Try the right-hand side."

"I can feel, there's nothing there."

"Just to please a silly old man."

Harry squeezed his fingers into the pocket. To his surprise there *was* something there. A piece of paper. He tugged it out. It was a five-pound note.

"It might buy you a Mars Bar or something," said the bald magician.

"Gosh, thanks!" Harry sat down. "How did you do it?"

Mr Tolly tapped the side of his nose. "Tricks of the trade." He broke a crusty roll and reached for the butter dish.

"But what happened to the knife and fork?" Auntie Florrie sat at his side.

"Oh, I'd forgotten about those. They vanished, didn't they.

I thought you must have them."

"Me! Of course I haven't."

"Didn't you put them in your handbag?"

"In my handbag! Whatever would I want to – " Her pretty red handbag lay between them. She snapped it open. "Oh, Mr Tolly!"

There lay the knife, fork and spoon, neatly wrapped in a clean table napkin.

Laughter and loud applause rose around the table.

"Really!" Auntie Florrie planted a big lipsticky kiss on his cheek. "I don't know how you do it."

"Ja, you get better – better!" said Huggy.

"Bravo! Bravo!" The second stranger at their table set down his wine glass and clapped enthusiastically.

Harry regarded him, a distinguished and kindly-looking man in an expensive suit and silk tie that bore the crest of some organization. He had thick silver hair, neatly oiled and parted, full cheeks and gapped teeth.

"Really excellent, Mr Tolly." His accent was difficult to place – West Country or Australian.

Harry guessed he might be a businessman or gentleman farmer.

"I don't believe we have been properly introduced," said Mr Tolly. "Mr – ?"

"Mann," said the stranger. "Edward Mann."

Aunt Bridget gave a little crow of laughter and clapped her hands.

Harry did not understand.

"And may I ask – what is that tie you're wearing?" Mr Tolly leaned forward. "H.O.H.C. does it say?"

"Homes for Orphans and Handicapped Children." Mr Mann produced his wallet and took out two cards. "My own," he passed one across, "and the charity I represent."

Mr Tolly examined them. "And the purpose of your visit?"

"We're arranging a series of Christmas concerts. A big charity drive for the season of goodwill. Local performers and professionals who give their services free. We're hoping to use the hall of one of your schools in town – Barleymow Junior School I believe it's called. I've arranged to see the headmaster on Monday. Now what's his name?"

"Mr Foggarty!" Harry exclaimed.

"That's the gentleman. Since we're a children's organization, we thought it would be nice to involve some of the pupils."

"That's my school," said Harry. "I go there."

"So I understand. Perhaps you'll be performing. Your teacher might organize a choir. I hope to meet her also on Monday. I've heard such a lot about her. Miss Lavipu? Do I have the name correct?"

Harry was startled.

"Lily Gestapo?"

Mr Mann's face was serious but the others were laughing.

"All right," said Aunt Bridget. "No need to tease the boy any more."

And before Harry's astonished gaze the stranger's face collapsed and changed. Off came the silver wig and eyebrows, out of the mouth came cheek pads and a set of gapped teeth, out of the eyes came a pair of blue contact lenses.

There sat Max, the same as always except that he had shaved off his pencil moustache and wore padding to give himself a stomach.

It was as magical as Mr Tolly's performance a few minutes earlier.

"Gosh! That's terrific!"

Max winked and tapped the side of his nose. "Tricks of the trade," he said in a perfect imitation of Mr Tolly's voice.

"Well, if you can take in Harry who's been living with you

for four months," said Aunt Bridget, "you can take in Priestly who hasn't seen you for years – except maybe through binoculars from the edge of the wood there."

"And Mr Foggarty and the teachers?" said Max.

"Absolutely, most convincing. At least I thought so." She looked round the table. "What about the rest of you?"

"Yeah, great!"

"Fantastic!"

"Specially with Angel's visiting cards." Auntie Florrie examined them. "Whose is the address?"

"The charity's real, it has to be," said Max. "I've been in touch with them for a while now. The other address, Lake Farm in Devon, that's my sister's. She's married to a farmer called George Mann. They can be trusted. I've stayed there a couple of times recently, posing as his brother Eddie back from New Zealand. If anyone checks up it's all covered, I think."

"Why did you laugh," Harry asked Aunt Bridget, "when he told you his name was Mr Mann?"

"Didn't you get it?" His aunt smiled. "Mr Edward Mann – Mr E. Mann?"

"Mystery man!" piped Dot.

"Oh, Max!"

"And remember, Harry," said Aunt Bridget, "if you see Mr Mann at school on Monday – or any time – you show no special interest, you know nothing about him except what your teachers tell you. And that's *important*."

Harry's heart thudded. "Is this the start of the plan – against Colonel Priestly?"

"That's right. Phase one. If all goes as it should, we'll make money for charity and there'll be a thoroughly enjoyable concert – in which your class will be performing. That means your teacher will be there. And if she's there, almost certainly her fiancé will be. Anyway, he's Chairman of the Board of Governors, so he should be there. And Max – or rather Mr Mann – will approach him for a donation. A man like Priestly won't miss the chance of parading his generosity in public. He'll be there all right. And when he is – !"

"What happens then?" said Harry.

"Ah!" Max toyed with the hair of his discarded wig. "You'll have to wait and see, won't you, young man."

Mr Tolly raised his eyebrows and smiled.

"Surprises!" said Aunt Bridget.

18
The Concert

A s autumn gave way to winter, giant posters appeared all over the town.

A MERRY CHRISTMAS TO ALL!

GRAND CHARITY CONCERT

STARS OF STAGE AND T.V.
LOCAL PERFORMERS
CHILDREN'S CHOIRS

BARLEYMOW JUNIOR SCHOOL HALL
FRIDAY 14th DECEMBER
7.30 pm
TICKETS: £5
CHILDREN AND OAPs: £2

ALL PROCEEDS TO HOMES FOR
ORPHANS AND HANDICAPPED CHILDREN

The demand for tickets was so great that the venue had to be changed from Barleymow School to the splendid Assembly Rooms. It promised to be a glittering occasion.

*   *   *

The evening arrived. There had been a light fall of snow. Golden light from the Assembly Rooms shone across the pavement and car park. Powdery avalanches fell from twigs and telephone wires upon the heads of concert-goers. Children arriving with their parents scooped snowballs from the tops of walls and threw them on to the white roofs.

Even before they entered the doors the night was magical.

Inside the Assembly Rooms all was bustle and expectancy. Christmas was in the air. Coloured streamers trailed overhead; gorgeous decorations – Santas, sledges, angels, holly – shone from each white pillar; a giant tree, glittering with lights and tinsel, stood near the stage; a big net full of balloons which would be released to the children at the end of the show, hung high above the audience.

In rooms behind the crimson stage curtains the nervous performers put on costumes and make-up, tuned their instruments, ran through jokes and routines. There was no room backstage for the children's choirs: chattering like jackdaws they sat in the front rows of seats, hair brushed and faces shining for the occasion.

Harry was not among them. Even if he had sung like an angel Gestapo Lil, who daily found some new way of persecuting him, would have found an excuse for not including him in the choir. Harry's singing voice, however, was more like a crow than a nightingale. Even Auntie Florrie had been forced to admit when he sang *Away in a Manger* to a small group in the kitchen: "Well, it's very nice, dear, lovely, but – "

"But what?" Harry had demanded.

"You sing all the wrong notes," Huggy said bluntly. "You sing like a tom-cat. You wrestle good, you sing like a tom-cat – a tom-cat that somevon is strangling."

Harry was cross but soon cheered up because Mr Foggarty chose Akku, Charlie and himself to be his special helpers, and that was better than being in the choir.

Now, clutching books of raffle tickets and a rattling money tin, they moved through the audience. Neatly turned out in their best trousers and shirts they were a vivid trio.

The money poured in.

At the end of the second row, centre-aisle, Gestapo Lil sat with her pupils – boys in blue shirts, girls in white blouses. She was immaculate, as always, in a dress of blue and ivory watered silk that complemented yet outshone the simple clothes of the children.

Harry looked up at the gallery. In the middle of the front row sat Colonel Priestly, surrounded by other local dignitaries. He wore one of the large-checked tweed suits of which he was so fond. His oiled hair, brushed flat, gleamed like copper. His red cheeks shone with good-natured laughter.

The hands of the big clock on the wall crept round. Seven thirty … seven thirty-five. The programme-sellers and ticket-sellers were called to the corridor exit; the last of the audience settled themselves comfortably; the lights dimmed. For half a minute the Christmas tree sparkled like fairyland. Then double spotlights hit the stage and focused together on the curtain. The heavy folds parted. Max, in his role as Mr Edward Mann, organizer of this gala occasion, stood centre-stage.

Briefly he welcomed the audience on such a wintry evening; told them something about the charity and the excellent use their money would be put to; gave a hint of the rich variety of pleasures on the programme; and handed over, amid warm applause, to the master of ceremonies.

The show began. Harry could not see the early acts because he was busy backstage with his friends, counting the money they had taken, tearing out the second halves of the raffle tickets, folding them and dropping them into a big white bucket. From afar he heard the singing and applause, the voices telling jokes and gales of laughter from the audience.

Max had persuaded a number of friends to appear – well-known actors and TV stars. It was an evening of quality entertainment into which the sweet voices of the children blended perfectly.

Max himself, under his stage name of Rosco Burbage, came out of retirement to play Scrooge in a scene from *A Christmas Carol*. He was magnificent. Harry, whose work was finished by that time, applauded wildly and joined in the cheers of the audience.

Lights came up for the interval. Time for the raffle. Akku went among the audience with the white bucket; Charlie ran back to Mr Foggarty with the tickets that were picked out; Harry carried the prizes – boxes of chocolates, dolls, games, bottles of port and whisky – to the delighted winners.

Angel, who sat in the stalls with the crowd from Lagg Hall, won a tin of chocolate biscuits and opened it immediately.

The lights were dimmed. An air of excitement filled the hall. As the master of ceremonies reappeared on stage, the audience greeted him with cheers and tumultuous applause.

Harry stayed behind the scenes because he was required to help in Mr Tolly's act.

Nutty had brought Tangle and Socrates to town in a small horse box. Tangle greeted Harry joyfully and was tied to a rail in the wings. Harry stood beside him, holding Socrates on a short halter, every now and then whispering in the donkey's long ears and clapping his woolly grey coat.

Two singers from the local operatic society performed duets. A famous impressionist went through his routine of jokes and well-known voices. Harry's class filed on stage and sang two Christmas songs.

The audience loved it all.

"And now," announced the master of ceremonies, "magic! You've seen his name in lights; you've seen him in the great theatres; you've seen him on television! Now he's here – to mesmerize you with a display that will make you disbelieve your own eyes! For this man the laws of Newton and Einstein cease to exist! Donkeys disappear, ladies float into mid-air, candles ignite themselves and leap into candelabra. Ladies and gentlemen, I give you the great, the amazing, the one and only – Autolycus!"

Mr Tolly stood in the wings at Harry's side, tugging his fingers nervously and refusing to talk. Now he took a deep breath, straightened his shoulders, smiled broadly and stepped forward into the spotlights.

Rapturous applause rose from the audience.

From head to foot Mr Tolly glittered. He wore a dark crimson suit with a cummerbund. About his shoulders hung a cape of midnight blue with a white lining. On his head was a top hat. Slowly he drew off white gloves and laid them on a table, tossed back the cape and drew up his sleeves. Then, standing centre-stage, he proceeded to dazzle the audience with the most wonderful display they had ever seen. One ping-pong ball became ten. Ten ping-pong balls became a bouquet of ostrich feathers. The bouquet of feathers became a fine shawl out of which fluttered one – two – three – four – five white doves. In a line they settled on a gilded perch.

The audience shouted and cheered.

Dot, with her circus background, was Mr Tolly's assistant. In a golden wig, spangled leotard and tights, she was petite and glamorous as she led Socrates on-stage and shut him in a gilded cage. She gave him half an apple, then locked the doors with a heavy chain and circled the cage, tapping it with a wand to show how solid the bars were. In full view of the audience Mr Tolly drew sky-blue curtains across the back, the sides, and finally the front of the cage. Giant mirrors enabled the audience to see all round. Then Dot struck a pose and Mr Tolly stepped forward.

"Adjo fiddly dum-ya kum!" he cried and made some magic passes with his hands.

Then, grasping a thick golden cord, he pulled it dramatically. The curtains fell to the boards. Socrates had gone. In his place was a curly mongrel: it was Tangle. Mr Tolly stepped into the cage, clipped a lead to his glittering collar, and led him before the audience.

"Aaahhh!" cried the children. Shouting and applause filled the hall.

At Mr Tolly's back the cage was removed.

"I wonder what happened to the donkey." He scratched his head. "Have any of you children seen him?"

"No-o-o-o!" came the response.

"Are you sure?"

"Ye-e-e-es!"

He looked down at Tangle. "Perhaps the dog ate him."

They shouted with laughter.

"Ah, well! Maybe he'll turn up before the end of the show." Mr Tolly gazed across the audience. "Now – I need a volunteer."

Eager hands shot into the air. Mr Tolly looked round uncertainly then fixed his eyes on the balcony.

"Colonel Priestly!" he said. "Thank you!" though the Colonel's arm was not raised. "Would you care to join me on stage?"

"No, no." Colonel Priestly gestured with a hand.

"Come, sir." Mr Tolly pressed him with good humour. "You're well-known for your charity work. Come and join the fun. Show us what a sport you are."

The Colonel's eyes slid sideways in desperation. He did not want to appear on stage with this magician. "No," he shook his head laughing.

"Go on!" came a voice from the audience.

"Be a sport!" cried someone else.

Six hundred faces were turned in his direction.

"There you are, sir. You hear them. They want you!" Mr Tolly beamed towards the gallery and beckoned. "Come on, give the town a chance to applaud your generosity."

Aunt Bridget stood at Harry's side. "Isn't he terrific!" she said.

"Ve vant Priestly!" came a deep cry.

It was taken up. "We want Priestly! We want Priestly!"

The pressure was too great to resist. Colonel Priestly rose, smiling to hide his hatred for the man who was making him do this thing.

The audience cheered.

"Thank you, sir. Thank you. Bravo!"

Mr Tolly turned back to the audience. "And now, while the sporting Colonel makes his way down," he threw out an arm, "I give you my assistant – the brilliant, the glamorous, the one and only – Dotty Skylark!"

She was a sensation! For two breathtaking minutes Dot zipped and cartwheeled and catapulted about the stage in a firework display of acrobatics that long before she had finished had the audience leaping in their seats, shouting and cheering. As a climax she sprang high into the air, so high she might have been on a trampoline, performed a double somersault, and came down in a perfect splits.

The audience was ecstatic! Bright as a doll, Dot bowed and waved.

Then, panting happily, she descended the steps and escorted Colonel Priestly to the stage.

"Anything go wrong here, Dotty Skylark," he smiled broadly, "and I'll make you sorry you were born! All of you. I'll squash you like a matchbox full of insects!"

"Ah!" Mr Tolly applauded briefly and greeted him with a

handshake. "Thank you for volunteering." He ushered Colonel Priestly into the centre-stage spotlights and turned to his assistant. "May I have the cards, please."

Dot carried them across, a giant pack almost a metre in length.

"And the scarf."

She laid a blue silk scarf on the magician's table.

"Thank you." Gallantly Mr Tolly kissed her hand.

Dot retreated into the wings.

Aunt Bridget beckoned. "Have you got them?"

"Yes." Glancing behind her to make sure they were unobserved, Dot revealed Colonel Priestly's wallet and pocket book.

"Good work." Aunt Bridget glanced up a flight of steps that led from the wings. "Up here, quick! You too, Harry."

They ran up the stairs and into a tiny dressing room, little more than a cupboard. Angel and Max, still wearing a big hooked nose and Scrooge's rags, were waiting for them.

A small camera was in Angel's hands.

"Right, Max, you go through that." Aunt Bridget thrust the wallet into his hands. "Anything interesting, anything at all, give it to Angel. I'll deal with the pocket book. Dot, you keep *cave*."

At once Dot posted herself at the door, looking up and down the corridor.

With quick fingers Aunt Bridget turned the pages of the small leather-bound notebook.

"Nothing ... nothing ... nothing. Aha! Angel – "

She spread the pages on a wobbly card-table. Angel leaned above them with his camera. Flash!

Aunt Bridget turned the page. "Again."

Flash!

"And again."

Flash!

Max flicked through a fat bundle of twenty-pound notes and put them back.

"A sheet here, Angel." He spread it on the green baize.

Flash!

Two minutes ticked by.

"Harry," said Aunt Bridget. "Downstairs and see how Mr Tolly's getting on. He'll give you a signal how long we've got left. Come straight back and let us know."

Harry galloped down the stairs. Standing in the wings he saw that Mr Tolly had been blindfolded with the blue scarf. Colonel Priestly was showing a giant card to the audience. Behind the Colonel's back Mr Tolly held up a tie. The audience roared with laughter. Puzzled, Colonel Priestly looked round but by then the tie had been tucked away.

Ah, he can't see me, thought Harry. I'll have to wait. Then Mr Tolly half turned towards him and raised a hand to adjust his top hat. For a split second two fingers flickered in the air – then the act went on.

Harry raced back up the stairs. "Two minutes," he panted.

"Long enough." Aunt Bridget was calm. "Another one here, Angel."

"And here," said Max behind Scrooge's straggly beard.

The camera flashed.

With thirty seconds in hand the work was complete.

"All in order, Max?" said Aunt Bridget.

"Yes, that's it." Max handed the wallet to Dot.

"And the pocket book," said Aunt Bridget. "Got them the right way round, Dot? Good, off you go. Harry, you're looking after Tangle and Socrates, remember. Angel and I will slip out the back way. Good work, everybody. See you after the show."

Dot's glittering leotard and bright wig were before Harry as they ran along the corridor and down the stairs. Tangle and

Socrates were tied to a rail at the bottom. Briefly Harry made a fuss of them and ran on. Just in time he arrived in the wings.

"And, sir, is *this* your card?" Still blindfolded, Mr Tolly held the card aloft. "The nine of diamonds?"

The audience burst into loud applause.

With a flourish Mr Tolly pulled the scarf from his eyes, stood splendidly triumphant for a moment, then handed scarf and cards to Dot who came running from the wings.

"And a big hand for Colonel Priestly." Mr Tolly rested a hand on his shoulder. "A jolly good sport."

With shouts and whistles the audience responded.

"Thank you very much."

"Not at all." Colonel Priestly made for the steps that led down from the stage into the audience.

"Oh, one moment. Before you go, sir. I wonder, have you lost anything?"

"No, I don't think so."

"I mean, you haven't missed anything since you came on to the stage?"

"No, I – !" Colonel Priestly's hand flew to his jacket. His wallet and pocket book were still there. "No, I don't think so. Not that I'm aware of."

"Not something made of – gold?"

The Colonel glanced down at his waistcoat. His valuable repeater watch and the fat gold chain that crossed his stomach had both gone. Rather crossly he looked up and saw them dangling from Mr Tolly's fingers.

The audience laughed. Watch and chain were returned.

Carrying them in his hand and trying to smile, Colonel Priestly turned again towards the steps.

A second time Mr Tolly called him back. "I'm so sorry. But you haven't by any chance lost something else? Say an article of clothing?"

Angry blotches of red shone on the Colonel's cheeks. "No, I, er – " The scarlet handkerchief was still in his breast pocket. "No, I don't think so."

"Not a Brigade of Guards tie?" It trailed from Mr Tolly's hand. "Perhaps not everyone knows," he stood beside the smaller man, "that the Colonel here was an officer in one of our most distinguished regiments – my old regiment as it happens – the Grenadier Guards."

"Wonderful!" Max laughed. "Look at him. More like a corporal in the Catering Corps. He's six inches too short for the guards."

"Will people know that?" said Harry.

"Of course. *And* Priestly knows it."

"See how red he's gone," said Dot.

To more applause the tie was returned.

"Was Mr Tolly really in the Grenadier Guards?" said Harry.

"He certainly was. Captured by the Nazis and escaped. Got the M.C. for bravery. You won't hear him mention it, though. Gentlemen don't boast about that sort of thing – or lie, like Priestly."

Watch and tie in hand, Colonel Priestly made his way down the steps into the audience. Finally it seemed he had made his escape from the stage. But Mr Tolly had one more surprise in store.

"Oh, Colonel! What will you think of me! I almost forgot." He patted his pockets as if searching for something. "One last little item."

Colonel Priestly was furious. Somehow, with hundreds of pairs of eyes upon him, he managed to force his crimson face into a smile. "This time I really don't think so."

"If you could return for one moment … I truly think you should."

"I have nothing else to lose." He patted his collar and pockets.

"My tie, my wallet and pocket book, my watch, my handkerchief. They're all here."

"Do *you* think he should?" Mr Tolly addressed the audience.

"Ye-e-e-es!"

"Please, sir."

As Colonel Priestly made his way back up the steps it was hard to tell whether he was smiling or snarling.

Mr Tolly, beaming warmly, waited for him centre-stage.

The Colonel reached the top of the steps and advanced into the spotlights. Then he appeared to stumble. Whether his heel struck an uneven board on the stage or his toe caught the turn-up of his trousers, it was hard to tell. What was certain, however, was that the next moment, without any warning, his trousers fell down. Colonel Priestly gave a cry and clutched at his waist, his knees – too late. The ginger tweed trousers lay in folds about his feet, revealing to the startled audience his shirt tail, thick white legs gripped by sock suspenders, and a giant pair of boxer shorts gaily patterned with girls in bikinis.

Quickly he bent to pull them up. In the confusion of the moment his shoe caught in the waistband. He staggered, he hopped, he clutched Mr Tolly for support.

Resplendent in his top hat, crimson suit and cape, Mr Tolly held out a pair of jazzy braces. "I'm so – !"

Furiously, as the first waves of laughter broke about the hall, Colonel Priestly hauled up his trousers, snatched his braces from Mr Tolly's hand, and stumbled into the wings. His face was livid with rage. To those who saw him close it appeared that he was about to burst a blood vessel.

Harry watched him pass.

The Colonel paused in his flight and stared at him venomously. "You laugh, boy!" he hissed. "I'll make you pay for this! You *and* your criminal friends. I'll make you rue the day you were born! All of you!"

"On your bike, Priestly." Max stood at Harry's side, long-whiskered, a few strands of grey wig scraped across his scalp. "Meddle with us and you'll find you've got a fight on your hands."

"Aarrggh!" Colonel Priestly raised a fist as if to strike him then thought better of it. "Geriatric old cons! You should all be put away!" Clutching his watch, tie and trousers, he ran off down the corridor.

Harry and Max watched him go.

"Oh, Mr Tolly! You beauty!" Max gazed across the stage to where the magician was still trying to make himself heard above the gales of laughter that rose from the audience. "He did us proud! Didn't he, boy?"

"I hope so," Harry said uncertainly.

19
Revenge at Dawn

At quarter to eight on Sunday morning Harry was woken by a commotion on the staircase below his bedroom. People were shouting. There was the noise of a scuffle.

It was still dark. Tousled and hot with sleep he switched on his bedside lamp. The light stabbed his eyes. Blinking, he saw Tangle at the gap in the door, staring down the well of the spiral stairs.

The shouting continued, the landing light came on. Tramping footsteps mounted towards his bedroom. Alarmed, Harry sat up and swung his feet to the floor.

Tangle began barking, bristling towards the intruders. The footsteps and voices reached the landing. The door swung wide.

A tall policeman entered first. He was followed by two women Harry had never seen: one thick-set and forty with the shadow of a moustache, the other young and spotty. Then came Aunt Bridget and Mrs Good, and at their backs another uniformed policeman.

"There's no argument," said the senior of the two women. "He's got to come with us. I've got a magistrate's order!"

"It's ridiculous!" Aunt Bridget wore a long woollen dressing gown. "This isn't a police state. You can see, he's got a perfectly good home here. He's neat, he's clean, he's healthy, he's happy, he's good-mannered, he goes to school regularly. What's wrong with the way we're bringing him up? Look at his bedroom."

They looked around the large chamber, from the flushed boy on the bed to the open beams, the beautiful *Gauguin* on the white wall, Angel's painting of him on the raspberry cart, the bag of schoolbooks by the table, his clothes hung on the back of a chair.

"Up in an old stone tower!" exclaimed the moustached woman. "All by himself! It's not natural. What if there's a fire?"

"There's a rope ladder under his bed. It's all been approved by the safety inspector."

"Got an old mongrel up here an' all!" said the spotty woman in a disagreeable voice. "Prob'ly got fleas. Sleepin' on his bed. It's not 'ealthy!"

"That's his pet!" said Mrs Good hotly. "You'll not find a nicer dog than Tangle this side of Timbuktu."

"That's not what we've heard," said the older woman. "Our report is that it attacked a local landowner and bit him quite severely. If he'd reported it at the time, it's very likely the dog would have had to be destroyed." She put a hand towards Tangle who backed away snarling. "See." She made a note on the pad she was carrying.

"Good dog." Aunt Bridget gave Tangle a reassuring pat. "Quite right."

The policemen seemed sympathetic. One, dark-haired, peered with interest from the high window and looked through a sheaf of Harry's drawings. The other shrugged apologetically. "I'm sorry, we've got no option. It's a magistrate's order. The boy's got to go with the social workers."

"It's for his own good," said the younger woman. "There's been complaints. A house full of ex-prisoners. All well-known criminals. All pensioners. It's not a fit place for a young boy to grow up."

"A bad influence," said the senior woman. "Bad moral example! Stands to reason."

"How dare you!" said Aunt Bridget. "How dare you say such things in this house! In what way are we not bringing him up properly? Lovely grounds to play in. Animals. A house full of people – every one of whom loves him like their own grandson. His homework's done regularly. There's not one shred of evidence that we've been a bad influence on the boy in any way. He came to us here at Lagg Hall when his parents died. We're delighted to have him. Words can't express the joy he's brought to us all. He has a loving, stable home here and you want to break it all up. It's wicked, that's what it is, plain wicked."

"We're not here to argue," said the thick-set woman. "From what we hear there's clear signs of ill-treatment as well. Covered with bruises sometimes." She consulted a document. "On his legs and his back."

"Ill-treatment! There's nobody in this house wouldn't die for him! Ill-treatment! If there's a few bruises it's from football. He's a lively boy. And Huggy – Miss Karsavina – is teaching him to wrestle. Maybe he got a few knocks there."

"Football! Wrestling! Is that what you call it? We'll see what the doctor has to say."

"And not everybody agrees he's the polite, well-brought-up boy you'd like us to believe," said her spotty companion. "Far from it."

"We know who you're talking about," said Mrs Good. "That horrible teacher of his, Miss McScrew."

"And our neighbour, Colonel Priestly," said Aunt Bridget. "We know all right. They're the ones behind it. He's the magistrate signed the order, isn't he?"

"His nasty revenge for what happened at the concert two nights ago!" said Mrs Good. "That's what it is. He can't touch the rest of us so he takes it out on the boy."

The social workers did not reply.

"I knew it. I knew the second I saw you," said Aunt Bridget. "Maybe you'll be hearing more about dear *Colonel* Priestly in the near future." She smiled grimly. "But what about Mr Foggarty, the headmaster, what does he say about the boy? What about the other teachers? What about the school bus driver?"

"Like I said," repeated the senior woman, "we're not here to argue, we're here to carry out the order of the magistrate. The boy's got to come with us – now."

"And the police are here to ensure we're not hindered in doing our duty," said her colleague. "So we don't want no trouble."

The young policemen shuffled their feet and looked uncomfortable.

"His safety and welfare is all we care about," continued the moustached woman. "The social services will see he's properly housed and taken care of while there's a thorough investigation. That's the time to argue and make any complaints you might have." She shuffled through some dog-eared papers. "Here's the order. It's the law!"

The word brought silence.

The spotty woman smiled and turned to Harry. "Come on, get yourself dressed. Have you got a suitcase?"

Harry looked at Mrs Good.

"No, we threw out the old thing he brought with him," she said.

"Oh, well, poly-bags will do." She rooted in the bag she was carrying and produced three crumpled supermarket bags. "Where's your spare clothes?"

"He is not carrying his clothes in those!" said Mrs Good firmly. "Wait here. You're not to touch a *thing*!"

Fifteen minutes later, tidily dressed and with a neat blue suitcase by his side, Harry stood on the gravelled forecourt. Most of the snow had gone, it was a clear frosty morning. The first glimpse of sun showed red through the trees. Two cars were drawn up, one a police car, the other belonging to the social workers.

"There's nothing we can do, Harry, not right now." With difficulty Aunt Bridget withheld her tears. "But I promise you, I will move heaven and earth to get you home as soon as possible."

"And that goes for all of us."

"'Ere, buy yersel' some sweeties wi' this." Fingers pressed a crumpled ten-pound note into his hand.

It was wrapped around something scrunchy and metallic. He looked down. It was the probes.

"Ssshhh! Careful!" Fingers' back was to the social workers. "'Appen they might come in 'andy."

"Yeah!" Harry's eyes were wide. "Thanks." He tucked them into his trouser pocket.

"All right," said Spotty in her unpleasant nasal voice. "No good puttin' it off, hangin' round here in the cold. Say your goodbyes an' we'll be on our way."

"You're sure he'll get a good breakfast?" said Mrs Good.

"I said so, didn't I," the thick-set woman replied crossly.

"You vatch your mouth or I fetch you von!" said Huggy ominously.

"Goodbye, dear." Wrapped in a fluffy pink dressing gown, her make-up a wreck, Auntie Florrie hugged him fiercely. "We'll have you back before you can say Percipops and Lavvy-Poo!"

The policemen climbed into their Panda car. The senior social worker pulled open the door of a dusty Volkswagen estate. A pile of blankets and children's secondhand clothes straggled across the back seat. She pushed them aside to make room for Harry.

He watched her. He did not want to get into that dingy car with those dingy women.

Suddenly, without thinking about it, he took to his heels. Across the gravel he fled, across the frosty lawn and into the trees.

At his back there was confused shouting:

"Stop! Come back! That's it, boy! No, Harry, no! Go on, go on, you'll lose 'em in the woods! You little devil! Catch 'im, catch 'im!"

Harry sprinted as if his feet had wings. But it was one thing to dodge Beastly Priestly and Gestapo Lil, quite another to outstrip a fit young policeman. Closer and closer came the thud of heavy shoes. He risked a glance over his shoulder. The policeman's hat had fallen off, he was running like the wind, overtaking Harry at every stride.

Soon they were deep among the trees, dodging this way and that through the thick trunks and bushes. The policeman was right at his back. Harry dug his foot in, turned like a hare and shot away in another direction. The dark-headed policeman gave a cry and skidded into a tangle of thorns.

Soon he was back on Harry's tail. A strong hand grabbed the shoulder of his anorak. Like an eel Harry slithered out of it, scrambled to his feet and raced back the way they had come.

Without warning his ankle was caught by a trailing stem of bramble. There was no staggering, no trying to keep his feet. At full speed he fell smack on his face, flat as a flounder. Gasping and winded he lay among the frosty leaves.

Next moment the policeman had him by an arm.

"My!" he panted. "You're some runner! School champion, are you?"

Harry looked up, struggling for breath.

The kindly policeman collapsed by his side. "It'll not be so bad... Don't worry yourself... With any luck you'll be back here afore you know it." He rubbed the sweat from his forehead and looked around. "Great place, this. I'd have loved it when I was a lad your age."

Harry managed a faint smile.

"Couple o' battleaxes, them social workers, eh?" said the policeman. "Wouldn't fancy being married to one o' that pair. Still, it's not them you'll be living with, is it."

They lay for a minute then rose and made their way back to the cars.

"A real nice lad," the policeman said to the social workers. "You canna blame him for trying. So no rows, all right? An' look after him well, mind. I'm going to take an interest in this one myself."

Anorak over his arm, Harry said goodbye to his friends and stepped into the stale cigarette smell of the brown Volkswagen. The door slammed shut. He tested the lock but it was child-proof. There was no way out except past the social workers.

"Fasten your seat belt!"

The engine started, the car drew away. Harry rubbed the fogged window at his side. Through the grimy glass he saw the small group standing on the pebbles. Behind them Lagg Hall was pink in the light of sunrise. They were there, they were gone, as the car swung in a semi-circle and jolted away down the drive.

Harry looked back and saw the Panda car following. He sank back against the upholstery, swamped by misery. Everything he loved was being left behind: his home, his friends, his dog, his schoolmates, the woods. Where were these horrible women taking him? Was it far away? Where would he live and sleep – in a friendly house or "a home for penniless orphan brats" as Gestapo Lil had threatened? Where would he go to school? Who would tell Akku and Charlie? When would he come home to Lagg Hall? Would he come back at all?

He could not bear it.

Then, thrusting his hands into his pockets, he felt the crumpled ten-pound note and smooth steel of the probes.

20
Felon Grange

For ten minutes the dusty brown Volkswagen bowled along country roads then turned into a stately entrance. Wrought-iron gates stood before them. Stone lions, griffins and other heraldic creatures stared down from an ancient arch. In ornate gold lettering a board proclaimed:

FELON GRANGE
PRIVATE

The spotty young social worker stepped from the car and spoke into an intercom set in the wall. Overhead a security camera followed her movements. The tall black gates hummed open to admit them and closed at their backs. Like some predatory insect, the camera followed their progress then returned to its eerie hunt for intruders.

Slumped on the back seat Harry had no eyes for the splendid gate or noticeboard and only slowly became aware that they had left the public lanes and were driving through parkland. On each side of the pink drive stood iron railings. Beyond lay landscaped pastures set with ancient oaks. White cattle with spreading horns watched them pass, steaming in the frosty air. Half a mile ahead, at the end of an avenue of beech trees, stood a magnificent white mansion.

He looked behind. The police car had returned to town. They were alone.

An ornate fountain stood in the middle of the forecourt. King Neptune held aloft a conch shell from which water cascaded over his limbs and splashed cherubs astride leaping dolphins. Some of the figures were sheathed in ice.

The grimy Volkswagen swung in a semi-circle and drew up before a tremendous portico with steps and tall fluted pillars.

"You stay here in case the kid tries anything."

The moustached social worker climbed the steps, passed between the white pillars, crossed the porch and rang a bell. After some time the door opened and a male servant appeared. They talked briefly. The door closed.

The social worker waited.

Harry watched.

After several minutes the door re-opened. A figure emerged. It was a man. He wore a green silk dressing gown and was smoking a cigar. Briefly he exchanged words with the social worker then advanced into the morning.

It was Colonel Priestly.

Smiling nastily he stood on the top step and looked down at the car. Harry's startled face gazed up from the window.

It was cold on the porch. The Colonel clutched the neck of his dressing gown. Again he spoke to the social worker then shouted behind him.

"Smithy! GBH!"

Almost at once two sturdy servants came running. The Colonel spoke to them, smiled down once more at Harry, then returned to the warmth of the house.

Followed by Smithy and GBH, the social worker descended to the car and gestured for her colleague to open the window.

"He wants to talk to us. Special arrangements for this one, he says." She lowered her voice. "Couple of hundred quid in it,

I reckon."

"What, each?"

"Yeah." She jerked a thumb. "These two are going to take care of – what's he called?"

The young woman consulted the magistrate's order. "Eugene Augustus Montgomery Harold Barton." She laughed.

"That's right. Eugene-Augustus. Stuck-up little brat. What a name!"

She opened Harry's door and caught his arm. "Come on, out. You're to go with them."

Harry resisted.

"None of that," she said, "it's too early in the morning. Out!"

"No!" Harry pressed back from the door. "Not with them."

"Oh, dear!" She sighed. "Look, we don't want to have to use force."

"Out the way, love." One of the servants, GBH, pushed her aside and leaned into the car. "You! Come 'ere!"

He seized Harry's arm and dragged him from the car. Harry resisted, bringing half the blankets and old clothes with him. They trailed across the frosty pink tarmac.

"An' quit yer strugglin' or I'll fetch yer one!" The man raised a beefy hand.

Harry struck at his face and kicked his leg. The next second his head was ringing from a heavy blow.

"'Ere, Smithy. You grab 'is legs. I'll take this end."

Harry bucked and wriggled like an eel but in their strong hands he was helpless. Shouting his resistance, he was carried up the steps, between the pillars, across the porch and in through the front door of Felon Grange.

Colonel Priestly stood in the hallway – richer and gloomier than Lagg Hall – warming his hands round a cup of coffee.

"What you want doin' with 'im, Colonel?" GBH had to shout to make himself heard above Harry's roars.

"Shut him up, for Pete's sake! Gag him!" A yellow duster lay on a polished table. "Here, use this."

The duster was rolled up and thrust into Harry's mouth.

"That's better. Hear yourself think now."

The social workers hovered on the porch. Colonel Priestly regarded them contemptuously.

"Look at them! Like two of the witches out of *Macbeth*! Come in, come in! Don't let all the heat out! Shut the door!"

They did as they were told.

Testily he pointed down a corridor. "Kitchen's along there. I'll be with you in a minute."

They departed.

"Nnnn! Ngggg! Ngggg!" struggled Harry.

"Sling 'im in the cellar, Colonel?" GBH took a better grip on Harry's jacket.

"What, with all my wine? Use your loaf." The Colonel thought. "No, put him in that empty dressing room on the first floor. The one with no windows. And lock the door. Then get on with your work." He looked down at Harry. "And you can sit up there and sweat while we decide what to do with you." He topped up his coffee from a silver pot. "Let's see: likely to run away ... that means locked up ... some kids' institution. Mmm! Grimthrash might do nicely. Charlie Hobnail owes me a favour." He looked back at Harry. "How d' you fancy that? Head shaved and locked up with a crowd of kids used to carrying knives and knuckledusters. Older than you. All convicted of robbery with violence – beating up teachers and old ladies. Murder!"

"Nnnn! Aggghh!"

"Ten days there while we get you made a ward of court. Then pack you off to the far end of the country. Some grotty orphanage. Or a couple of ignorant, ratty foster-parents. Broken windows and walls covered in graffiti. One of my *special* probation officers to keep an eye on you." He snorted. "That ought to take care of you – little toe-rag! That'll teach you to throw eggs and make a fool of *me*! I warned you not to play games with Percy Priestly."

"Nnnn! Nggggg!"

"Hah!" The Colonel sipped his coffee with obvious enjoyment. "Take him away."

Harry was carried up the splendid staircase past oil paintings of distinguished men and women and along the richly-carpeted corridor above. Through half-open doors he saw luxurious bedrooms with long curtains and satin bedspreads. Reaching a closed door, Smithy dropped Harry's legs and turned a brass key. The door opened to reveal a small unlit room. Harry's grip was torn from GBH's jacket and he was thrust sprawling inside. He spat the duster from his mouth and sprang back but before he could reach it the door swung shut. The key clicked in the lock.

All was black as midnight.

He hammered on the panels.

"Less o' that!" GBH's tone was threatening. "You stay there till we come for yer."

"'S right. Any more o' that 'ammerin' or shoutin'," Smithy added his voice, "I'll come in an' give yer a good 'idin'. You've got my word for that. Think on!"

Harry's ear still burned from the blow GBH had given him outside. Their voices retreated.

He stood in darkness. Dim light filtered round the edge of the door. Somewhere there must be a light switch. His hand groped across the wall and found it. The dazzle of a naked bulb flooded the room.

It had gold-flock wallpaper and a thick green carpet. There were two pieces of furniture, a reproduction chest of drawers and a wardrobe. Harry examined them. Both were empty except for a checked tweed suit on a hanger. There was no doubt who it belonged to. Throwing jacket and trousers to the floor, he stood on them with both feet and heaved. With a satisfying r-r-r-r-ip! the trousers split down the leg, the jacket tore up the back. He threw them like rags into the bottom of the wardrobe.

Taking the probes from his pocket, he selected the strongest and raked it across the chest of drawers. Deep scratches scarred the glossy veneer. He did the same to the door and the walls, circling the room with the point pressed hard. The paper tore, plaster crumbled to the carpet.

These acts of vandalism, the first and last Harry was ever to commit, stopped him from thinking. When they were finished, the awfulness of his situation rose inside him like a tide. Sinking to the floor, back against the wall, he stared across the room in despair.

But not for long.

Rising, he crossed to the door and pressed his ear to a panel. From far away came the noise of hoovering. Otherwise all was silent.

He peered into the keyhole. Among the probes was a tool for removing a key. He inserted it. Fine claws gripped the metal. He turned it, exerting gentle pressure. In half a minute the key slipped from the lock and landed with a soft thud on the corridor carpet.

Harry removed the implement and again examined the keyhole. He selected a probe. Briefly it scratched. The tumblers were raised: with a well-oiled *click* the lock snapped open. He returned the probes to his pocket and took off his shoes. All was quiet. Inch at a time he eased open the door and looked out.

The corridor was deserted. Shoes in hand, soft as a wraith, he flitted to the nearest bedroom – cream and gilt – pulled the door shut at his back and hurried past the big bed to the window. It was a long way down, too far to jump. He opened the window and peered along the wall of the house. No drain-pipe was within reach. Disappointed and very frightened, he pulled the window shut.

A second bedroom – shades of apricot – was the same. And a third.

Harry grimaced. It would have to be the stairs.

The corridor was still empty. The thick carpet muffled his feet as he ran to the landing and peered down. The hall, too, was deserted. A distant sound of voices and brief laughter came to his ears. Clutching the banister, he crept down the broad staircase.

With no warning, no noise of footsteps, a young servant appeared below him. His head was shaved to stubble, he wore jeans and a plastic apron. Harry shrank back and froze. Believing himself unobserved, the youth picked up a packet of slim cigars that Colonel Priestly had left on a table and slipped some into his shirt pocket. With a jaunty step he passed on out of sight.

Harry continued to the bottom of the stairs, glanced right and left along corridors, and ran across the hall to the stained-glass doors of the lobby. They closed behind him. He hurried to the massive front door and cautiously pulled it open. The tremendous portico was clear. Nobody moved in the forecourt. Then beyond the fountain he saw a scarlet sports car speeding up the avenue of beech trees.

Gestapo Lil!

There was no chance of escaping unseen. And the road was almost a mile away. Once the alarm was raised, GBH and Smithy would be on him long before he reached it. Harry ducked back into the house and pulled the door shut.

The hall was still empty. He looked to left and right then dashed off, silent in stockinged feet, along the corridor. Perhaps he could climb out of a window at the back.

A door stood half open. Harry darted through and found himself in a big cupboard. He emerged and ran on.

A stone-flagged scullery appeared to be for dogs. As he looked in, two ferocious creatures were eating their breakfasts. One was a Dobermann, the other an Alsatian. Thick chains ran from their collars to ring-bolts in the wall. Briefly they looked up, eyes savage, then resumed wolfing down the bowls of red meat. Harry felt the hair rise on his neck.

Sudden laughter came from a door close at hand. Standing in the shadows, he peered in. It was the servants' kitchen-cum-dining-room. GBH and Smithy sat with the two social workers having breakfast. GBH had his feet on the table. Something he said made the younger woman shriek and slap his leg.

"What a thing to say!" she crowed. "Oh, you're awful!"

"I know," he said. "Give us a kiss."

Harry crept away and ran back through the hall. Beyond the stained-glass of the lobby the front door was opening. Through the distorting panes he saw Gestapo Lil silhouetted in the entrance. There was not a second to lose. He dashed on down the far corridor.

The rooms here were larger. One door stood ajar. He glimpsed a white cloth and cut-glass jar of marmalade. There was a smell of bacon and toast.

Thirty metres behind him the lobby door swung wide. A panelled door was at his side. Harry had no option. Seizing the handle, he pushed the door open and slipped into the room.

It was a library, parquet-floored and panelled like the hall. Rich rugs lay before a comfortable leather suite. A bright fire glowed in the hearth. Half the walls were lined by shelves of books. A voice, savage as the dogs, snarled in the silence:

"Are you a fool! I told you never – never! – to disturb me in here without knocking!"

Colonel Priestly stood at one end of the shelves, his back to the room. Heavy books were in his hands.

Harry ducked behind the settee.

The Colonel replaced the books and turned. The library appeared empty. "What the – !" Then he saw Harry's head. "You! How the hell – ?" He rushed across the room, hands outstretched.

Harry sprang out of hiding and ran to the door.

"Come here! I'll break every – "

Harry flung the door wide and dashed into the corridor.

Gestapo Lil stood in the hallway staring towards the commotion.

Harry raced away in the other direction. The Colonel's roars were at his heels.

Another door stood open. It was a sun-lounge. Beyond French windows he saw wintry flower-beds and lawns. He ran across and seized the handles. The doors were locked. A key was in the lock. He turned it and tugged again. The doors were bolted!

Snorting like a wild pig, Colonel Priestly charged across the room towards him. Harry ran behind a cane armchair. The Colonel flung it aside. Harry fled to the settee and grabbed an arm. The Colonel seized the opposite arm and tugged. Harry resisted. With all his might the Colonel heaved. The settee was torn from Harry's grasp. Cushions flew in the air. Colonel Priestly staggered backwards and fell, pulling the cane settee on top of himself. Furious curses issued from the tangle of arms and legs.

Harry fled back into the corridor.

Gestapo Lil was upon him, her painted face twisted with fury. Her handbag thudded against the side of his head, her red nails seized his collar. Desperately he twisted and struggled but she was strong – as he remembered only too well. She had him by the back of the neck. He lost his footing and fell. The sudden weight of his body broke her grip. Scrabbling on hands and knees, he crawled free. She seized his jacket. He tore it from her grasp and stumbled away. She gave a cry and leaped after him.

Behind her the corridor was full of people: Colonel Priestly, his hair wild and dressing gown flying, Smithy, GBH, and the two social workers, buttered toast still in their hands.

Like a hunted rabbit, Harry dashed away with the crowd in pursuit.

The corridor turned at right angles. Skidding, he ran on. A narrow flight of stairs rose at his side. Two at a time he sprang up them.

Gestapo Lil was too close. She flung herself at his heels. Her clutching fingers caught the end of a trouser leg. Her other hand closed about his ankle. "Aaahhhh!" Full-length, Harry fell upon the stairs. Desperately he grasped the edge of the thin carpet. His grip was not strong enough. Helplessly he was dragged back. His free foot kicked out. He wedged a leg across the stairs. Gestapo Lil heaved. His body twisted. The leg buckled beneath him. It hurt. Something in his knee went *crack*! Harry cried aloud and let go with his hands. Head over heels he tumbled backwards into Gestapo Lil. She lost her balance. One on top of the other, mixed up as fighting cats, they crashed to the bottom of the stairs.

In a tangled heap they lay in the corridor, surrounded by the crowd.

Gestapo Lil was not hurt though her clothes were dishevelled. Her grip upon his ankle was unbroken. Releasing it, she seized him triumphantly by the neck of his jacket.

Harry gritted his teeth. Something terrible was wrong with his knee. Swamped by pain and despair, he looked up at the grinning faces above him.

21
Grimthrash Jail

Seafield Young Offenders' Institution was a hundred miles from Lagg Hall and stood on the edge of a great industrial city. It was a stern nineteenth-century building that had once been a prison and was surrounded by a towering wall of sooty stone. Every window was covered by bars and the thick doors were strapped with iron. In recent years muddy playing fields had been laid out at one side. They were ringed by electrified fences of heavy mesh topped with coils of razor-wire.

Why it had been renamed Seafield was hard to imagine, for the only field in sight – apart from its own trampled plots – was a littered eyesore of waste ground beyond one of the walls, and the nearest it came to the sea was a pile of sandy rubble dumped there following the demolition of a nearby gasworks. For three hundred and sixty-four days of the year the sky was leaden grey and a north wind whipped dust and litter into the faces of the inhabitants. No one ever called it Seafield. Universally it was known by its old name – GRIMTHRASH JAIL.

Harry's room was on the third floor, high above the exercise yard. The walls were white, the metal bed was covered by a red duvet. A covered bucket stood in one corner for use as a lavatory during the night. The light was protected by thick glass and metal hoops to prevent any boy from hurting himself. On a shelf stood a few books and a small radio which could not be turned up loud. There was a plain table and chair. From the window he looked above the wall to a wilderness of shabby streets and a skyline of steelworks, factories and smoking chimneys.

On his arrival that Sunday lunchtime Harry had been whisked into another car and driven straight to the city hospital. His knee, plainly, was dislocated. It was x-rayed and then, while nurses held him firmly on the table, snapped back into place by a doctor.

"It'll be stiff for a while," the doctor told him, "but I don't think anything's torn. Wear this knee support and keep off it as much as you can. You'll be all right." He ruffled Harry's hair. "People will think you're a footballer."

On his return Harry's clothes and lockpicking tools were taken away and he was made to take a shower, even though he had spent an hour in the bath the previous evening. Then he was given a freshly-laundered uniform: black shoes, thick navy-blue trousers, blue shirt and a navy-blue jersey with the initials S.Y.O.I. on the left breast. As he pulled the shirt over his head, Harry wondered about the boy who had worn it last. Next he was taken to the barber's shop where his hair was examined for lice and cropped short. After this he was shown his room and left there with a sandwich and tea, the first food he had eaten that day. Finally, a guard escorted him to the common room.

Harry had been dreading it – youngest in a prison of young criminals!

He need not have feared. Whatever their pasts, the boys – big boys with broken voices and hair on their upper lips – made him welcome and looked after him like a younger brother. They asked why he was there and in return told him their own stories. They lent him comics and invited him to play draughts and Monopoly. They told him terrible jokes and talked about football. Because he limped and his knee was sore they stopped others from jostling him in the dining-hall.

"'Ere, watch where yer goin'! Nearly knocked into my mate 'Arry, yer did. Do that again an' I'll black yer eyes for yer!" And turning to Harry, "All right, mate? This do yer? Come on, you lot, make a bit o' space."

In return, when they went to the schoolroom, Harry showed them how computers worked and helped them with their maths. They called him Einstein.

Although the boys were kind – and if his knee had been strong he could have played football with them in the yard – Harry hated it. He hated being dragged away from Lagg Hall. He hated the two women who had brought him to this place. He hated Mr Hobnail, the Governor, with his thick hairy hands and scented breath that smelled of cachous. He hated the way the guards shouted at them for no reason. He hated being locked in. He hated his bucket and the view from his barred window. He hated the thought that Beastly Priestly and Gestapo Lil had beaten him; that his whereabouts were being kept secret from his friends; and that while he waited helplessly, his future was being decided by the malevolent Colonel and people under his influence.

Ten days, they had said. Ten days in Grimthrash. It seemed like a life-sentence.

On his third night Harry could not sleep. He felt headachy and had not been able to eat his supper. For a time he thought he would be sick. His legs and back ran with sweat.

As usual the door of his room had been locked at nine o'clock. At ten the light was extinguished. In thick Grimthrash pyjamas he lay unhappily and watched the lights of distant cars cross the ceiling. It was a wild night. A December gale rushed and roared in the bars of his high window. Somewhere, beyond the noise of the wind, a train hooted, an ambulance raced to an emergency, police sirens wailed in the darkness.

A church clock struck one. Harry eased his knee and pulled the duvet about his neck.

Memories stopped him from brooding: his parents' parties at Hampstead; riding Chalky in the paddock; Ol' Goggly; roaring through the lanes on the Norton; summer fishing; Mr Tolly on stage; football with Akku and –

Suddenly, above the rush of wind, there was a sound.

Tap tap.

Harry was startled. He propped himself on his elbows and looked round. Where had the noise come from? Not the window, he was three floors up. Not the door, he was sure. Perhaps it had been imagination.

He sank back. If only –

Tap tap!

This time there was no doubt. Harry threw back the duvet and swung his legs to the floor.

Tap tap tap!

It came from the window. There was something outside, a dark shape silhouetted against the lights of the city. What was it? He was fifteen metres from the ground!

The vinyl was chill against his bare feet. Nervously he crossed the room.

"Harry!"

There was a face at the window. A little face like a walnut. A halo of white hair protruding from a woolly hat.

"Dot!"

"Ssshhh!" She put a finger to her lips and mouthed the words: "Can you open the window?"

He pulled it wide. The bitter gale burst into his room. Curtains billowed and comics went flying.

Harry shivered. "How did you know I was here? They said – "

"That copper told us." She was dressed in black. A tough little hand gripped the bars. "Look, we're going to – "

"How did you know which was my window?"

She jerked a thumb. "I've been perched on a roof over there half the night with a pair of binoculars. Bit parky! Saw you at bedtime. Look, we're going to – "

"How did you get up?" He looked down – the walls were sheer.

"Well they don't call me the Eiffel Spider for nothing, dear. But there's no time for all that now, will you *listen*! We're going to get you out. Fingers and Huggy are with me, your aunties are waiting in the car. Now I want you to get dressed straight away. And tell me, if we cut one bar out can you squeeze through the gap?"

Harry did not need to think about it. "Yes," he said.

"Good. Well I've got a rope, we'll pull up the nylon ladder. There'll be no problem. I want you to shut the window and when you're dressed press a blanket or something over it. There won't be much noise but there's no point taking chances. Now go."

She lifted a coil of light rope from her shoulders, looped it round two bars and dropped an end.

"Go!"

Harry shut the window. In two minutes he was dressed. Already the nylon ladder was secured and Dot had gone. As he heaved the duvet from his bed, Fingers appeared in her place. Barely discernible in the darkness he gave a cocky grin and thumbs-up, then pulled from his pockets an oilcan and small hacksaw.

A soft *eeh – aah – eeh – aah* came through the glass as he commenced work on the middle bar.

Standing on the chair, Harry pressed his quilt across the window. The noise was muffled. Certainly no guard would hear it through his door. He hoped none of the young offenders would be disturbed and raise the alarm.

As he stood there he felt sick again and dizzy. Briefly he closed his eyes.

For five minutes the sound continued then there was a little *chink* and silence. Harry waited a few moments then risked a peep. Fingers was gone. He examined the bar. In the darkness he could see no damage. A bright dust of iron filings shone on the window-ledge.

He eased the window open and tried to hear above the rush of the wind. The rope ladder was taut, somebody was climbing. He peered down but the bars got in the way.

Slowly a mountainous figure appeared, blacking out the lights of the city.

"Oh, my!" Huggy gasped. "Is easier for a little sqvirrel like Dot than a big Russian bear like me! Hello, Harry! Vot you doing in this clink, this horrible black-hole chokey? Ve have you out in no time. Stand back."

Bracing her feet, she grasped a side-bar with her left hand and the bar Fingers had sawn through with her right. Her muscles bulged, a little grunt of effort escaped from her nose. Slowly the thick iron bar bent outwards and upwards. She shifted her grip. "Mmmmmnnnhhhh!" Higher and higher went the bar until it stuck out from the wall like a long peg.

A big gap had appeared in the middle of his window.

"Right! You first," whispered Huggy. "I sqveeze aside. Climb past me. I vipe the fingerprints and fix the ropes so ve bring the ladder vith us."

Harry thrust his shoulders through the gap. The bent bar gave him a good handhold. He heaved.

"Aaahhh!" His bad leg twisted and burned like fire.

"You all right?"

"My knee! ... Let go! I can manage!"

Gritting his teeth, Harry pulled himself clear of the window. He felt weak and was sweating. For a moment he hung by his hands, high above the ground. The icy gale swung him like a pendulum, tore at his clothes, roared in his ears – but froze away the dizziness. His hurt leg dangled uselessly. With his good leg he cast about desperately for the nylon ladder and set his foot on a rung. Briefly he clung tight. Then fast as he could, he began to descend.

Only then did Harry realize that faces were pressed to the bars of the windows all around him. Some signal had passed from cell to cell. The young villains who had become his friends had watched every stage of the rescue, overheard the whispered conversations. No one had given the game away.

"Good on yer, Einstein!" they called softly. "T'ra. See y' about! Send yer mates back for me! Send us in a couple o' dolly-birds, OK? Watch how you go!"

"Thanks!" Harry smiled up and waved. "Good luck!"

Then gritting his teeth once more and battered by the wind, he resumed his descent of the prison wall.

Soon he stood in the exercise yard, pressed into a shadowy corner with Dot and Fingers. The ladder shook as the vast bulk of Huggy descended. Then Dot pulled a hanging line. The knot at Harry's window came unfastened. With a rustle and soft thud the nylon ladder fell to the cobbles.

He looked up. The grim wall towered above them. Like strange white insects a score of hands fluttered from the bars.

His knee throbbed and felt like jelly. Now that he was still the bitter wind chilled the sweat on his back. He shivered.

"Come on," said Fingers. "Now!"

The four hunched figures flitted across the lamplit yard to the shadow of the wall. Dot slung the coiled line about her shoulders and reached up. Tough fingers seized a protuberance, climbing shoes found a tiny ledge. She was half a metre from the ground ... a metre ... three metres. As if her hands and feet were spread with glue she clung to the wall.

A minute later, like a windblown pixie, she sat on top and dropped an end of rope. Fingers tied it to the nylon ladder. Someone on the far side hauled it up.

They waited.

"Right," Dot whispered. "All secure. Up you come."

"Harry, you first," said Huggy. "Both hands. You make it OK."

He looked up and took a determined breath, then seized the hand-lines and began to pull himself up. Heave with his arms, foot on the rung. Heave with his arms, foot on the rung.

Halfway up he was exhausted.

Huggy held the ladder away from the wall to make it easier.

"Come on!" Dot urged from above. "You're doing fine. Heave! That's it. Heave!"

"Up you go, boy," Fingers called softly. "Almost there."

Then Dot gripped his shoulders. With an effort Harry swung his leg across.

For a minute he could not speak.

The wall had protected him from the gale. Now it buffeted and roared about them. The sweat turned icy cold in his cropped hair. He pulled the dark prison jacket about his throat. He felt very exposed, perched on top of a prison wall in the middle of the night. On one side were the black windows of Grimthrash, on the other the streetlamps of the grimy city. It seemed impossible they would not be spotted.

A rubbish-strewn lane ran beneath the prison wall, separating it from a patch of waste ground, a derelict slum area with scrubby trees and piles of rubble. The old Mercedes, showing no lights, was pulled up below them. Dot's rope had been tied to the fender.

Aunt Bridget and Auntie Florrie stood in the lane gazing up. If they were tense their manner did not show it.

"Hello, dear!" called Auntie Florrie. "My word, what an

adventure! So exciting!"

"Quite like the old days," said Aunt Bridget. "Most invigorating!"

"Dot says you've hurt your leg. Never mind, soon get you patched up."

"What happened?"

"I twisted my knee. They took me to Felon Grange and – "

"What!"

"Yeah, those two women. Priestly paid them. I reckon they weren't proper social workers."

There was time for no more. Huggy and Fingers had arrived beside them.

"Heads below!" Dot pulled the ladder up one side and dropped the end down the other.

"I hold," said Huggy, "you go down. Harry, you first."

He grasped the handlines and slid from the wall. Compared with the effort of climbing it was easy. Half a minute later he stood in the lane by the Mercedes.

He was free!

Aunt Bridget nodded briskly. "Tomorrow morning you tell me *everything*!"

Unsuccessfully he tried to dodge Auntie Florrie's embrace and clouds of Chanel.

"Mmmm – mmm! What have they been *doing* to you? Those horrible women! And that *Beastly* Priestly! And in *prison*! Never mind, Auntie Florrie's got you now."

She let go. "Do you like the new number-plate? Nutty made it up specially for tonight."

Harry limped to the front of the car. In the dim street lights he read : GET 1M. Shakily he laughed.

Dot and Fingers stood beside them. Huggy alone remained on the wall, six metres above the cobbled lane. She dropped the ladder.

Harry gasped. "How's she going to get down?"

"You'll see," said Aunt Bridget. "Don't worry about Huggy."

Above them the huge woman, like an orang-outang, had shifted both legs to their side of the wall.

"Vatch out below!" she called in her bulldog voice. "Unless you vant be sqvished like ripe tomatoes. Here I come!"

Like a two-hundredweight sack of turnips she slid from the wall and came hurtling to the ground. Her arms flew up, her skirts blew high. The by-standers had a glimpse of two trunk-like legs and a tremendous pair of polka-dotted bloomers. Then she hit the cobbles and went bowling along the lane, head over heels like a beach-ball.

"Are you all right?" Harry hurried forward.

Huggy sat up among the old cans and newspapers. "Of course I all right! Vhy I not all right?" She straightened her clothes.

"Well, a great success, I'm sure." Auntie Florrie opened the car. "Time to be going home. Huggy, you in the front. The rest in the back."

They piled in. Harry found himself squashed between Aunt Bridget and Fingers. One smelled of clean soap, the other of tobacco. With a smooth roar the engine sprang into life, the headlamps came on.

For fifty metres they drove alongside the stern wall of Grimthrash then turned down a lane through the waste ground.

"Could you slow down a minute," Harry said. "Open the window."

Leaning across Aunt Bridget he waved to the pyjama-clad figures at the high windows of the prison. Pale arms waved back through the bars.

Auntie Florrie drove on. The Mercedes turned a second corner – and a third. They were among slums and tenements.

And when Harry looked back again, Grimthrash was hidden from view.

22
Folly in the Woods

The gale had become a storm. As they made their way through the woods the wind roared like an angry sea. No light penetrated the lowering clouds. In the beams of their torches the branches tossed and shaggy evergreens shook like nightmare.

Mrs Good, well wrapped up in a raincoat and waterproof hat, went first, then Harry, then Aunt Bridget. Tangle brought up the rear.

It was four o'clock in the morning.

Harry remembered the time he had gone hunting for Ol' Goggly. But then the trees had been in full leaf, it was a moonlit summer night and he was exploring. Then he had felt fit and strong. Now it was winter and the woods were inhospitable: the earth was a quagmire and the trees thrashed stinging twigs in his face. Now he was on the run – from Grimthrash Jail and the police. Now he felt sick: his bones ached, his head ached, his throat was sore. At every step pain shot through his knee.

Tangle trotted to Harry's side and touched him with his nose. For the twentieth time he rubbed the ragged coat. "Who's my lovely boy!" he whispered hoarsely. "Yes! You going to guard me, then, are you?" And Tangle's tail stood straight up with happiness.

Deeper and deeper they advanced into the Lagg Woods. The roar of the wind rose to a scream. Harry shone his torch into the branches overhead. Wildly they tossed against the black sky.

"What drama!" cried Aunt Bridget. "Isn't it wonderful!"

Mrs Good ignored her. "How are you feeling now?" she shouted, close to Harry.

"OK," he shouted back. But when her torch was turned away he shivered convulsively and closed his eyes with dizziness.

"Soon be there!" called Aunt Bridget. "Not far now."

Torch thrust forward and shielding her face with an arm, she pressed on into the wilderness.

Head lowered and feet squelching, Harry followed.

Five more minutes brought them to their destination. A short distance ahead a ghostly shape appeared through the trees. As they drew closer it materialized into the white folly Harry had visited so often during the summer. Swamped in vegetation and hung about by swaying branches, it now resembled a haunt for Count Dracula more than the romantic little temple he had painted.

A scatter of rain came on the wind. They ran the last few metres. Rotting leaves made the steps slippery. Twigs and fir cones crunched in the porch.

"We've swept out the inside," said Mrs Good, "and put in a couple of paraffin heaters."

She pushed open the door. A warm, pleasantly fumy scent wafted out at them. They entered and pulled the door shut. After the wildness of the night it was suddenly still, like a tomb, while the wind moaned about the dome and branches rattled on the roof like bones. The beams of their torches flashed across the darkness.

Mrs Good crossed to a ledge where a box of matches lay beside an oil lamp. She removed the chimney and put a fluttering match to the wick, replaced the chimney and adjusted the flame. The draughts made it leap, casting shadows about the marble walls and darkening the glass with little coils of smoke.

In the yellow lamplight Harry saw that a bed had been made up against one wall. A thick quilt was spread upon it, and on an upturned box alongside lay a number of games and this week's football magazines. A second box had been made into a bed for Tangle.

"I hope you'll be warm enough," Mrs Good was saying. "You're not at all well. I wouldn't have brought you out if it hadn't been absolutely necessary. But the bed's well-aired, Nutty fetched it across this afternoon. And I've put in a couple of hot-water bottles."

Harry did not care. He began pulling off his clothes, dropping them on the floor.

She took out his warm pyjamas. "And you won't mind being alone, just for tonight. You won't be frightened."

"I'll be all right." Harry buttoned the jacket she handed him.

"It's the best we can do for the moment. We hadn't reckoned on you being ill." Aunt Bridget gathered up his discarded clothes. "The minute they find your cell's empty, or see that bar sticking out from the wall, the police will be round here like flies." She smiled. "Priestly will be hopping mad!"

Harry climbed into bed and clutched a hot-water bottle to his chest. A wild gust of wind made the lamp gutter.

"It won't be for long," said Aunt Bridget. "Only a day or two till the heat's died down. Then we'll make other arrangements."

Harry closed his eyes.

"We'll try to have somebody here all the time," said Mrs Good. "Except tonight – because the police might want to see us all." She tucked the duvet about his legs. "There'll be a torch beside your bed but I'm turning off the lamp, don't want any light showing at the windows. I'll leave it over there in case of an accident."

"Mmm!"

"We'll stay for a few minutes to see you're comfortable."

"And Auntie Florrie or I will be back first thing in the morning," said Aunt Bridget.

"Mm."

Tangle stood watching the bed with bright eyes then cocked his eyebrows in the direction of the two women. Taking a chance, he jumped up by Harry's feet and curled up quickly before they could say no.

Dimly Harry felt the bed rock. Aunt Bridget was talking: something about Colonel Priestly – a gang – a date for delivery. He did not listen. Her voice was slipping away, along with Grimthrash, the storm, the folly, and the rest of that extraordinary night.

"He's worn out, poor lad."

"No wonder."

Harry heard the words but did not respond.

"Let him sleep now."

And ten seconds later – he did.

When Harry opened his eyes it was daylight. He had been dreaming. All was fever and confusion. For a moment he imagined he was dead, or buried alive in some chill marble vault. Grey light filtered from choked-up windows. A rushing, roaring sound filled the air. Dead hands were tap – tap – tapping above him, scraping to get in.

Then two shaggy paws clumped beside his head and Tangle was panting into his face. Abruptly Harry remembered. He was in the folly. The terrible feeling wasn't death, he was going to be sick! Jumping from bed he ran barefoot to the door, down the steps and into the trees.

Just in time.

It was awful! Icy rain saturated his head and back. His

stomach heaved. His chest ran with sweat.

Afterwards he felt better. Wiping his lips, Harry stood in the half-shelter of a bush and looked about him – blond and crop-headed in blue-striped pyjamas.

The storm was at its height. Wind screamed in the high branches. From a dim dark sky rain lashed through the trees and turned the earth to a swamp that spurted between his toes.

What time was it – morning or midday? There was no way of knowing.

He shuddered. The pyjamas clung to his whippet-thin body. Hunched against the rain he limped back to the steps. Sticks and fir-cones stabbed the soles of his feet.

Boom! The door shut with an echo, plunging the folly into gloom. Harry peeled off his sodden pyjamas and pulled on the trousers and jersey he had worn the night before. The material was scratchy against his skin. Standing by one of the heaters, he scrubbed his hair with his shirt and vest. Then, pulling both heaters close to the bed, he plumped his pillows, climbed in and pulled the quilt to his ears.

Harry shivered and was lonely. His head ached, his feet were like ice. Lying on his back, he gazed up into the dome and around the walls with their frosty memorials. He listened to the storm beating the wood.

A plate of red apples and tangerines stood on the box beside his bed. There was a can of juice, a large bar of fruit and nut chocolate, and a thermos flask. He was not hungry.

A note lay beside them:

> *Harry*
> *Have to go back to the Hall.*
> *Back as soon as poss. Keep*
> *warm. Love,*
> > *Auntie Florrie*

He laid it aside. Why had she hurried away, he wondered. Was there some trouble? Colonel Priestly? The horrible Mr Hobnail? The police with handcuffs?

There was nothing he could do, anyway.

For a while he lay on the edge of sleep then rose and lit the oil lamp. Several matches guttered in the draughts and blew out. He turned up the wick. It burned up smoky and blackened the glass. He adjusted it and wiped some of the soot away with his shirt, then carried the lamp to his bedside.

Tangle watched from the foot of the bed.

Despite the heaters it was bitterly cold. Harry's breath smoked in the lamplight.

Slowly, curled up beneath the quilt, he began to warm through. With little interest he reached for a football magazine and read a page. His eyes, smudged with tiredness, kept closing. He read another page. The magazine slid to the floor. Tucking his fingers beneath his chin and pulling up his knees, Harry gave a deep sigh and drifted away into a land of fevered dreams and perspiration.

When he woke again it was night. The windows had been covered and the lamp, a single point of light in the dark folly, burned cheerfully.

Huggy sat on a box with a huge piece of knitting.

"Ah, you vake up." She spoke gently, her big face beamed. "How you feeling now?"

Harry examined himself without moving. "A bit better."

"Is good. My, how you sleep! The best healer in the vorld for you."

"What time is it?"

"Eight o'clock." She examined her watch. "Qvarter past."

Harry lay comfortably, limply. He listened. The storm sounded less violent.

"You vant something to eat?"

He considered. "Yes, in a while."

"No hurry. You lie there. Vhen you ready I change the bed – you hot. Then see vhat you fancy." She indicated a basket on the floor. "I bring things vith me."

A dying gust rattled the door and made the lamp-flame leap.

"My, vhat vind! It nearly blow even *me* avay!" Her eyes opened wide. "But Dot – you know vhat *she* do? She dress up varm and go climbing the trees. In that storm! She mad!"

Harry smiled. He raised his head and saw Tangle. The tip of a tail wagged in greeting.

"Did the police come round?"

"The police! The police, you say! My, vhat activity! Police, social vorkers! They search the place – tvice! All through the attics, the sheds – everyvhere!"

"What did they do then?"

"Vhat can they do? They find no Harry Barton. No trace of us at that dreadful prison – vhat you call it?"

"Grimthrash."

"Ja. No trace of us at Grimthrash. The young prisoners – they see nothing, they hear nothing." She shrugged.

"But they must know you did it."

"Unless you some kind of Superboy! Ja, they know ve did it. But they have no proof. So they go avay."

Harry thought. "But they'll come back."

"Naturally. That vhy you stay here a few days. Until you qvite better. Then you join the rest of us – for Christmas!"

"How long's that now? I've lost track."

"Today the – nineteenth? My goodness, only six days to go! And I bought no presents yet!"

Harry eased himself on the pillows. Suddenly the cold, tree-strangled folly felt almost homely.

"Did you make out your list yet – for Santa Claus?"

"What list?"

"Vhat list! You mean you never make no list? Vhat presents you vant, of course! From Santa's vorkshop!"

He shook his head.

"Oh, my vord! Vell, I leave you a pencil and paper. No, better, ve do it now. Together." She rummaged in her handbag. "Then I take it back vith me and ve vhoosh it up the chimney to the North Pole!"

He smiled. "Gestapo Lil says I'm too old for Santa Claus."

"Too old! Vhat she know about it? Even *I* not too old for Santa Claus!" She laid aside her knitting. "Before ve start, vhy you not eat something. A nice orange? A piece of chocolate? A sandvich – your favourite, tinned salmon? A cup of hot soup?"

"What kind of soup?"

"Chicken. Goody make it special. You like some chicken soup?"

"Mmm!" Harry struggled up against his pillows. A smell of sweat and fever wafted from beneath the duvet.

"Is good." Carefully Huggy poured the soup from a flask and set a buttered roll beside him.

Harry warmed his hands around the mug and took a sip.

Huggy beamed again. She pulled a magazine on to her knee and rested an old envelope on top. "Now!" She sucked the end of a broken biro. "Vhat you vant from Santa Claus?"

Harry nibbled a corner of the roll. His tired eyes shone. "Well, I'd like a…"

23
The Snowy Return

The storm blew itself out and was followed by days of bitter cold. First came frost that turned the earth to iron. Then heavy snow which transformed the wood into a magical land.

For two days Harry stayed in bed. Then he was better – or almost. Sitting by the heaters with friends from the Hall, he played countless hands of poker and other cut-throat gambling games. With his Swiss army knife he carved sticks into sailing ships with masts and cotton rigging. Still limping, he romped in the snow with Tangle. And late at night he lost himself in adventure stories that transported him far away to desert islands, strange galaxies and the throb of Formula One racing pits.

All these were enjoyable but by the time five days had passed Harry was bored. Hiding out in the folly, on the run from prison and the police, might be a real adventure but it had lost its fun. He wanted to go back to the Hall, to lie in a hot bath and sit in Mrs Good's kitchen.

Late one morning he took his chance.

Nutty had been sitting with him, sharing a flask of coffee and a bag of Danish pastries.

"Aye, well." The bald handyman stood up. "I'd best be gettin' back. There's a spray job wanted on the car, dark winders, an' yer auntie wants the engine in special trim. Somethin' comin' up after Christmas, I understand. To do wi' yon Priestly. I daresay she'll tell y' aboot it when she comes round wi' yer lunch." With a big hand he rubbed Tangle's ears. "Ta-ra, well."

A trail of footprints wound through the trees. Harry watched the gawky figure disappear then hurried back inside. Quickly he straightened his bed, made the heaters safe and pulled on his anorak. Tearing a sheet from the scoring pad – page after page filled with doodles and columns of figures – he wrote a note:

> *In case you come and I'm not here.*
> *Nutty has just gone and I'm going*
> *to the hall – a diffrent way.*
> *Harry*
> *PS I'll take care nobody see's me.*

He left it on the box beside his bed, called Tangle and ran out into the white morning.

Abruptly he halted. A figure stood on the snowy trail. A policeman in uniform. Only twenty metres away.

Both froze, staring.

Harry's heart raced, his knee gave a twinge. He couldn't run. They had him!

Then something extraordinary happened. The policeman raised a finger to his lips – a silent *Ssshhh!* – and pulled off his hat. Harry recognized the dark-haired constable who had chased him through the woods a week before. The same constable who had told the social workers to look after him. The constable who had telephoned his aunts to tell them he had been taken to Grimthrash Jail.

The young man did not speak but pointed a finger back over his shoulder. Harry understood that other policemen were not far off. Then he pointed directly at Harry and away in the other direction.

Harry stared and did not move.

The man repeated his signals, urgently.

Harry nodded. *Thanks!* He mouthed the word and raised a hand. Beckoning Tangle, he set off through the trees in the direction the policeman had indicated.

Snow swished to the top of his wellingtons and fell from the branches in powdery cascades. After a couple of minutes he looked back. The kindly constable had vanished among the trees.

"Nothing here, sarge!" His faint call drifted on the air. "I reckon it's a wild goose chase."

There was a reply but Harry could not distinguish the words. He pressed on.

The men's voices receded.

The wood was beautiful and unreal, a tangled fairyland. White branches against a clear blue sky; coils of bramble turned to ice; spiders' webs thick as string. He clambered over snowy trunks and pushed through thickets. The midday sun, fat as an orange, hung among the trees.

His breath smoked. The cold was so intense that snowballs crumbled. He put his fingers in his mouth to ease the pain.

Harry's route took him past the lake, frozen now, a white and silver plain. He circled the shore. The rowing boat was crusted with ice and half full of snowdrift.

Five more minutes brought him within sight of Lagg Hall, warm and solid with smoke curling from the high chimneys. Two police cars were drawn up on the forecourt. Harry stayed back among the trees and watched.

Aunt Bridget came to the door of the conservatory. A man dressed in a warm jacket left one of the cars to speak to her. He entered the conservatory and the door closed.

A uniformed policeman appeared from the tower and crossed to the second car. Briefly he spoke into a radio then stepped in and pulled the door shut. The car did not drive away.

Harry shivered. His head ached. He was not as fit as he had thought.

Tangle looked up. What was happening next, he wanted to know.

It seemed the policemen were going to be there for some time. Harry retreated down the track to Chalky's paddock. The white horse snorted, steaming like an engine in the frosty air, and trotted to meet him. Harry climbed the fence and rubbed his silky muzzle then crossed to the wooden stable. It smelled cosily of dry dung and straw and horse sweat. Briefly he patted Socrates' woolly neck then raked some straw together and made himself comfortable.

An hour passed. Wild creatures looked in from the wood – a mouse, some chaffinches, a weasel. Tangle romped in covered with snow and cleaned himself with a noisy tongue. Chalky joined them and the warm, horsy smell grew stronger.

Harry dozed.

The cold woke him. He rose, stretching cramped muscles, and looked from the stable entrance. All seemed clear. He retraced his steps across the paddock and down the track. The cars had gone. Perhaps, however, police remained in the house. It would not be sensible to walk boldly to the front door. Turning aside, he circled through two hundred metres of woodland, emerged beyond the kitchen garden and descended to the back of the house.

A light burned in the kitchen. Softly Harry crept to the window and peered through. Mrs Good was washing up the lunch dishes. Nutty was helping her, a striped tea-towel slung over his shoulder.

Harry tapped on the glass. They looked up and saw his white face. Mrs Good flew to the window.

"Have they gone?" Harry whispered.

"Yes, love, all away. Come on round, the door's open." Her eyes grew troubled. "Ee, you look fair frozen. All done in."

"No, I'm fine." He started along the path. "Come on, Tangle. We're home!"

24
Christmas at Lagg Hall

For as long as Harry could remember, his parents had spent Christmas at Klosters, a beautiful and expensive ski resort in Switzerland. There they had many friends. They realized, of course, that Christmas was also a time for children and every year sent Harry expensive gifts – or to be precise, telephoned the leading toyshop in London, named a sum, and told them to choose and deliver whatever toys were most popular with boys at that time. This telephone call plus a big card that said

> *To Harry*
> *MERRY CHRISTMAS!*
> *Lots of love*
> *Mummy and Daddy*
> *x x x x x*
> *See you soon*

meant that their duties to their son were happily concluded and they were free to party and celebrate – to ski and laugh and dance and dine and drink champagne – with clear consciences.

Harry, meanwhile, with Gestapo Lil for company, played with his toys in the loneliness of that big house in Hampstead and longed for school to start again.

This year was different. This year Christmas was
WONDERFUL!

It was not safe for him to sleep in the tower, or any other room in the Hall, so Nutty knocked up a giant hay box in the old cart shed where he had his workbench and the air was sweet with the smell of logs. It had a lid with holes in it, a lid which could be pulled down in case of emergency and fastened with a hook.

On Christmas Eve Harry lay there in a sleeping bag, the lid up, reading a comic by the light of a small electric lamp. An enormous red stocking, specially knitted by Huggy, hung from a nail in a nearby post.

The door scraped and Mrs Good bustled in. In one hand she carried a torch, in the other a mug of hot milk. Three biscuits were in her apron pocket.

"Are you comfortable, love?"

Harry smiled up in the lamplight. "Yes, fine."

"Sure you're warm enough?"

"Warm as toast. It's nice in here."

"That's good. Well, drink your milk while it's hot, then lights out. Else Santa Claus won't come. Nothing but a stocking full of cinders for boys that leave the lights on too late." She kissed him on the forehead. "And pull down the lid before you go to sleep. Just in case."

"I will."

"Night-night, then. Sleep well. Big day tomorrow."

Her kindly face shone.

"Are you all going out later?"

"To the Watch Night Service, that's right. We go every year. But your Aunt Bridget's staying behind – and Mr Tolly. So you'll not be alone."

Harry thought about it. "Happy Christmas, Goody."

"Happy Christmas, love."

She returned down the shed. The door opened. "It's like *Silent Night* out here. Bright moon and everything." Her footsteps receded, crunching in the snow.

Harry slept soundly.

And suddenly it was Christmas Day!

Christmas Day with Huggy's red stocking overflowing with toys and books and sweets and nuts and fruit.

Christmas Day with the woods sparkling and rabbit tracks on the lawn.

Christmas Day with streamers across the hall, holly above the pictures, and a magical tree spreading its branches above a mountain of parcels in the drawing-room.

Christmas Day with a stolen *glug* of sherry when no one was looking and Harry giggling half-drunkenly on the big settee.

Christmas Day with Tangle's mouth watering like a tap, glorious steamy smells issuing from the kitchen, and the big dining-room table glittering for a feast.

Christmas Day with the Queen's speech and everybody snoozing while Harry watched an adventure film on television.

Christmas Day with reindeer pulling a laden sledge across the icing of an enormous cake.

Christmas Day with a giant jigsaw and charades and dressing up, the whole house ringing with shouts and laughter.

It was the happiest and most exciting day of Harry's life. He felt well again, his knee was almost better. His aunts had given him a computer. He wore tracksuit trousers and a new football jersey.

It was wonderful!

But one person was missing.

"It was that notebook we photographed the night of the concert," Aunt Bridget explained.

They sat roasting chestnuts on Christmas evening. The pine-log fire glowed and crackled.

"You remember – when Mr Tolly had the Beast on stage. Just one little entry."

She reached for a big brown envelope and shuffled through a bundle of enlarged photographs.

"Look." She passed one to Harry.

A thick red rectangle had been drawn around four lines.

```
20 Dec.    M H Oak–
Del. F G      1 wk +
Lge consg.
T-s   4 Jan.     Yar.
```

"I don't know what it all means," Harry said.

"How could you?" said Aunt Bridget. "But look. *M H Oak–*. If you read this week's *Gazette* you'll see there was a huge burglary at Marsh House, the Earl of Mallow's place at Oakborough, on the twentieth of December, just five days ago. Now if *Del.* stands for 'delivery', what do you think *F G* is?"

"Felon Grange!" Harry exclaimed.

"Good boy! I told you he was a receiver of stolen goods."

"A fence," Harry said.

She nodded.

"And *1 wk +* means a bit over a week later!"

"That's right! You see, he'll wait until the hue and cry has died down a bit, then quietly slip the loot up to his house for sorting out. You met Smithy and GBH, those two women, that boy who stole his cigars: his servants are all like that, a collection of rather nasty crooks." She returned to the photograph. "Then *large consignment*."

"What's a consignment?"

"A load, a stack of goods. It means there'll be a big pile of loot – pictures and silver, antiques, family heirlooms, that sort of thing. A van-full we reckon."

Harry consulted the photograph. "Then something's going to happen on the fourth of January. What does *T-s* stand for? And *Yar*?"

"Trans-shipment at Yarmouth. You see, he can't sell that sort of thing in this country. It's so valuable it would have to go to one of the big auction houses – Sotheby's or Christie's – and it would be recognized in a minute. So he has to send it out of the country, sell it in Rome or Tokyo or New York. So after he's sorted it out he'll make up a van-load, maybe with stuff from other robberies, and send it on to Great Yarmouth. There they'll pack it up in big wooden crates, stencil *Bathroom Fittings* or *Pine Furniture* on the outside, and load it aboard a boat for the continent. Bye-bye the Earl of Mallow's beautiful antiques."

Harry thought. "So you're watching to find out when it's delivered to Felon Grange."

"That's right. And when it is we'll wait until it's all safely unloaded, so they can't swish it away in a minute, then tell the police."

"Will they go – the police – him being a magistrate and all that?"

"They'll have to. Information from the public – they daren't ignore it."

"So that'll be – "

"The end of Beastly Priestly! Isn't it wonderful! And with any luck your Gestapo Lil as well."

Harry's face scorched in the heat of the flames. "What if it's delivered at night?"

"I thought you knew about all this. That's where Angel is right now, keeping a lookout."

"At Felon Grange?"

"Not in the grounds, no." She turned the chestnuts. "Nutty's built a hide near that big gateway, hidden among the trees. You can see everybody who comes and goes. And Dot's fixed a camera high up – with a night film and a button so's you can operate it from inside the hide. And Nutty ran a wire to the telephone cables, so we can talk to whoever's on watch from here."

"Can I give him a ring?"

"Of course." She told him the number.

Harry ran into the hall and dialled. An unfamiliar purring note came from the receiver at the other end. It was picked up. There was a furious electrical crackling then Angel's voice exploded into his ear.

"Hello! What d'ye want? What's wrong?"

"Nothing. It's Harry. I just thought I'd give you a ring."

"Eh? Oh! That's kind o' ye, laddie. Are y' all havin' a grand time doon there?"

"Yes, we're roasting chestnuts."

"Well, ye wouldna dae much roastin' up here, I can tell ye. It's cold enough tae – tae turn yer toes black an' make yer ears drop off like figs. I dinna think I'll ever hold a paintbrush again."

"Is there any sign of the van?"

"The van? Oh, ye mean the swag. No. But I've bin watchin' a wee herd o' deer. An' there's a bonny half moon."

Harry pictured Angel with his wild whiskers and thick glasses, peering from the hide. "It sounds nice."

"Aye, if yer fond o' the North Pole. What time is it?"

The grandfather clock was crowned with holly. "Half-past eight."

"Oh, good."

"Why?"

"Only half an hour tae go. Max comes on at nine."

"Will he take the Merc?"

"Aye, to a hidey-place, then a wee tramp through the trees. We're takin' it in turns, the eight o' us. Two hours on an' fourteen hours off. I'm glad I'm no' startin' at three in the mornin'."

"Can I come up?"

"Wi' Max? Surely. Ye canna stay, mind, no' when yer just oot yer sick bed. Better ask yer auntie, anyway."

"I will."

"Aye, well. See ye in half an hour, then. Ta-ta."

The phone went dead.

Harry ran back into the drawing-room.

The tree glittered, the fire blazed. The air was rich with the scent of roasting chestnuts.

25
The Black Van

More snow fell and lay unmelting. Cloudless days were followed by nights of bitter frost.

As Harry recovered he kept watch with his friends in the hide. It was a canvas igloo, camouflaged with branches. The earth was covered with rugs and slits in the walls gave a clear view up and down the lane. Beyond the stone arch they could see Felon Grange, small as a doll's house at the end of its long avenue of beech trees. A telephone cable trailed away through snowy scrub. On a branch overhead Dot's camera, operated by a red button within the hide, was focused on the wrought-iron gates.

Above the stone lions the security camera, eerie as a Martian or a praying mantis, swung this way and that, searching for intruders. By tramping across a quarter mile of tussocky grass and ducking through woodland, they were able to come and go from the hide without being detected.

Harry loved it there. Through the slits he spied on visitors and tradesmen, saw Gestapo Lil arrive in her red Aston Martin and Colonel Priestly drive off in his big yellow Rolls-Royce. And when the road was clear he watched hares and deer, saw birds feeding on berries and perching on the snowy branches. Mrs Good kept him well supplied with scones and flasks of hot blackcurrant. Sitting cross-legged on the rugs he listened to stories of life in the circus, and theatre, and racing-pits, and Oxford University – and the criminal underworld.

Late in the evening of December the thirtieth he went to the hide with Auntie Florrie. It had been snowing again but now the sky was clear. Although the little camping stove was turned up full, it was wickedly cold.

Peering up through the slits Harry identified the constellations he had learned during the past few nights: there was the Plough pointing to the North Star; the Seven Sisters; Orion the hunter with his three-star belt. A full moon, brightening from orange to white, rose above the trees.

Far down the lane the lights of a car, as yet unseen, illuminated the side of a hill.

"Car coming, Auntie Florrie." He stood back to let her see.

"So there is, dear." Her curls were silhouetted against the moonlight. "Well, hundredth time lucky. Can you find the camera button?"

"Yes, it's here."

"You handle that, then. Press it if I give you the word."

The note of an engine became audible in the silence.

"It's not a car, anyway," Harry said. "Too big."

"Mmm. A small lorry." Auntie Florrie listened intently. "Sounds like a Leyland. I think this could be it!"

The headlights appeared, half a mile distant. The engine note grew louder.

"Yes, definitely! A Leyland *Roadrunner*, 150 BHP."

They scrambled to the lookout slits which faced Felon Grange. Two pairs of eyes glinted in the moonlight.

The vehicle drew close, headlights on full beam. As it reached the snowy gateway it slowed, turned in and stopped. In the reflected light they could see it plainly, a black removal van with smoked windows and no name on the side. A man jumped down from the passenger door and crossed to the intercom in the wall.

"Now!" whispered Auntie Florrie.

Harry pressed the red button. A tiny click and whirr came from overhead.

"Again," she said.

The man called back to the van. The driver climbed down and joined him by the intercom. The headlights were full upon them. One wore a leather jacket and tight jeans, the other a black donkey-jacket. Together they spoke into the electronic grille.

"Again!"

Click! overhead.

Auntie Florrie pressed a pair of powerful binoculars to her eyes.

One of the men lit a cigarette. They returned to the vehicle.

Click!

The wrought-iron gates swung open. The engine revved and the van drove through, wheels crunching in the snow.

Click! Click!

The gates hummed shut. Crash!

The van drew away up the moonlit avenue.

Click!

"That's enough, dear. Better keep a few for when it returns."

Harry relinquished the red button.

"Well, that's what I call a success!" Auntie Florrie set down the binoculars. "Do you know who that was? Sammy the Stoat, one of Fat Monty's Mob, a very nasty piece of work. And the other looked like Hydraulic Jack, one of the biggest robbers in the business. I'd no idea Percy P. was working with them. I wonder what Bridget and the others will make of it?"

"Shall I give them a ring?"

"Would you, dear? That would be nice. Yes, you get Bridget on the phone and let me have a word with her."

Harry dialled the Lagg Hall number. His breath smoked in the pencil beam of a torch.

"Hello?... That you, Fingers? It's Harry... Yeah, freezing!... Yes, it's arrived... Mmm! Fantastic! Look, Auntie Florrie wants to speak to Aunt Bridget... Yes, right."

He passed the receiver across. "Fingers is getting her."

"Thank you, dear. My, what warm hands you have. Hello, Bridget?... Yes, two or three minutes ago... A Leyland *Roadrunner*, sixteen-footer, black with smoked windows... Yes, for what it's worth, HRM 393... You'll never guess who was in it! Sammy the Stoat and Hydraulic Jack!... I know, a real turn-up for the books... Well, I'd wait half an hour until they're in the middle of unloading then phone the fuzz... That's right, knee-deep in loot!... Yes, of course... Bye."

She hung up. "That Beastly Priestly, dear, I can't tell you *how* I dislike him. Well, let's hope we've settled his hash this time!" She laughed girlishly. "Where's that box of chocolates? After all that I think we deserve one!"

"Or two," Harry said.

"Precisely, dear. Let's have a real gorge!"

Early the next morning Harry climbed to the roof of the tower and looked down on a wild white world. New Year's Eve and it was blowing a blizzard. A million snowflakes whirled about him and patted his cheeks with icy paws. A bitter north-east wind piled the snow into drifts, carved it into sculptures, plastered tree-trunks and windows. All was dim and mysterious and exciting. A morning to wrap up warmly and plunge off on journeys of exploration, then return like a snowman to Mrs Good's glowing kitchen.

Suddenly all thoughts of adventure were driven from his mind. Two cars, headlights blazing, had turned from the road and were accelerating up the winding drive. Instantly he ducked and watched through the castellations of the parapet.

The cars drew closer, half-hidden by the trees. Harry drew in his breath sharply. One was a striped police car with a flashing blue light. The other was enormous, expensive and bright yellow.

They swung into the forecourt and drew to a halt. The doors opened. From the jam butty stepped two senior-looking police officers. From the Rolls emerged Colonel Priestly and Gestapo Lil. The doors slammed. Purposefully they tramped through the whirling snow.

Rat-tat-tat! Impatient knuckles rapped on the front door. Trrrr-inngggg! Rat-tat-tat-tat-tat!

The door opened. Angry voices rose to Harry on the roof. There was a calmer reply. More angry words flew in the air. The door opened wider, a golden glow from the front hall spread across the snow. He peered down. The four visitors vanished inside.

Harry tugged his hood about his ears. It was unlikely they were searching for him; two cars full of uniformed constables had raced up the previous day and searched Lagg Hall from top to bottom. No, this visit was because of Aunt Bridget's telephone call. Anonymously, thirty minutes after the arrival of the black van, she had rung police headquarters in Oakborough and told them about Sammy the Stoat, Hydraulic Jack and the delivery to Felon Grange. She had not given her name for several reasons: she did not wish to attract attention; Colonel Priestly had powerful friends including the local police chief; and she did not want to involve Mr Tolly who was just out of jail.

Fast as his feet would carry him in wellingtons, Harry clattered down the spiral stairs. Past his bedroom he went, round and round, one hand clinging to the wall, and spun dizzily out of the studded door into the blizzard.

Briefly he waited for the world to stand still then ran off through snowdrifts along the back of the house. Drainpipes descended the wall by the bathroom window. Harry had climbed them with Dot, standing on the brackets, bracing his feet against the rough stonework. Never, however, in wellingtons. Quickly he kicked off the snow, grasped a freezing pipe and started to climb.

His feet skidded, his knee hurt, his fingers ached – but a minute later Harry stood on the snowy window-sill. Panting, he pushed down the top window and slid through headfirst. Briefly he hung by the waist, legs kicking in the air, then his hands reached the top of the lavatory cistern. It was a bumpy landing but no one was close enough to hear. Quickly he pushed up the window, tugged off his boots and threw them into the bathroom cupboard.

The door stood ajar. Raised voices came to his ears. The visitors were in the hall. He pulled the door wider. The coast was clear. Softly he flitted down three steps and along the corridor.

Half a minute later Harry crouched on the landing and peered down through the banisters, past balloons and streamers and big paper bells, at the scene below.

Six people stood in the hall: his two aunts and the four visitors.

Colonel Priestly wore a long tweed coat of his favourite ginger check. He had not removed his hat, a deerstalker of the same material. He was furious.

"I *know* it was you! And I notice you don't deny it. Who else would be mad enough to tell the police a thing like that?"

Aunt Bridget, looking very stately in a long, richly-coloured kaftan, did not reply.

"As if a man in my position – high-court judge, magistrate, owner of a beautiful estate like Felon Grange – would jeopardize all that by involving himself with a crowd of criminals! Fat Monty! Hydraulic Jack! Sammy the Stoat! Why not Jack the Ripper and be done with it! I ask you!"

"Ah, but that's where you've been so clever," said Aunt Bridget. "Who would *suspect* a man in your position?"

"And the grander you've grown, the more secure your position has become." Auntie Florrie's house-coat was a cloud of rose-pink chiffon. She had found time to tidy her curls and apply a dazzling slash of lipstick.

"Precisely," said Aunt Bridget. "But one wonders where you got the money to buy a place like Felon Grange. One point five million? You didn't have it when you put the Sapphire girls away, we know that. Are judges *that* well paid? How can you afford the upkeep?"

"Not to mention the yacht and racehorses and personalized Rolls-Royce," said Auntie Florrie. "And the roulette tables at Monte Carlo, and buying your way into high society with all those big parties and donations to charity."

"You see, we've been taking an interest in you, Percy Priestly. We've got our ears to the ground."

"We know what we know!" said Auntie Florrie darkly.

"And if you're hoping to trick us into making accusations in front of witnesses, before we're ready to prove them," said Aunt Bridget, "so that you can threaten us with libel, then think again. But this much I *will* say. These police officers and their men may have searched Felon Grange from cellar to attic and found no trace of any stolen goods, I cannot deny that. But – and with all due respect, Chief Inspector – I believe that because of your reputation and connections some of them may not have searched very thoroughly. More importantly, however, I believe that for ten years you have been a top operator and fence for one of the most notorious gangs in this country. I believe that you habitually consort with criminals and use your position to their and your advantage. And I believe that the removal van with dark windows which we saw last night was driven by two of the villains you named and contained the proceeds of the robbery at the Earl of Mallow's estate on the twentieth of this month. I am convinced of these things – but make no accusations. You cannot touch me for what I think."

Colonel Priestly hopped with rage. His face was crimson, his eyes popped, his fat hands clenched into fists. Harry was sure he was going to hit Aunt Bridget.

"She's a mad woman!" he spluttered to the two policemen. "You're a mad woman! You're all mad! Ga-ga! Everyone knows it! What van? There *was* no van!"

"We saw it," Aunt Bridget said calmly.

"We? A bunch of geriatrics! A crowd of ex-cons that have it in for me because I put most of you away – and very rightly too. You should all be put away! For keeps! Lock the door and throw away the key! What do you think your word's worth compared with mine?"

"We photographed it going through the gate," said Auntie Florrie. "And Hydraulic Jack and Sammy the Stoat."

"You photographed – ! I don't believe you."

"It's still on the reel. If you wait I'll get Mr McGregor to develop it and print an enlargement." She turned to the senior police officer and smiled winningly. "A Leyland *Roadrunner*, 150 BHP, if you're interested, Chief Inspector. Sixteen-footer. Black with smoked windows. No lettering or logo. HRM 393."

"Photographs!" blustered Colonel Priestly. "Have you been spying on me?"

"Spying?" The baby-blue eyes opened wide with innocence. "What reason could we have for spying? And even if we did – what harm? An eminent man like you. Living such a worthy and respectable life."

"Ahem!" The senior police officer turned to Aunt Bridget.

"These claims you make, Miss – er – Barton. Very serious, you know."

"Of course," said Aunt Bridget. "Why else would I make them? But I'm afraid I'm in a position to say no more at the moment, Chief Inspector."

He stared at her hard. "Well, let me assure you again that acting upon information received, twelve police officers searched Felon Grange from top to bottom with a fine tooth comb. Colonel Priestly was understandably annoyed, being disturbed in the middle of the night like that, but after we had explained he co-operated in a very public-spirited manner. Nothing was discovered which in any way linked him or his home with the robbery at Marsh House."

Aunt Bridget remained silent.

Colonel Priestly smiled.

The Chief Inspector turned to him. "But about this van, sir. I understood you to say that there was no van."

"Well there wasn't, not so far as I was aware. But if these loonies have photographed one I suppose there must have been. Friends of one of my servants, I imagine. Party time and all that." He felt for a half-smoked cigar and struck a heavy gold lighter. "I don't encourage friends," puff-puff, "but you can't keep track of everybody." Clouds of smoke rose about his head. "Get to the bottom of it when we go back."

"But Percipops, there's no need." Gestapo Lil wore a black snow-suit with a blood-red belt and blood-red boots. Her corn-gold hair shone in the light. "What are we talking about here? A van! It *might* have been friends of one of the servants; it *might* have been delivering hot pizzas; it *might* have lost its way in all these snowy lanes. What possible reason is there to suggest it was filled with the proceeds of a robbery? The idea's preposterous! And anyway, you don't have to prove it *wasn't*, they have to prove it *was*."

She twined her arm in that of Colonel Priestly.

"You refer to two low-life criminals, Miss Barton. The names mean nothing to me. Nor, I'm sure – unless he's had to deal with them in court – do they mean anything to my fiancé."

Harry thought of the entry in Colonel Priestly's pocket-book – but Mr Tolly had stolen that. And Sammy the Stoat and Hydraulic Jack had been a long way off, perhaps too far to photograph clearly.

Aunt Bridget and Auntie Florrie remained silent.

"You see!" Gestapo Lil smiled triumphantly. "They have no proof. The whole thing's nothing but a fantasy dreamed up by a crowd of vindictive old wrinklies. Like these two witches here."

"What language!" said Auntie Florrie. "And in our own home too. Geriatrics! Mad women! Cons! Wrinklies! Loonies! Witches! Very nice, I'm sure! And you're the woman who was nurse and housekeeper to our nephew. Now you're his teacher! Really, I'm shocked!"

"Ah, yes. Your missing nephew," said Colonel Priestly. "The first time you've mentioned him. I wonder how much you know about that? I wonder where he is now?"

A tiny movement in the hall mirror caught Auntie Florrie's eye. Glancing up, she saw Harry reflected at the top of the stairs. Engrossed by the scene below, he had allowed his head and shoulder to come out of hiding. Her eyes widened. The others had only to look up and he would be spotted. Behind her back she flapped a hand for him to get out of sight.

"I wonder many things about our missing nephew," Aunt Bridget was saying. "I wonder why he was taken away in a dawn raid. I wonder why he was taken away at all. I wonder why social workers took him straight to Felon Grange, why he was imprisoned there, and how he came to be injured. I wonder why he was driven a hundred miles with a dislocated knee and locked up like a criminal in Grimthrash Jail."

"Those questions are answered easily enough," said Colonel Priestly. "The boy was running away. When he was apprehended he had professional lock-picking tools in his pocket. I'm the magistrate who signed – "

"Just a minute, Percikins." Gestapo Lil let go of his arm. She was staring at Auntie Florrie. "Why are you flapping your hand like that? What are you doing – signalling to somebody? Is there somebody there?" Her eyes flew about the hall. "That nephew of yours! Is he – ?" She ran to the stairs.

Harry drew back just in time.

"What are you talking about?" protested Auntie Florrie. "I have a sore wrist."

Gestapo Lil ignored her. "He's up there, isn't he! I know it!"

She raced up the broad staircase.

As Harry took to his heels along the corridor, Huggy was emerging from her bedroom. When she rose each morning, in preference to a housecoat or floppy tracksuit, Huggy pulled on one of her old wrestling costumes. Today she wore a Japanese karate outfit with trousers, a sash and a tremendous dragon on the back.

Harry dashed past her and dived under the bed.

Huggy was startled but no words were necessary for a moment later Gestapo Lil appeared at the head of the stairs.

"I'll get you, you little beast!" she cried in her shrill nasal voice. "I'll ferret you out!"

Briefly she looked this way and that then started down the corridor in pursuit.

Huggy pulled her door shut. Knees bent and hands hanging she blocked the corridor – a sight that had struck fear into a thousand opponents.

"Ah!" she exclaimed, her voice as deep as a man. "You! I vant see you vhat you did Harry! Come here!" She beckoned. "I break both your legs! I pull your arms off!"

Gestapo Lil hesitated.

They stared at each other.

Neither moved.

Suddenly Huggy darted forward.

With a shriek Gestapo Lil fled, pursued by the ferocious dragon.

"Aarrgghh!" Huggy leaned over the banister and shook an enormous fist. "You vait! If I not get you now, I get you sometime!"

"Percy! He-elp!"

Gestapo Lil stumbled headlong down the stairs. Near the bottom she lost her balance completely. "Aaahhh!" Head over heels she crashed to the floor.

Startled, Colonel Priestly stared past his fiancée at the terrifying figure on the landing.

"Hah!" Huggy gazed down. "A pretty pair!"

Flat beneath the bed Harry heard their cries. Huggy to the rescue! With a sigh of relief he rolled on his back and stared up at the strong bedsprings. Then thrust a hand into his pocket and felt for a toffee.

26
Blizzard

"Ah, come on, Auntie Florrie. Let's go and join them. Please!"

It was New Year's Eve. The snow, which had eased during the day, was falling thickly again, driven by the north-east wind, piling against the doors, swirling in the light that shone from curtained windows.

The clock on the mantelpiece chimed ten-thirty.

Harry sat with Auntie Florrie in the festive drawing-room. Christmas cards stood on every shelf, the big tree shone in one corner. A Monopoly board scattered with red hotels had been pushed aside. A pack of cards and piles of coloured counters lay on the coffee table between them – a small pile before Harry, a huge pile before Auntie Florrie. The wind moaned in the chimney, sucking sparks and hot flames from the fire. Apart from Mrs Good, who had just left to do something in the kitchen, they were alone in the house.

"But it's not fair!" Harry exclaimed. "If anyone went it should have been me! I'm the only one who's been in Felon Grange. If they're going to raid the place you'd think that would be useful!"

Auntie Florrie tapped the ash from her cigar. "I know you're dying to go, dear, but don't keep asking. Bridget did explain it all. The Beast's having this big New Year party and Max has got himself invited as the brother of that actor friend of his: you know, what's-his-name, always on the TV. So he's going to case the joint, suss everything out and leave a couple of windows off the latch for the others."

"Yes, I know all that," Harry said impatiently. "And when the guests have driven away and everybody's gone to bed they're going to break in and hunt for that loot the police couldn't find."

"Or *said* they couldn't find, dear."

"Yes, all right. But that makes it even better – and I want to be there! So do you! It's an adventure. A snowstorm and every-thing! And I'd have thought the fact that I've actually *been* through the house – upstairs, downstairs, back-stairs, kitchen, hall, library, sun-lounge, bedrooms – you'd think all that would be *useful*!"

"I know, dear, it does sound reasonable. But you heard what Bridget said about being caught. She doesn't want you to get involved. And she's in charge."

"But they're not going to get caught. And whether I'm there or not, what difference does it make? I *am* involved. I'm on the run from the police. If they're caught and get into trouble I'll never be allowed to come back here, will I. So I might as well be there helping them. It's all because of me to start with. I should be there!"

"You're so persuasive, dear." Auntie Florrie took a fortifying mouthful of Bosun Blinder. "It does make sense. But supposing we did decide to join them, how could we get there now? They've taken the car."

"The *Commando*!" Harry jumped to his feet. "It would be fantastic! In the snow! And the gates are open because of the party! People will be coming and going all night. Hide it in the bushes and go round the meadows. Nobody will see us because of the blizzard. Then come down the back and join the others in the car."

"Yes, but where *is* the car?"

"You *know*! Aunt Bridget *said*! There'll be servants looking after the guests' cars. When Max goes into the house he's going to take them with him. As soon as the coast's clear, the rest drive on up the track to the stables without any lights and pull the Merc back among the trees. That's why Nutty had to spray it white – and put in dark windows. If anyone spots it they're going to pretend it's a courting couple from the party."

He giggled.

"It's very tempting." Thoughtfully she drew on the cigar, her cheeks flushed with the fire.

"Come on, Auntie Florrie! Please!" Harry seized her arm. "On the bike! In the snow! At midnight on New Year's Eve! Get our own back on Beastly Priestly and Gestapo Lil. It'll be brilliant!"

"Oh dear! I'm just a fool!" She looked up, her blue eyes reckless. "All right, then. In for a penny, in for a pound. Go and get yourself ready."

"Ya-hoo!" Harry grabbed a chocolate, bounded over the settee and rushed towards the door.

At the same moment the door swung wide and Mrs Good entered, bearing a tray on which rested a big jug of cocoa and a plate piled high with hot buttered toast. There was nearly a terrific collision.

"My, that's a more cheerful face I see!" she exclaimed. "What's come over you all of a sudden?"

"We're going to join the others!" Harry shouted. "On the bike!"

"You never are!" She stopped in her tracks and frowned disapprovingly. "Surely you've got more sense!"

Auntie Florrie smiled guiltily.

"Well I never!" exclaimed Mrs Good. "On that motorbike in a blizzard like this! You want your heads looking at." She cleared the cards from the table. "Still, I can't say I'm surprised. I suppose I should be grateful you're not tobogganing down the roof on this tea-tray."

Auntie Florrie made a face.

"But nobody ever listens to me." Mrs Good clattered the cups and saucers. "Come on, Harry – and you, Florrie. Sit down. Before you set one foot outside that door you'll get this good toast and cocoa inside you."

Harry and his auntie did as they were told.

The snow was blinding. For the sixth time in a minute Harry put up a glove and rubbed the flakes from his goggles.

The powerful motorbike snaked and slithered through deep drifts in the drive, then leaped as the tyres hit earth in the shelter of trees. Harry's feet hovered on the footrests, ready to go down. On main beam the headlamp revealed nothing but a wall of white, a billion feathers rushing at them out of the dark. Auntie Florrie set it to dip, illuminating the snowdrifts and smoothed-over tyre tracks twenty metres ahead.

Snow-ploughs had cleared the road. Lorries had scattered grit and salt. The driving snow obliterated their efforts. In an hour it was an inch deep. In two the drifts were building up at field gates and gaps in the hedgerows.

Auntie Florrie scraped snow from the face of the speedometer. The needle swung between twenty and thirty miles an hour. They hit a drift. The bike slewed sideways. She throttled back and turned expertly into the skid.

When Florrie Barton won the Isle of Man T.T. she had beaten the best riders in the world.

Harry's nose and mouth were covered by a scarf. Only his cheekbones were exposed. They froze and ached. He did not care and leaned forward.

"It's fantastic!"

Her reply was lost in the blizzard.

They hit a bigger drift. Harry was thrown forward. The back wheel ploughed in an arc. The front wheel bucked as it hit the verge. Two feet went down. Auntie Florrie swung back into the road. On they roared.

Ten minutes brought them to the lane which led past Felon Grange. A red tractor with a snow-plough attached was reversing at the junction. One of Colonel Priestly's workers was keeping the road open for guests. Auntie Florrie squeezed past and accelerated away between the tumbled banks of snow.

They drew up, engine running, at the entrance gates. The ancient arch was capped with white, the wrought-iron gates stood open. Above the lions and mythological carvings the security camera was still, a blob of snow in the beam of the headlamp.

Auntie Florrie rubbed her visor and looked around. "Like you said, dear, we'd better leave the bike here. A bit obvious if we drive right up to the house."

Beyond the arch, at the start of the long drive, was a shrubbery, a patch of lawn set with large evergreens and summer-flowering bushes.

"Just the spot." She switched off the headlamp. At once they were plunged into a world of darkness, whirling snow and confusion. She clicked the *Commando* into first and nosed through the gate then turned aside, weaving between tall laurels and azalea.

A car was approaching up the lane. She switched off the engine. It swung through the entrance – a Range Rover. In a swirl of snow it drew away up the beech avenue and vanished into the blizzard.

All was silent save for the whining of the wind.

Auntie Florrie risked the headlamp again. Big bushes, heavy with snow, pressed close on every side. "We should be safe enough here." She kicked down the stand. "The ground's frozen."

They tugged off their helmets and beat the snow from their jackets. Auntie Florrie produced a battered leather balaclava from one pocket and a heavy torch from the other. Harry pulled on the woollen hat with a bobble which Huggy had knitted him for Christmas.

"Well, dear, which way? Across the fields or up the avenue and hide behind the trees?"

"Across the fields," Harry said. "It's safer."

"And wilder." The balaclava gave her the appearance of an early aviator. "All right, lead on, Macduff."

Harry led the way up the drive to the start of the meadow. The snow whirled about him. When he switched on the torch nothing could be seen but dazzling flakes and a grey, snow-plastered tree-trunk. He trudged across the verge and ducked through railings into the field.

Away from the shelter of the trees the wind was stronger. Harry tugged up his collar, pulled down the rim of his hat and lowered his head into the blizzard. Thigh-deep he ploughed through the drifts. Snowflakes clung to his lips and eyelashes. His cheeks froze in the arctic wind.

After five minutes he was totally lost.

"A bit more to the left, dear," Auntie Florrie called cheerily. "Goodness, a bit of a wintry old night, isn't it. Here, hang on a minute. Have a mint."

It was a wild tramp. They tumbled across a ditch and clambered through a barbed-wire fence. A second meadow lay before them. Nothing was to be seen but snow and occasionally a dim, twisted tree.

After a long time they reached a hedge and hunted along it for a gate. A herd of white cattle blocked their path, tearing at hay in a wooden rack. Harry turned the torch upon them. Despite their fearsome horns they were gentle creatures. Curiously they regarded the two intruders. Their breath and bodies steamed in the cold.

Harry and Auntie Florrie picked a path through the herd and climbed the gate. A third great meadow lay before them. The cattle were left behind.

"Hang on a minute, dear."

Harry stopped.

"Give me the torch."

Auntie Florrie knocked the snow from a sleeve and examined her wrist-watch.

"Ten past twelve. Happy New Year, darling!"

Harry gazed around at the driving snow. "Happy New Year, Auntie Florrie."

The snow-plastered aviator laughed and planted an icy kiss on his cheek.

"Let's make a New Year resolution. Death to the Beast! Well, get rid of him, anyway."

Her eyes were gay but her make-up was a wreck. Black streams of mascara ran down to her chin. She rubbed them away with a glove.

"Death to the Beast!" Harry cried. "And Gestapo Lil!"

"Good for you!" said his auntie.

They trudged on.

A while later it became apparent that the snow was easing. Harry greeted it with relief. From a totally unexpected direction – almost at their backs – a dim glow appeared through the gloom. They headed towards it.

The windows of Felon Grange were ablaze with light. Despite the blizzard the courtyard and end of the drive were packed with cars – expensive cars.

Harry and Auntie Florrie stood in the shelter of a pine-clump and watched the last flakes drift past. An arctic wilderness had been transformed into a scene from a Christmas card.

"Well, we're going to stand out like a couple of old scarecrows now, aren't we, dear," said Auntie Florrie. "And the stables are on the far side. Best keep well back."

Ducking behind walls and hedges and small rises in the land, they circled the house and crept down a track towards the shadowy stables.

"Can you see anything?"

A patch of woodland lay ahead.

"No."

They advanced.

The stables stood on their left, the trees on their right.

The branches were black, the ground white. As Harry stared, he thought he detected a more solid patch of white among the tree-trunks. Was it? He peered.

"Auntie Florrie. Over here."

It was a car.

Cautiously they crept towards it. A rotten branch snapped beneath the snow.

The driver's window was wound down. "Here, what do you want?"

Harry sprang back, ready for flight. This was a stranger's voice – annoyed, aggressive.

"Can't a fellow have five minutes with his girl without you snooping round and sticking your nose in. Buzz off!"

"Oh, shut up, Mr Tolly," said Auntie Florrie. "It's Harry and me. Come on, open up. It's like Siberia out here!"

27
Moonlight Raiders

"Come on, Harry."

"Mmm."

"Wake up!"

"Mmm – what?"

"Do you want to come with us or are you going to sleep?"

"I want – " Harry struggled to a sitting position. He was stiff and confused. It was dark. A crush of people was all about him. "Where – ?"

Abruptly he remembered. The back seat of the Merc. He must have fallen asleep.

"What time is it?" He rubbed his face.

"Just coming up to four." Aunt Bridget was brisk and businesslike.

"Four o'clock! Has everybody – ?"

"Yes, the guests have all gone – apart from two couples who are staying the night. The last light went off half an hour ago."

The back door opened. A bitter gust swirled through the car. Huggy and some others were standing in the snow. They had been waiting in the stables.

"Come on, Harry, where's your jacket? I don't suppose you thought to bring trainers."

"No."

"You'll have to wear your wellies, then, but kick them off before you go through the window. Don't want you clumping up and down the corridors like a fisherman."

They gathered beside the car. The sky was clear. A full moon cast shadows on the snow.

"Well, you all know what we're after." Aunt Bridget spoke softly but decisively. "The haul from the Marsh House job. That and nothing else. So no sticky fingers, all right? No wasting time over cash and trinkets. We have one purpose and one only: to rid the district of Percy Priestly and his ghastly fiancée. Tonight's our big chance to show the world what a two-faced crook he really is."

"And bring dear Harry back to Lagg Hall," said Auntie Florrie.

"That goes without saying," continued her sister. "Now, the loot's probably stacked away in some strong room or hidden chamber. You all know what to look for: locked doors, finger-marked panels, trapdoors, scratch marks – that sort of thing. It won't necessarily be in the big house, so I want four of you to check all the outhouses: the stables, sheds, garages, places like that. The best group, I think, will be Florrie, Dot, Mr Tolly and Nutty: he'll be back in a moment, he's away dealing with the guard dogs just now."

"Here he comes," Max said. "Right on cue."

The stooped figure trudged towards them up the track. At his heels trotted the Dobermann and Alsatian that Harry had seen wolfing red meat in the kitchen. Then they had been ferocious beasts. Nutty's gentle words had transformed them into gambolling pets.

He rubbed the Dobermann's chest. "Who's a good boy, then?"

The fearsome dog rolled in the snow and kicked its legs like a puppy.

"No problems?" said Aunt Bridget.

"See for yersel'," said Nutty. "A canny couple o' dogs. But I'd better keep 'em wi' me – just in case."

"Good. Well, let's get cracking. We'll leave you four, the outside group, to work the way you want. The rest of us – " She turned. "OK, Max. Lead on, McBeauguss! Show us the way in."

It was very cold. The powdery snow squeaked beneath their feet as they walked down the track. Clouds of breath rose about their heads. The guests' cars had gone, all but three which stood abandoned in the drive. In the grand forecourt the fountain was stilled, the balustrades piled with snow. As they emerged into the open, Harry felt very exposed. The full moon shone upon them like a searchlight.

Only reflections and a Christmas tree lit the black windows of Felon Grange. The great house towered before them against the sky.

"This way." Max turned down a path.

They followed him into the moon-shadow and after a short walk stopped by a small-paned sash window. Max brushed snow from the sill.

"'Ere, what abaht the alarms?" said Fingers.

"Switched off for the guests." Max spread his fingers against the window-frame and pushed up. It did not move. He pushed again. "Damn, I hope they haven't locked it."

"Prob'ly just frozen," said Fingers. "Winders that won't open – story o' my life. People should 'ave more consideration. 'Ere, shift across. Mebbe if the pair of us – "

Together they strained. The window resisted. They grunted with effort. With a sudden *crack* it broke free of the ice and shot up, jamming Fingers' hand.

"Aahhh! Aahhh! Quick!"

He was released.

"Ohhh! Aahhh! Cor blimey!" He shook his few remaining fingers.

"Shut up!" hissed Huggy. "You vant the whole countryside should hear you?"

He stared at her reproachfully and popped the fingers into his mouth.

A breath of warm air wafted into their faces.

"Excellent!" said Aunt Bridget. "Well done!" She looked round. "Right, then, everybody ready? In we go."

Harry kicked off his wellingtons and tugged up his socks.

One after the other, setting their feet in cupped hands and kneeling on bent backs, they crawled through the window. Soon all six – Aunt Bridget, Huggy, Max, Angel, Fingers and Harry – stood in the dark laundry-room of Felon Grange. Max slid the window shut behind them.

It was a relief to be out of the bitter night air.

Beyond a tumble-drier and piles of washing the door stood ajar. Fingers eased it wider and peered to right and left along the corridor. All was dark, no sounds disturbed the peace.

"All clear."

Everyone carried a pencil torch. In single file they left the laundry room and tiptoed along the corridor – past the kitchen where Smithy and GBH had sat with the social workers, past the dogs' room, past the cupboard into which Harry had strayed by mistake. The air smelled of cigarettes and wine and perfume and rich foods.

Reaching the panelled hall they halted. Moonlight shone through the high, frosted windows. A sound could now be heard, low and rhythmic. In a distant bedroom, beyond the grand staircase and far along the upper corridor, somebody was snoring.

"Cor, listen to that!"

"Percy Pig in the land of dreams," said Aunt Bridget.

"I go up and smother him." Huggy's eyes shone in the torch-light. "Then ve go home. Ja?"

"No!" said Aunt Bridget. "Behave yourself, Huggy!"

Angel's beard jutted above a red muffler. He flashed his torch across the brown portraits and one or two modern paintings on the walls. "Will ye look at yon! Tryin' tae gie himsel' a set o' ancestors. An' look like a patron o' the arts forbye." He snorted. "Naethin' but a load o' tatt! I wouldna gie them house room. Except for one."

His torch spotlit the portrait of a rich old lady in embroidered sky-blue silk and carrying a dog.

"I like that," said Aunt Bridget.

"Aye, so ye should. It's a Gainsborough. I wonder what he paid for it."

"A fortune, I should think."

"I hope so. Heh–heh–heh! 'Cause it's one o' mine! I did it about fifteen year ago. Am I no' a bonny painter!"

They laughed softly.

Above their heads a big bunch of mistletoe hung from a chandelier.

"'Ere, 'Uggy." Fingers glanced up. "'Appy New Year!" Gallantly he embraced her and stood on tiptoe to plant a kiss on her soft, whiskery cheek.

"That's right. Happy New Year! Happy New Year!"

For a minute there was a party atmosphere of hugging and hand-shaking. Fingers flung his arms in the air and snapped his two or three fingers like a Spanish dancer, while Huggy, who wore a gigantic purple snow-suit, did some very fancy footwork and twitched imaginary Russian skirts. The beams of their torches flashed about the hall.

"Shush, everybody! Ssshhh!" Aunt Bridget waved her hands in alarm and the party died down.

Harry's feet were frozen. He shivered, remembering all that had happened on his last visit to Felon Grange: how he had vandalized the dressing room; crept down the stairs; seen

Gestapo Lil drive up; fled from the library and sun-lounge; been dragged down the back stairs by an ankle; the pain in his knee; the drive to Grimthrash Jail. Only a fortnight ago – it seemed longer.

He gave his attention to Aunt Bridget.

"Now this is where we split up into two groups," she was saying. "Huggy, Angel and Max. I want you to take the hall and stairs here, the cellars – them particularly – and the kitchens. All right? Fingers, Harry and I will cover the rest of the ground floor. We'll meet you back here in," she checked her watch, "forty-five minutes. Then, if we've had no luck, we'll tackle the upstairs."

As they turned away, Harry's heart was thudding. The shadows seemed full of eyes. Their torches were very bright.

Aunt Bridget pushed open a door. A strong scent of cigars and food and spirits greeted them as they entered.

This was the largest room in Felon Grange and clearly had been the heart of the New Year party. A big Christmas tree shone in the window; a dying fire glowed in the grate; tables had been pushed back for dancing. Some clearing up had been done but the room was still a mess. Bottles and glasses stood everywhere – champagne glasses, whisky glasses, wine glasses, beer mugs – some half full, others toppled and fallen to the carpet. Ashtrays overflowed. Half-eaten plates of food lay about on ledges.

"Well, a good time was had by all," Aunt Bridget remarked drily.

"Uhhhh!" A sudden noise made them freeze. "Nnnnn!"

A dark shape lay between the tables. They seized weapons: a bottle, a chair, a heavy candlestick. Cautiously they approached and shone a torch.

A man lay sleeping, dead drunk. He was young and wore a dinner jacket with silk lapels. His black bow tie hung loose, the top button of his shirt was unfastened. As they looked down he began to snore.

"Well, he'll not be bothering us." Aunt Bridget set down her chair and turned to Harry. "Forget the party, what we're looking for is any sign of a trapdoor or secret chamber. This is a fitted carpet," she inspected the edge, "so there won't be anything in the floor. But possibly the walls or one of the alcoves."

"'Sright." Fingers spoke through a mouthful of cashew nuts. "Any cracks, like, that shows where there's a slidin' panel or somefing. Or maybe there's an 'idden safe."

They spread out and circled the room, testing shelves and mirrors, peering into corners, tugging at the beading with fingernails.

As Harry passed a buffet and plates of nibbles he helped himself to crisps and vol-au-vents, twiglets and tiny sausage rolls. He ate chocolate mints and rum truffles, and scooped up garlic dip on fingers of celery. When Aunt Bridget wasn't watching he took a quick swig from a bottle of flat champagne.

In five minutes their winkling torches had revealed nothing.

"No point in goin' on 'ere," said Fingers.

"I agree," said Aunt Bridget. "Big drawing room like this, picture windows, expensive carpet – most unlikely. The library's a better bet." She looked round, trying to get her bearings. "That should be – "

"I'll show you." Harry led the way. "It's just down here."

He ran along the corridor and skidded to a stop at the big polished door. No light shone round the edge. He put an eye to the keyhole. All was dark.

"All clear?"

He burped and nodded.

"In we go, then. Quietly, mind."

Softly Harry grasped the handle and turned. The door did not open. He pushed.

"It's locked!"

"'Ere, let's 'ave a dekko." Fingers took over. "'E's right, it is locked. Flippin' security lock! 'Eavy door an' all. Well, what d'ye make o' that? What's naughty ol' Perce got to 'ide from 'is mates?" He felt for his spare set of probes. "Come on, let the dog see the rabbit."

Briefly the probes scratched. He exerted some pressure. The lock snapped open.

"There y'are, Bridget. Open Sesame! Sinbad does it again."

He turned the handle and the door swung wide.

"A genius!" Aunt Bridget planted a kiss on his lined forehead and led the way into the room.

Harry pulled the door shut at their backs.

The library was exactly as he remembered except that now the fire was dead and the curtains were drawn. No glimmer of moonlight appeared round the heavy folds.

"Well, this is more promising." Aunt Bridget flashed her torch from the leather suite to the crowded bookshelves and fine oak panelling. "A heavy door locked, brocade curtains. Mmm... Right! Harry, you check the floor – under all these rugs and the table and the three-piece suite. Fingers, you take the panelling. I'll search the shelves."

Eagerly Harry did as he was told. The floor was covered with polished parquet blocks, golden-brown. One after another he swished the Afghan rugs aside. No trapdoor was revealed. Exerting his strength, he pushed back the heavy settee and armchairs. On hands and knees he crawled beneath the table. Like Sherlock Holmes – except that he had no magnifying glass – he examined the hearth and fireplace.

The others were having no better luck. Fingers' torch pried into every corner of the panelling. Aunt Bridget hunted shelf after shelf of law books from the floor to the ceiling.

Nothing.

She pushed the hair from her forehead and glanced at her wrist-watch. "It's here somewhere, I can feel it."

"Yeah, me too." Fingers hitched his baggy trousers. "I got that prickly feelin' up the back of me neck, an' me 'ands are all sweaty. Dead cert, that is. There's a safe somewhere nearby, an' all."

"But where!"

Harry remembered something. "Aunt Bridget, you know when I was here the last time, and I ran in, and Colonel Priestly was angry. I told you."

Aunt Bridget was listening.

"Well, he was doing something over there, just past the fireplace." He shone his torch and crossed the room. "He had these books out here. His back was to the door so I couldn't see properly. But he was mad!"

"My darling boy! I wonder – " She flew to his side. "What, these books here?"

"I think so. Or maybe the ones underneath."

"Here, hang on to these." She passed half a metre of heavy books across and bent to peer into the recess. "No, nothing there. Just a minute." She crouched lower. "No. Unless – " She poked a finger into the corner then looked round. "Harry, you didn't notice him carrying anything else? A pen, say?"

Harry thought. "Not that I remember."

"Because there's a knot-hole in the wood here. You get knot-holes in pine – the rest of the shelves are made of oak. I wonder." Her torch roamed the library. "Look on the table, see if you can find a biro or a pencil, something thin."

Harry set down the books. A cut-glass tray of pens stood on the big library table. Most were expensive but among them lay a cheap blue BIC. He carried it across.

"Perfect."

Harry peered past her shoulder. High up in the end of the

shelf, right in the middle and hidden by the shelf above, was a small knot-hole. The rest of the wood, though a little dusty behind the books, was polished and smooth-grained.

Grasping the BIC firmly, button-end forward, Aunt Bridget poked it into the knot-hole.

Harry held his breath.

Nothing.

She pushed.

Still nothing.

She pushed harder.

Click!

The tall bookcase shivered. The edge moved beneath her hand.

"That's it!" Aunt Bridget looked up. Her eyes were wild. "Harry! We've got it!"

She rose.

Three pairs of hands grasped the shelves.

"Gently! Gently!"

They pulled. Smooth as silk more than a metre of books swung open. Beyond lay a space black as midnight. A breath of cool air flowed into their faces.

Fingers shone his torch through the gap. Harry gasped.

It was an Aladdin's cave. A feast of colour and brilliance. A chamber half as big as the library stacked to the roof with valuables. The thin beam moved across fabulous ornaments, a forest of winking silver. Chandeliers, glittering like a hundred tiaras, trailed across paintings. Golden salvers lay scattered upon chests and tables. There were wonderful clocks and jewel-encrusted swords, violins and tapestries. Ropes of pearl, opal and turquoise spilled from an open casket. There were leather-bound books and scrolls of yellowing parchment. On a crumpled velvet cloth a jumble of necklaces, rings, brooches and other trinkets flashed white and ruby fire.

"Cor blimey!" Fingers' voice was reverential. "Did you ever in your puff!"

"Open Sesame indeed!" Aunt Bridget smiled and touched the cameo beneath her scarf.

They swung the bookcase wide and advanced into the hoard of treasure.

28
Villains in Pyjamas

Harry was sent to fetch the others. On tiptoe he ran through the silent house. The moonlit snow at the windows made the shadows more intense. In every corner, behind every door, he saw crouching villains: GBH and Gestapo Lil, stranglers with cords, cut-throats with knives. Poised for flight, he peered into the kitchen and pitch-black cupboards. With wide eyes he descended steps into the cellars.

The walls were of stone like a dungeon. The air smelled of dust and wine. Chamber followed chamber. He passed a workbench, old bicycles, a pile of logs, hanging bunches of traps – gin traps, mole traps, pole traps, snares – broken one-arm bandits, shrivelled raincoats.

"Huggy!" His voice was a croak. "Angel!"

Their torches came on. Max, his glossy hair streaked with cobwebs, peered through the bars of a wine rack. Angel rose amid sacks of potatoes.

"What's up?"

"We've found it!"

"What!"

"Yeah! In the library. It's fantastic! Aunt Bridget says you're to come."

Huggy appeared through a stone arch.

They returned to the hall. Moonbeams slanted through high windows. Harry led the way followed by Angel, squat and whiskery, Max in his dinner jacket, and Huggy like a purple ogre.

He opened the library door. Spellbound they stood at the entrance.

"What d'ye make o' this, then?" Fingers greeted them. "I never seen nuffin like it!"

They shut the door and joined the others in the secret chamber.

"Obviously it's not all the Marsh House job," Aunt Bridget was saying. She pointed. "Those candlesticks, for instance. I know for a fact they come from Lord Turtle's place. And that's the famous Scorpion brooch from the Fitz-Holland collection. They vanished months ago."

"Yeah, I rec'nize a few bits an' all," said Fingers. "That's the Kilallan diamond. An' them rings an' that gold plate – they come from Mrs Simmons' place up York way."

"Never mind diamonds," said Angel. "Will ye look at these paintin's. Feast yer eyes!" He shone his torch. "Modigliani – Cézanne – Braque – Turner. It's a one-man gallery. See yon Fra Angelico – that vanished in Rome. Gorgeous! Worth millions." He scrubbed his spectacles with a grubby handkerchief. "Nowhere in the world ye could sell these. Nae gallery would touch them. Have to go tae private collectors."

Harry stared. "But I know that one!" He pointed. "It was in our house in Hampstead. It used to hang on the landing. And that one over there – it was halfway up the stairs."

"Yer jokin'!" Angel's eyes swam like blue fish.

"No, really! They were there till … just before I came away."

Angel was silent. He looked at Aunt Bridget.

She stared back, her eyes bright as sapphires. "What are they?"

"Well, yon's a Stubbs. An' that landscape over there's a Corot."

"Oh, my goodness!"

Harry looked from one to the other. "Are they valuable?"

Angel put a hand on his shoulder. "Corot didnae paint it to be worth a lot o' money, he painted it to be beautiful. Look at it!"

"Yeah, yeah! All right, it's beautiful," said Fingers impatiently. "Flippin' artists! What the kid wants to know is – is it worth a lot o' bread?"

Aunt Bridget flashed a look at Angel. "We'll not know that until other experts have had a look at them," she said quickly. "Harry's father died bankrupt, remember. There are a lot of debts."

Huggy heard only part of the conversation. "These pictures, you mean they are *yours*?" She moved to Harry's shoulder. "That voman, she steal them from your house and bring them here?"

"Looks like it," Max said.

"Ohhh! Vorse and vorse. And his mother and father just dead! Vot a bitch! I tell you – "

CRASH!

The library door burst open.

Harry's heart leaped.

They spun round.

The lights came on, blinding after the darkness and thin beams of torchlight.

Colonel Priestly stood in the doorway. In his hands was a double-barrelled shotgun. At his back the corridor was crowded with servants.

"Bridget Barton!" He spat the words. "I should have known! It had to be you!"

He advanced into the library. The servants followed.

"Damn you! You *and* your interfering cronies!"

"Well, Percy!" Aunt Bridget's granny glasses flashed in the light. Tall and erect, she stepped from the treasure chamber. "I love your jambies!"

His ginger hair was dishevelled. He wore a pair of yellow silk pyjamas with a leaping tiger on the chest.

"Never mind about that!" He spotted Max. "What are you doing here? I thought you were the brother of that – "

"Alas, no." Max smiled regretfully.

"Perhaps you know him better as Mr Edward Mann, concert organizer," said Aunt Bridget. "And Scrooge. But as you say, never mind about that. This is much more interesting." She looked at the stack of loot behind her, shining and winking in the light. "Naughty old Perce! What *have* you been getting up to?"

His face was livid, blotched red and white. His hot little eyes popped. His cheeks quivered.

"Won't your friends be *surprised*!" Aunt Bridget went on. "Colonel Priestly, high-court judge, magistrate, tireless worker for charity, big landowner and socialite, friend of the famous."

"I warn you!" He thrust forward the shotgun.

"Goodness, *won't* the papers have a field-day."

There were, Harry saw, eight servants. They too wore pyjamas and dressing gowns and carried weapons – sticks, bottles, carving-knives. He recognized Smithy and GBH. They looked a gang of villains.

Colonel Priestly controlled himself. "And what makes you so sure the papers are *going* to hear of it?"

"Well, you can hardly expect six of us to keep quiet," said Aunt Bridget. "Not to mention these charming workers of yours. You might just as well face it, Percy. This time the game's up."

"Is that right? Well, so far as these men are concerned," Colonel Priestly glanced behind him, "they won't say a word. Will you, boys?"

They shook their villainous heads. "Nah! Never! Not on your chuff!"

"You see. And as for the rest of you – well!" He smiled nastily. "Ways and means, Miss Barton. Ways and means."

"And what precisely do you mean by that?"

"That a solution to our little problem isn't too hard to find."

"No?"

"Well, three answers spring to mind immediately."

"And they are – ?"

"One hears so much about road accidents these days," he said sadly. "I presume you came in a car. And all this snow – slippery lanes, treacherous corners. There could so easily be a nasty crash. Not much left after a car fire, they tell me. Especially with a full tank of petrol."

"You never would! What, six of us! With all these witnesses!"

Beneath the tiger his stomach resembled a beach-ball.

"You don't know what I'm capable of." He jerked a thumb backwards. "And they wouldn't turn a hair."

Their smiles showed that he spoke the truth.

"But it would be a bit public and we're not savages. There's no need for that sort of violence." He smoothed the bristles of his moustache. "Much easier to give you all a jab, knock you out for a few days. Crate you up like that loot there and ship you off overseas. Foreign governments do it all the time... Bit of nasty weather, the crates might fall overboard." He opened his eyes wide. "No, officer, they never came here. Sorry, I can't help you at all."

Smithy laughed.

"'Ere, they're a load o' loonies!" said Fingers.

"Don't say that!" Colonel Priestly shifted the shotgun.

"And the third way?"

"You have young Harry Barton with you, I see. Come here, boy."

Harry hung back.

"Come here! Or do you want me to use the first barrel on your auntie?"

Harry shuffled forward, crop-headed, his clothes damp with melted snow.

Colonel Priestly yanked him by the jacket. "This is my best security for your silence, I think. The boy. The police don't know where he is. Already he's a missing person. I shall take him away. I know places, in this country and overseas, from which he'll *never* escape. Africa! South America! There he'll be kept safe – unless one of you blabs about tonight's work. The minute the police come asking – " He drew a finger across his throat. "Kkkkk!"

There was silence.

Harry trembled and stared about him. Two servants stood between him and the door.

"Now, what to do with you all for the time being?" Colonel Priestly thought. "Tie you up and gag you, I suppose. GBH," he turned, "you'll find a roll of cord and a pocket knife in that drawer over there. Moxy, fetch half a dozen napkins from the dining-room. They'll do for gags."

"Aaaahhhh! Aaaahhhh!" Fingers began to shout. "Aaaahhhh!"

"Stop that! Stop that noise!" Colonel Priestly snarled.

"Aaaahhhh!"

Max's eyes shone. "Aaahhhhh! Aaahhhhh!" He added his voice.

"Aaaahhhh!" cried Angel.

"Stop it! Stop it!" Colonel Priestly danced with fury.

"Orrrhhhh!" roared Huggy, louder and deeper than the men. "Orrrhhhh!"

"Aaaaahhhhhh!" screamed Aunt Bridget.

The noise was deafening.

"Stop it! Stop it!" Scarcely knowing what he did, Colonel Priestly fired a warning barrel above their heads.

BANG!

The pictures jumped. The charge of shot whammed into the ceiling, tearing a huge ragged hole. Great slabs of plaster shivered off and fell about their shoulders. Dust and smoke and the sharp smell of cordite filled the air.

Max regarded him with reckless eyes. "Aaahhhhh!" he bellowed again. "Aaahhhhh!"

"Orrrhhhh!"

"Aaaahhh! Aaaahhh!"

"Aaaaahhhhhh!"

All was confusion. The servants did not know what to do.

Harry saw his chance. Twisting like an eel, he grabbed a club from the man at his back, ducked, dived past a waist, lashed out at a grabbing arm and sprinted for the door.

There was a cry of pain.

"Get him! Get him!" shouted the Colonel.

"Go on, Harry!" cried voices. "Run! Run!"

"Aaaahhhh! Aaaahhhh!"

BANG!

At Harry's back the second barrel of the shotgun went off.

What had happened he did not know. Headlong he raced down the corridor. GBH and Moxy were right at his heels – one in striped pyjamas, the other in boxer shorts and hairy-chested as a gorilla.

As he reached the hall a small crowd of people came running down the stairs. They were Colonel Priestly's guests who had been disturbed.

"What on earth's going on?" cried the man in the lead.

"Stop 'im!" GBH cried. "Burglars! The boy's with 'em! Quick! Grab 'old of 'im!"

Harry's socks skidded on the polished boards. He drew back his club and whacked the guest on the shoulder.

He cried aloud and clutched his arm.

But a second man was right at his back. Before Harry could deliver another blow he was seized by the jacket and flung to the floor. The club was wrenched from his grasp.

"Great, sir! Thanks!" GBH stood above him. "Try that again, you young villain, and see what you get!" He dragged Harry to his feet. "You come alonga me. Back to the library. The Colonel wants to 'ave a word wi' you!"

"But what's happening?" cried the first man, nursing his arm.

From the library came the noise of a tremendous fight – cries and screams and thuds. Furniture smashed, glass splintered, a bottle flew through the open door and exploded against the corridor wall.

"I'll fix you for that!"

"Aahh!"

"Take that!"

"Let go! Let go!"

CRASH!

"No! No!"

WALLOP! THUD!

"You rat! You beast!"

Fingers whizzed through the door on his back, regained his feet, tugged up his baggy trousers and shot back into the fray.

From the corner of his eye Harry spotted a movement near the top of the staircase. It was Gestapo Lil in a slinky red dressing gown. Sly as a stoat she ran back up and vanished along the corridor.

"A gang of burglars!" cried the guests in the hall. "Poor Colonel Priestly! We must go and help him!"

Harry recognized the man he had hit. He saw his face on the television every night. He was a famous newscaster.

"It's them that's the robbers!" he cried shrilly. "Colonel Priestly's one of the biggest – "

"Shut up, you!" GBH's fist clumped the side of his head.

Moxy addressed the visitors. "It's all in hand, sir. You just go back to your beds."

"No, I think we really must – " Shrugging his sore shoulder, the newscaster ran off with his companion towards the fighting.

"Wait 'ere!" GBH shouted at their wives. "Come on, you!" Dragging Harry by the jacket, he hurried in pursuit.

The library was a scene of devastation: the heavy furniture lay overturned, shelves and curtains had been torn down, a thousand books littered the floor.

Among the debris lay bodies, some motionless, others nursing broken heads.

Above these casualties, standing on tables and the backs of chairs, those still fighting waved clubs and table-lamps, priceless vases and sets of fire-irons.

Aunt Bridget, legs set like a boxer, delivered a tremendous right hook, left overarm cross and uppercut to a passing servant. His head snapped backwards, his eyes glazed with astonishment. Like a stringless puppet his joints gave way.

In the heart of the battle Huggy was supreme.

"Right! You! Come here!" She caught Smithy by an arm.

"No!" he cried. "No! Please!"

"But yes!" In one flowing movement Huggy stepped side-ways, dropped her hip, straightened and tugged. Like a missile, Smithy flew through the air and hit a picture halfway up the wall. Together, man and shattered picture crashed to the floor.

Huggy dusted her hands. "Right! Who's next?"

"Nobody's next!" An icy voice at the door made everyone freeze.

Gestapo Lil stood in the entrance. Her golden hair was immaculate. She wore the slinky red dressing gown with a hem of ostrich feathers which Harry had seen on the stairs, and scarlet slippers to match. In the fingers of her left hand she carried a cigarette in a long ruby holder. In her right arm she cradled a machine-gun.

Her finger was on the trigger.

29
Black-Eyed Warrior

"That's enough games for one night, boys," Gestapo Lil said softly. "Now, if you'll all pick yourselves up and carry the wounded, we'll make our way to the hall. You have guests waiting, Percy. We'll sort this out there." She looked Aunt Bridget in the eye. "And if you think I won't use this little toy – !" Half-turning she squeezed the trigger.

TAT-TAT-TAT! TAT-TAT-TAT-TAT-TAT!

The noise was deafening. A series of holes stitched itself across the library wall.

"All right?" She drew on her cigarette. Blue smoke drifted from her nostrils. "This way, please."

She stood aside.

Hobbling and winded, swollen-eyed and broken-toothed, the combatants filed past her. It was only then Harry realized that all the figures stretched out on the floor and sprawled across the furniture were from Felon Grange. In the eyes of the Lagg Hall warriors was the light of battle. Servants, their buttons popped and pyjamas in rags, crawled to their knees and heaved up unconscious comrades.

Soon everybody, a crowd of more than twenty, stood and lay in the grand hall. All the lights had been switched on. Streamers and bunches of balloons stirred in the draught about the stairs.

"What's all this about?" demanded the newscaster for the third time. "What's that room stuffed full of valuables?"

A babble of shouts answered his question:

"Gang of thieves … the police … roomful o' loot … ex-cons … dirty rotten liar … Jekyll and Hyde … plain crook … prison where he belongs…"

TAT-TAT-TAT-TAT-TAT!

Another burst of machine-gun fire brought silence. Smoking cartridge cases bounced across the hall.

"Button up! The lot of you!" Gestapo Lil gestured with the barrel. "Percy – over here beside me. The rest of you – on the stairs."

GBH walked towards her.

"You too."

"But we're on your side, darlin'." He scratched his chest. "We've just been – "

"On the stairs, saphead! You lot too, all the guests – with the rest. That's right, wives as well. Percy and me here – everybody else there. Got it?"

Colonel Priestly was a sorry sight. One eye was shut, the result of a tremendous punch from Aunt Bridget, and he limped heavily. With one hand he clutched the waist of his pyjamas for the elastic had snapped. But his vicious spirit was not broken. Malevolently, with one ratlike eye, he surveyed the crowd on the broad stairs.

"Game's up, Percy," said Gestapo Lil. "Have to face it. And all because of that little weasel over there: Eugene-Augustus Barton!" She sketched a circle around Harry's chest with the barrel of the machine-gun. "How I hate him! I've a good mind to blow him away right now."

She raised the sights. The deafening chatter of the machine-gun filled the hall. Three metres of banister disintegrated in a hail of bullets. Clouds of cordite smoke rose in the air, sharp-smelling as fireworks.

"But I'll tell you what we're going to do." She ejected the end of her cigarette and tucked the holder into her dressing gown pocket. "You," she indicated the crowd on the stairs, "are going down into the cellars for a while. Meanwhile Percy and I are going for a little drive."

They watched her as a rabbit watches a stoat.

Harry stood at the back with Aunt Bridget.

She touched his hand. "Don't look up!" Her lips did not move.

For several seconds he froze then risked a glance beneath his eyebrows.

Dot stood on the landing. One leg was hooked over the banister. Directly below her stood Gestapo Lil.

Colonel Priestly smiled. "That's right, a little drive. We may meet again – peasants! Old lags! But I doubt it. Hah! Had an escape route planned since the first day I started operating. Five million tucked away in Swiss bank accounts. Who wants to live in Britain anyway – miserable, boring, old Britain? Always cold and wet. Time for a change: Australia, South America, one of the Pacific Islands. Warm seas, sunshine – fabulous!"

"So," Gestapo Lil gestured to the servant who stood nearest the cellar door. "If you'd be so good."

He crossed the floor and opened it.

"Down you go."

With a resentful glance he disappeared down the steps.

"Good." She smiled thinly. "Now, one at a time. And if you want to see if I'm bluffing about the gun – try me."

In single file, several metres apart, they crossed the hall, ducked through the cellar door and descended into darkness.

Suddenly, beyond the lobby, there was a thunderous knocking at the front door.

"Come on, open up! Police!"

Everyone was startled. Gestapo Lil swung round. At the same instant Dot threw her second leg over the banister, balanced, and dropped four metres like a monkey, straight on to the shoulders of the unsuspecting woman below.

Gestapo Lil gave a loud cry and fell to the ground. The machine-gun leaped in her outstretched hand.

TAT-TAT-TAT-TAT-TAT-TAT-TAT!

A stream of bullets went whipping and whistling and ricocheting away down the corridor.

Faster than Harry would have believed possible, Aunt Bridget leaped down the stairs and seized the smoking weapon, wrenching it from Gestapo Lil's grasp. With the butt of her hand she unclipped the magazine of ammunition. Two, three, four times she smashed the machine-gun against a corner. The mechanism crumpled, the hot barrel bent. With all her strength she flung it away.

At the front door, meanwhile, the knocking had ceased and there was a crash of glass.

"Thank heavens, the police! A bit of sanity." The newscaster strode across the hall and pulled open the stained-glass door of the lobby.

A long window beside the front door had been broken. Clambering through it was an extraordinary old lady in studded-leather motor-cycling gear. On her head was an ancient flying-helmet from which a halo of bright yellow curls escaped about her face. She paused in the gap, regarding him with big baby-blue eyes, then smiled.

"Good evening."

She jumped down into the lobby and turned to open the front door. A huge bald man stood at the entrance, and a stooped gangly figure with two ferocious-looking dogs at his heels.

The newscaster peered past them into the snow. "Where are the police?"

"Oh, there aren't any *police,* dear," said Auntie Florrie. "Just us."

Nutty had the dogs on ropes. "Now behave yersel's!" he said firmly, but beyond the lobby doors another riot had broken out. Fists and weapons flew, figures struggled on the floor, bodies came tumbling down the stairs. It was too much for the guard dogs. With one bound they tore the ropes from Nutty's hand.

The newscaster was knocked aside as the huge Alsatian and Dobermann sprang past him into the heart of the battle.

Woof! Woof! Grrrrr! Agggrrrhhh!

The dogs were like demons – snarling, snapping, shredding sleeves and pyjama trousers.

The fighting turned to panic. "Aaahhh! Get off, you brute! My leg! Stop it, stop it!"

All was pandemonium.

For one moment, in the midst of the chaos, Colonel Priestly and Gestapo Lil found themselves unguarded.

"Percy!" She flashed her eyes down the corridor. "Quick!"

They scrambled to their feet. Violently she thrust two figures aside. One, two, three times his pink fist clumped down on Auntie Florrie's balaclava. Side by side they scuttled back towards the library, one in a slinky red dressing gown, the other in yellow silk pyjamas with a tiger on the chest.

Harry was first to see them go. He stood on the staircase, one eye blacked and knuckles sore.

"Stop them!" He waved a walking stick and raced down the stairs. "They're getting away!"

Aunt Bridget and others heard his shrill cry. Instantly they let go of their adversaries, dodged the leaping dogs and gave chase.

But Colonel Priestly and Gestapo Lil had a good start. The library door stood open. They ran through and slammed it at their backs.

Harry crashed against the panels. In one movement he seized

the handle and pushed. The heavy door stayed shut. Someone at the far side was resisting. He strained against it, feet skidding.

In the library something heavy was being dragged. The door suddenly opened several centimetres then banged shut.

Aunt Bridget and the others arrived beside him. She grabbed the handle. A dozen hands planted themselves against the wood. They pushed. Still the door would not open. They pushed harder.

Within the library there was a noise of frantic activity.

"Shoulders!" cried Aunt Bridget. "All together – heave!"

The door stayed shut.

"They jammed one o' them big chairs or somefing under the 'andle," said Fingers.

"No problem." Huggy smiled with tombstone teeth. "I fix."

She set her feet, drew back an arm, and punched a fist through the panel above the lock. The wood splintered. She tore the hole bigger, reached inside and pushed back the big leather settee.

They burst through the door.

At the same moment the bookshelves at the far side of the library swung shut. For a split second Harry saw Colonel Priestly and Gestapo Lil scrambling in the treasure chamber – then bang! the bookshelves clashed together and they were locked behind the heavy oak boards.

"We'll soon have them out of there!" exclaimed Aunt Bridget. "Harry, where's that pen?"

But the library was such a chaos of overturned furniture, books and torn-down curtains that the blue BIC had disappeared.

"Something thin – anything!" cried Aunt Bridget.

Everyone hunted.

"What about this?" Auntie Florrie held out a toasting fork.

"Yes, that might do." Aunt Bridget tried to screw off the end but it was soldered on.

"There's a pen 'ere."

"Too thick!"

"I've got it! I've got it!" Dot ran forward with the cheap biro.

"Good work!" Aunt Bridget crouched to the empty shelf. Carefully she inserted the BIC into the little knot-hole and pushed.

Nothing happened.

She pushed again – hard.

Still nothing.

"It's locked! They can lock it from the inside!"

"Ve get you! Don't you vorry!" Huggy roared through the bookshelves. "Ve drag you out of there like vinkles!"

"There's a pile o' logs in the cellar." Angel's beard jutted ferociously. "I think I saw an axe."

He ran off and returned clutching a long-handled axe and a sledgehammer.

"Ah!" Huggy seized the axe and pulled up her sleeves. "Vatch your heads!"

She swung the heavy blade. A shelf disintegrated. She swung again. Splinters flew from the edge of the knot-hole.

Angel, his Highland blood roused, attacked the back of the bookcase with the sledgehammer. More shelves crashed to the floor. Wallop! Smash! The hammer-head buried itself in the oak. He tugged it free and swung again. A board burst loose. Light shone through the gap.

Nutty, meanwhile, had tempted the dogs with bowls of meat and locked them in their scullery room. Apart from two figures who lay bound and another who sat on the stairs nursing a broken head, the hall was empty. The servants had fled. Everyone else had gathered in the library.

They did not see, therefore, beyond the kitchen, far down at the end of the corridor, a slinky red arm emerge from a doorway and lift a coat and jacket from a peg. They did not see, beneath it, a yellow arm collect two pairs of wellington boots.

"We'll soon have them now!" cried Auntie Florrie. "Just a minute, Huggy." She pulled some broken wood from the lock.

Thud! Crash! Angel's hammer continued its work of demolition. He kicked in a board. Then another.

There was a gap big enough to squeeze through.

"'Ere, Angel, mind me napper." Fingers inserted his head and looked round.

The shining roomful of loot lay before him. An overhead lamp swung on a cable. No missiles flew about his head. No desperate figures lunged at him with antique sword and candlestick. He slid through the opening.

The chamber was deserted.

"'Ere, Bridget! Don't want to alarm yer – but they've gone!"

"What!"

It was the work of a moment to release the lock. The shattered bookshelves swung open.

Fingers was right. Beyond the stack of treasure a second door stood wide.

"Look, the jewels have gone! The Scorpion brooch, the Kilallan diamond, the pearls, the rubies – everything!"

"Don't look at me! I ain't touched 'em!" said Fingers.

Harry ran round the chamber and out through the open door. Beyond lay a junk room: stuffed birds in dusty glass cases, a rocking horse, tea-chests of unused china, a lopsided suit of armour.

He ran out into a passage. All was black and deserted.

Suddenly at his back there was a shout and a familiar sound: *Tootle-tootle!*

As fast as the treasure would allow, he scrambled back to the library.

Everyone had run to the window. He jumped on a chair and

stared over their heads. Powerful headlamps illuminated the snow.

Tootle-tootle-tootle-tootle!

The yellow Rolls-Royce swept past. A hand waved at the window, a laughing face gazed towards them.

The next moment it was gone. The headlights vanished, the sound of the engine faded towards the drive.

Tootle-tootle!

The triple horn mocked them from the night.

Tootle-tootle-tootle-tootle-tee!

30
The Ancient Gate

"**M**ax, you're fastest." Aunt Bridget didn't waste a second. "The car – quick! We'll meet you on the front porch."

Nutty gave him the keys.

"Hurry!"

Max pushed up the library window and jumped down into the snow. His legs disappeared in a drift. He fell. Snow smothered his dinner jacket and silk bow tie. Hastily he brushed himself black, ploughed through the drift and set off running up the moonlit track.

"The phone!" said Aunt Bridget. "Where's the phone?"

Harry found it buried under books behind the overturned table.

"Dial 999!"

He put the receiver to his ear. "It's dead!" He rattled the rest.

"Here, let me see." Aunt Bridget listened. "Right, run up to the hall. See if that one's working."

Harry sprinted up the corridor. Miraculously the telephone still hung on the wall. He snatched it up. That, too, was dead.

"Must be the snow." Aunt Bridget stood beside him. "Or they've cut the line. Right, that means we'll have to stop them ourselves." She looked round. "Dot, you and Mr Tolly, Nutty and Angel – stay here. Keep an eye on the loot and see this lot are safely tied up, we need them for witnesses. If any of the other thugs come back, let them have it. You can handle them." She turned to the house guests. "As for you four, if you want to do something useful – make some coffee and fetch the police."

"But the telephone lines are – "

"You've got a car, haven't you! Knock up a neighbour, drive into town. Use your initiative!" She rested a hand on Harry's shoulder. "Come on, then, everybody else into our car."

They ran out through the lobby. After his exertions and the warmth of the house Harry was sweating. The bitter night air gripped his face. All around him the massive pillars of the porch were silhouetted against the sky. Frosty stars glittered above the snow.

Far down the drive the Rolls-Royce had stopped at the gate. Its red tail-lights shone in the night. In the opposite direction the headlights of the Mercedes sprang out among the trees.

Harry dashed off round the house to collect his boots which he had left beneath the window. One of his socks came off in a drift. Briefly he hunted then left it and ran on bare-footed.

He arrived back at the porch at the same time as the Mercedes. Auntie Florrie took the wheel and the rest piled in. The tyres spun in the snow, the car slewed sideways, then with an acceleration that threw them back in their seats, they took off down the avenue.

In the full beam of the headlights the drive was dazzling. There had been a fresh fall of snow while they were in the house, covering the tyre tracks left by departing guests. The twin tracks of the Rolls ran ahead of them, tumbled and deep. The steering wheel leaped in Auntie Florrie's hands. Snow whirled from the bonnet, plastering the windscreen, and was swept aside by the wipers.

The Rolls-Royce was still at the gate. As Harry stared, the brake-lights went off, the headlights swung and the big car turned away down the lane. Briefly the treetops were illuminated. A distant *tootle-tootle* reached his ears above the noise of the Mercedes.

And then it was gone.

The wrought-iron gates were shut. Auntie Florrie drew up and everyone piled out.

"Your scene, Fingers," said Aunt Bridget. "Can you open them?"

"Need a magic eye, really. Still, see what we can do." He rubbed his hands. "Cor, a bit parky, innit?" He took out his torch and crouched by the control box. "Oh, dear! He's scuppered it. Look!"

The side of the plastic control box had been smashed in.

Aunt Bridget looked round at the gates. "They're not unlocked are they?"

Max gave the bars a heave. The tall gates rattled.

"Won't budge. Look, he's put a lock and chain round them just in case."

"Damn! Damn!" said Aunt Bridget.

"Well, 'Arry can pick the lock easy enough an' I can fix the box. But it'll take ten – mebbe fifteen minutes."

"Too long! They'll be away!" She thought. "I suppose you couldn't ram a way through, Florrie?"

Auntie Florrie shook her head. "Not with that thick chain. Anyway, heavy gates like that would smash up the radiator."

There was silence. Beastly Priestly and Gestapo Lil were getting away. Failure stared them in the face.

"I can't *stand* it!" said Aunt Bridget.

"There's still a way," said Fingers. "Quick an' all."

"What?"

"Oh, my vord!" Huggy exclaimed. "He blow them open! I getting out of here!"

"How quick?" said Aunt Bridget.

"Minute an' a 'alf – two minutes."

Aunt Bridget did not hesitate. "Right, on you go. Do you need a hand?"

"Nah! Take the car back a few metres, that's all. 'Arry, fetch me bag o' tools from the boot."

Harry ran to the car and returned carrying a black canvas holdall.

Fingers was waiting at the gate. "'Ere, 'old me torch."

He unzipped the bag and rooted through the jumbled contents: coils of wire, metal punches, scraps of cloth, a hammer, glass cutters, rolls of carpet tape, chisels and jemmies, a tangled stethoscope, a black woollen balaclava and much more. The biggest item was wrapped in newspaper. Fingers unfolded it to reveal a bundle of red sticks like giant fireworks, each with a cord protruding from the end.

"Dynamite," he said briefly. "'Ow many d'yer reckon? One for each 'inge? Yeah, that should do it – an' one for the lock."

He extracted five of the red cylinders and tucked the others away.

"'Ere." He handed one to Harry and tore off a length of carpet tape with his teeth. "'S all right, can't go off. Strap that to them middle bars, alongside the chain."

By the time Harry was finished, Fingers had attached four more.

"Right, everyone back be'ind them bushes. 'Eads down an' put yer 'ands over yer lugs." He handed Harry a box of matches. "Thirty second fuses, OK? When I say the word put a light to the one I give yer an' run like 'ell! Back among them bushes wi' the others. No fallin' in the snow, right?"

"Right."

Fingers prepared to light his own sticks. "Are yer ready?"

"Yes."

"OK. Light 'er *now*!"

Harry struck his match and touched the flame to the cord. At once it ignited, fizzing and smoking in the moonlight.

He scampered back up the drive and dived through the shrubbery. Heart thudding, he crouched in the snow beside Auntie Florrie and Aunt Bridget, closed his eyes and pressed his hands over his ears.

There was not long to wait. A splitting, earth-heaving roar broke the New Year peace. Even beyond the thick bushes the shock waves punched Harry like a giant hand. There was a heavy rumble and a moment later a loud metallic CRASH! The air was full of whirling snow and leaves. The explosion echoed and re-echoed, rolling across the sleeping countryside.

They rose, smothered in snow, coughing with the smoke, and made their way back to the drive.

The dynamite had done its work well. The gates were open. Indeed the gates were not there at all. One had disappeared. The other, like a huge metal wing, rose into the air from the roof of the Mercedes. Like a giant spear it had flown thirty metres and sliced down through the windscreen and engine.

"Oh my goodness!" Fingers was stricken.

"Terrific shot! Now you see vhy they call him H-Bomb!" said Huggy. "Vhy all his fingers missing. Ve lucky he have two arms and a head!"

Harry stared. Not only had the blast removed the gates, it had brought down the ancient stone arch. Huge blocks of masonry littered the drive. A shattered shield lay face-up to the sky. Half a stone lion stared into the headlights of the Mercedes.

"Take a bulldozer to shift that lot," Fingers said gloomily. "No way through. The road's blocked." He looked round. "Sorry, everybody."

"Ah, well." The rest were sympathetic. "Just rotten luck! He'd scuppered the gates anyway. Maybe the police will catch them."

"No they won't. They've got away!"

"Auntie Florrie!" Harry pulled her sleeve. "What about the bike?"

"What, dear?"

"The bike!"

"Of course! Good boy!" Excitedly she turned to the others. "We've got the Norton! That can get through!"

"Where?" said Aunt Bridget.

"Just behind those bushes!" Auntie Florrie pointed. "Harry, get your helmet on."

"No, not Harry!" said Aunt Bridget. "Take Huggy – or me."

"Not in this snow." Auntie Florrie halted halfway. "It's going to be slippery enough as it is. Has to be someone light, used to the bike. Harry's good."

The blast had blown the *Commando* on to its side. Auntie Florrie heaved it upright and brushed off the snow. In a minute they were ready. She kicked the motorcycle into life and wove through the torn shrubbery.

"You fetch the police." VROOM! VROOM! "Tell them which way we're heading."

"Will do. Good luck! Take care!"

Auntie Florrie waved a cheery hand and drove the few metres to the fallen arch. Harry lifted his feet as they squeezed left and right through the great blocks of masonry. Then the open road lay before them.

"All set?"

"Yeah." He smeared the condensation from his goggles and rested gloved hands on Auntie Florrie's waist.

"Then off we go!"

31
The Fight in the Lane

The motorbike picked up speed. The engine roared, a plume of snow sprayed from the back wheel. Down the lane they sped. In the full beam of the headlamp the fresh snow was brilliant. Fence posts flashed past.

Felon Woods closed about them and formed a wintry tunnel. Down the middle they roared. Rabbits scampered for cover, rooks flew off in alarm and sent avalanches from the high branches.

RRAARRGGHH!

Then they were out once more among open fields. High in the south-west the full moon sailed among clouds. No light disturbed the miles of sleeping countryside.

Auntie Florrie switched off the headlamp. The moon lit the white road like a searchlight. If necessary it would be possible to ride without the headlamp. She switched on again.

They reached a junction. Auntie Florrie slowed, the bike leaned over and skidded. Two boots went down. They were round. The bike straightened. Picking up speed, they roared on through the snow and slanting drifts.

For the first miles there was no doubt about direction. As fast as she dared on such treacherous roads, slithering sometimes for fifty metres, Auntie Florrie gave chase.

RRRRRRRRRR!

The bitter wind froze Harry's cheeks. They passed farms – dropped into a valley – ran alongside a frozen river – crossed a hump-backed bridge – roared through a village – ignored the red light at some road works – slithered round a long series of S-bends – passed more farms – climbed through a plantation of conifers – mounted to the crest of a hill.

Suddenly, as they topped the ridge, there, not half a mile distant, were the twin red lights of a car. Instantly Auntie Florrie switched off the headlamp.

"This could be them!"

The *Commando* surged as she opened the throttle another centimetre. Harry shuffled his balance and gazed past her shoulder.

It was a district of rolling farmland with dark copses and cottages at the roadside.

Steadily the car drew nearer. Harry could tell that it was pale and big – the rear lights prevented him from seeing more. Soon they were close on its tail. Whether the driver had seen them he could not tell.

"Right! Hang on to your helmet!" Auntie Florrie pressed the horn – BEEEEP! – and switched on the headlamp.

Instantly the huge yellow Rolls-Royce sprang out of the night. Colonel Priestly swerved with shock as the full beam hit him from the driving mirror.

He accelerated, as if to draw ahead, but Auntie Florrie remained on his tail.

He slowed and switched on his left indicator to let the rider past – for there was no reason to think, after ten miles, that this motorcycle had anything to do with Lagg Hall. Still Auntie Florrie stayed behind, headlamp blazing.

Again the Rolls accelerated. Again it slowed. Finally it stopped.

Ten metres behind, the motorcycle had stopped also. Colonel Priestly pressed a button and the window hummed down. He looked back, blinded by the headlamp.

"What do you think you're playing at!" he snarled. "You want past or don't you?"

Auntie Florrie eased the heavy torch in her pocket. "Get ready," she murmured to Harry.

"Nobody ever tell you about dipping your headlights!"

There was no answer.

"Come on, Percy," said Gestapo Lil. "Leave him. It's just some teenager playing games. Probably drunk. We've got to get on. And shut that window, it's freezing!" She tugged the collar of a thin white raincoat about her neck.

"This'll only take a second." He threw open the door. "I'm going to sort him out."

He wore short green wellingtons, yellow silk pyjamas and a donkey-jacket.

Heedless of his cold fiancée, he left the door wide and strode back to the motorcycle.

"You looking for a thick ear, son? Switch that headlight off!"

Suddenly, from out of the dazzle, a furious figure rushed at him, brandishing a torch the size of a club. For a split second he had an impression of studded leathers and a big helmet, then the torch bounced off the side of his head. Luckily he put up an arm or it would have laid him senseless in the snow. The figure was shouting:

"You beast! You liar! We'll settle your hash for you! Come on, Harry, get him!"

A second figure sprang forward, smaller and even fiercer than the first. A black helmet with a gold wing above each ear butted him in the stomach. Gloved fists battered his chest and shoulders.

Dazed and defending himself, Colonel Priestly staggered

back to the car. Hands clung to his jacket. He wrenched them off and gave a hard push. This gave him the second he needed to scramble through the door and slam it shut behind him.

At once the terrifying figures were at the window. A fist flew through and hit him on the ear. He pressed a button and the glass hummed up.

"We'll get you, Priestly!" shouted the attacker with the torch. Don't think you'll escape that easy!" A boot thudded against the door.

It was a woman's voice. Beyond the visor a straggle of curls had fallen over big blue eyes.

"Florrie Fox!" he exclaimed. "And it's that boy with her!"

"What!" Gestapo Lil spun in her seat.

"They've followed us from the Grange!"

"Oh, full marks!" She gazed out venomously.

Harry had pulled off his helmet to use as a weapon and pushed the goggles to his forehead. His bright face, one eye blackened and nearly closed, gazed into the car.

"Put down that window an inch, Percy."

Fingers squeezed through the gap.

"You listen to me – orphan brat!" She had lost her composure. "There's no one here to protect you now. If I come out there it'll be curtains! For both of you!" Her golden braid hung from the pins and began to unravel.

Hands rocked the car. A barrage of kicks drummed against the door.

"Stop it!" she cried. "Stop it!"

Auntie Florrie ran round to the bonnet. Drawing back her torch she hammered at the headlight. It resisted. She battered again. The glass shattered, the light was extinguished. She ran to the far side.

"Percy!" screamed Gestapo Lil.

Colonel Priestly switched on the engine and flung it into gear.

Auntie Florrie sprang aside.

As the Rolls-Royce pulled away, Harry drew back his helmet and swung it at the windscreen.

BANG!

The glass shattered into a thousand dazzling fragments. It did not collapse but hung like a windscreen of diamonds, impossible to see through.

Colonel Priestly braked. He had driven thirty metres.

"Good boy!" Auntie Florrie scampered up the road and started banging at the second headlight.

It did not break so easily.

Colonel Priestly punched a hole in the windscreen with his fist. Fragments of glass rained down into the car like pebbles. He made the hole bigger.

Bang! Bang! Bang! Auntie Florrie hammered at the headlight.

Colonel Priestly set off fast. If Auntie Florrie had not been quick he would have run her over.

"Come on! Back to the bike!"

They ran through the snow.

VROOM – VROOM!

In two minutes they were back on the tail of the big yellow car.

Inside the Rolls it was freezing. An icy wind rushed through the hole in the windscreen. Colonel Priestly stared into the gale, his eyes watering. Gestapo Lil clutched the thin coat to her throat and knees.

Every snowdrift, every pothole, brought fragments of glass rattling down on to the dashboard like hailstones. The passenger side of the windscreen sagged. Gestapo Lil supported it with her fingertips. To no avail. Suddenly the whole windscreen collapsed. Nothing remained but a rim of crystals.

Now the wind blasted through the car. Colonel Priestly gritted his teeth and pressed down on the accelerator. Fifty miles an hour – sixty – seventy! In midsummer it would have been too fast for those country roads. In the snow it was suicidal. The Rolls-Royce bucked and slewed and snaked. Snow whirled house-high. And always at their back came the powerful motorbike, headlamp blazing.

Riding in the slipstream of the car, Auntie Florrie could hardly see. The spindrift was blinding. She and Harry became snowmen. Every few seconds a hand went up to clear visor or goggles.

Colonel Priestly could not feel his fingers. His eyelashes were frosted. He could not control the car. Clearly he was not going to shake off that wretched Florrie Fox and her nephew. His foot eased on the accelerator.

Sixty miles an hour – fifty – forty.

A road sign indicating a right-hand bend was plastered with snow. Frozen to the bone and vision blurred, Colonel Priestly failed to spot it.

A narrow farm track lay ahead.

Straight on he drove.

He discovered his error at once for the car started to leap and buck uncontrollably. The track had not been cleared. Between hedge and drystone wall the snow lay half a metre deep, more than twice that in drifts. The radiator buffed up solid white clouds which blew in upon them. He jammed his foot on the brake.

It was fatal. The wheels locked, the car slewed sideways and bounded off the verge, slewed the other way and hit a hidden root, bounced back and demolished several metres of wall, then shot across the track, tilted to one side and buried its proud yellow nose in the ditch.

Colonel Priestly and his fiancée were not hurt but were considerably shaken. For a minute they sat still, collecting their wits, then loosened the restraining seat belts.

"Percy!" Gestapo Lil gave a heart-rending cry. "The brooch!

The diamonds!"

The famous Scorpion brooch, together with rings, ropes of pearl and ruby, and a velvet clothful of jewels, had nestled on the dashboard shelf. The crash sent them flying. Now they lay scattered throughout the car, covered by snow and scarcely distinguishable from ten thousand pebbles of shining windscreen.

"Forget about them," snarled Colonel Priestly. "Let's get out of here!"

The car lay half on its side, one headlight blazing into the icy ditch. Awkwardly, jabbing elbows, knees and rubber boots into his furious fiancée, he clambered to the door. It had jammed. He tugged and pushed, using language that should never be on the lips of any gentleman. The door remained immovable.

It would have to be the windscreen. Standing, he thrust his head and shoulders through the gap. Stinging fragments of glass tumbled inside his pyjamas and lodged at the string that held up his trousers. He set his knees on the dashboard and crawled out. The bonnet was covered with snow. He inched towards the bank. Without warning his hands skidded. Sidelong he slid down the yellow bonnet and crashed into a thicket of gorse bushes.

"Oh! Ow! Ooh!" The sharp spikes stabbed through his thin pyjamas. "Ooooh! Ooww!"

Auntie Florrie had parked the *Commando* fifteen metres down the track. The dazzling headlamp illuminated the scene; indicators flashed to attract any passing motorist. Torch in hand she stood with Harry above the Rolls-Royce, ready to do battle.

The sight of Colonel Priestly trapped in the thorns made them laugh.

"Help! Give us a hand!" He reached towards them. "Owww!"

"Not on your life!" Auntie Florrie gathered a snowball. SPLOSH!

"Aahh! Wait till I – ! Owww!"

"Did it stab you in the bum? Good!"

Harry loved it.

"Come on, Percy!" Gestapo Lil stared malevolently from the broken windscreen. "You're not a child. Pull yourself together."

With a great effort and more cries of anguish, he stretched across the bonnet, set a foot on the Rolls-Royce crest and managed to drag himself free.

"Aahhh!" Standing on the snowy bank he began to pull out a hundred daggers of gorse.

Gestapo Lil was more cautious. Unseen by the others, her groping fingers had found the Scorpion brooch and a flashing red necklace. Safely they nestled in her raincoat pocket. In the hope of picking up some of the scattered gems she had stuffed the other pocket with pebbles of windscreen. Now, abandoning her fiancé, she planned to make a run for it – through the hedge at the far side of the ditch, across a moonlit field and into some woodland.

On hands and knees, steering well clear of the gorse bushes, she crawled through the windscreen and crossed the slippery bonnet. Reaching the silver crest, she set the instep of her boot against it and sprang for the bank of the ditch.

Her jump was not quite far enough. Diamonds and bright pebbles of windscreen cascaded from her pocket as she flew through the air and landed on the snowy slope. Red fingernails clawed at the tussocks of grass, wellingtons kicked for a toe-hold. To no avail. Slowly she slipped backwards – down, down and down into the ditch. Momentarily the ice supported her – then broke. Knee-deep she plunged into the mud and weed and icy water beneath.

"Aah! Aah!" She gasped at the cold.

But Gestapo Lil was a fighter. Headlong she plunged away down the ditch. The ice smashed before her. Her boots were full and nameless things squidged between her toes. The ostrich-feather hem of her slinky red dressing gown trailed in her wake, heavy with ditch-water. Her white raincoat was streaked with mud.

There was no way up for the far bank was choked with thorn bushes: brambles and gorse, hawthorn and wild briar. After twenty metres she halted and glared up with furious eyes. Long hair straggled over one shoulder. Her white teeth showed in a snarl.

A clump of young ash trees grew on the near bank. A farmer had cut them back. Catching hold of a stump, Gestapo Lil hauled herself out of the muddy ditch and crawled back to the track. Chopped-off branches protruded from the snow. She pulled out a length as thick as her wrist to use as a weapon.

The others had followed her progress. Lit by the moon, the crashed Rolls-Royce and the motorbike, the four antagonists faced each other on the lonely track.

"Right, Percy," said Gestapo Lil. "You deal with the batty old bird in leathers. I'll take care of the boy." She broke off the twiggy end of her branch under a boot. "It'll be a pleasure. I've been waiting a lifetime."

Harry watched her.

"Don't listen to her!" said Auntie Florrie. "You threw Huggy, didn't you. You can handle a nasty piece of – "

Colonel Priestly rushed at her like a wild bull. Auntie Florrie, her reactions like quicksilver, sprang aside and clonked him across the head with her torch.

At the same moment Gestapo Lil threw herself on Harry. He was taken by surprise. Forgetting everything Huggy had taught him, he fell backwards into the snow like any schoolboy. Gestapo Lil drew back the heavy stick. He saw her mad eyes, her clenched teeth. In that split second all those mornings of training on the lawns at Lagg Hall came back to him. Rolling towards her he took the blow on his shoulder, caught her wrist, threw up a leg – and using her own power, catapulted her right over his head. Gestapo Lil gave a cry of surprise as she flew through the air into a deep snowdrift. She landed on her back with a thump that knocked the air from her lungs and half a pocketful of glass and jewels from her raincoat.

For a moment she lay gasping, head buried in the snow, legs kicking in the air. Then she rolled over and pulled herself to her feet. The clublike stick was still in her hand.

Knees bent, arms hanging by his sides, Harry stood waiting.

"Aaaahhhh!" Swinging the stick and screaming, she rushed in.

Harry ducked inside the stick, caught her arm, turned sideways, straightened his legs and heaved.

The throw was so successful he could not believe it. Gestapo Lil – who had made his life unhappy for so long and was still fifteen centimetres taller and much stronger than himself – sailed through the air, bounced on the snowy verge and vanished back into the ditch.

At the same moment he became aware of a gasping cry. Auntie Florrie had been winded and Colonel Priestly was legging it down the track towards the motorcycle.

"Stop him!" she panted. "He'll get away! The key's in the ignition!"

At once Harry gave chase. He ran faster than the wheezing, overweight Colonel, but the man had a long lead. By the time Harry caught up with him he was sitting astride the beautiful *Commando*. He flipped out the kick-start and kicked it into life.

The engine roared.

The sight made Harry furious. Without pausing, he ran at Colonel Priestly and gave him a hard push. Man and motorbike toppled sideways into the snow.

For a moment the Colonel was trapped. Ignoring him, Harry

reached across and switched off the engine, removed the key, and tucked it beneath his motorcycling clothes, deep into the pocket of his jeans.

Colonel Priestly tugged his leg free, dusted off the icy snow and ran at him. Harry dodged aside. The Colonel rushed again. Harry caught his outstretched arm, ducked, turned sideways, tugged and straightened. Like a dream the fat Colonel flew over his back.

In the beam of the helpless Rolls-Royce, meanwhile, Gestapo Lil was crawling from the ditch. Gone was the immaculate grooming of old. Muddy hair hung over her face, weed stuck to her shoulders, her white raincoat was fouled, and the red satin dressing gown clung about her legs. All over she was covered with lumps of snow.

Shuddering with cold she rose to her feet. Thoughts of escape battled with the longing for revenge. She eased a hand into her sodden pocket. It was empty! The Scorpion brooch! The necklace! They were gone! Frantically she scrabbled in the snow. The ditch was choked with undergrowth; slabs of ice bobbed above weeds and muddy water. She felt in the other pocket. A few gravelly fragments of glass were all that remained.

Gestapo Lil gave a loud cry of despair. All was lost! Like a cornered rat she stared along the track.

Colonel Priestly had struggled to his feet.

"Lavvy!" he called. "The boy! He's got the key for the motorbike! Grab him!"

From each side they converged upon Harry. He ran towards one – then the other. They drew closer.

Still Auntie Florrie was not up.

He adopted the wrestling attitude. Knees bent and eyes watchful he shuffled from side to side.

"Go on, Percy!" urged Gestapo Lil. "You can handle a little weasel his age!"

The Colonel rushed forward. Like lightning Harry stepped aside, caught an outstretched arm and twisted. Head over heels Colonel Priestly went bowling along the track. His pyjama trousers parted company from the string that supported them. The moon shone on his bare bottom. He tried to rise, tripped and sat in a snowdrift.

Harry had no time to laugh for Gestapo Lil was upon him. The fury of her attack bowled him to the ground. Her fingers sought a hold on his hair but it was too short. Her sharp engagement ring scratched his ear. Her muddy hair flapped in his face.

Trying to remember what he had been taught, Harry caught her waist in a scissor grip, hooked an arm around her neck, grabbed her wrist and heaved. They rolled sideways off the track. All at once he was sitting on top of her. Seizing handfuls of snow, he crammed them into her face.

The next moment he was knocked sideways by a blow to the head and Colonel Priestly, having re-fastened his pyjamas, was kneeling astride him, pressing his arms to the ground.

"Quick, Lavvy! Get the key! It's in his jeans."

On hands and knees she crawled across. Harry bucked and struggled – to no avail. Her long-nailed fingers forced a way into his tight pocket and tugged out the precious key.

"Got it!" Triumphantly she held the key aloft. "Now tie up the revolting little reptile and sling him in the ditch!"

"Better strip off his jacket and over-trousers first," said Colonel Priestly. "Need them."

"And from the old bat!" said Gestapo Lil.

"Then on to the motorbike and away!" His piggy face sneered down at Harry.

Abruptly they were hit by a whirlwind. The key for the *Commando* was snatched from Gestapo Lil's fingers and flung away into the thorns and bushes beyond the ditch. CLONK!

For the third time the heavy torch bounced off Colonel Priestly's ginger hair. Gestapo Lil's raincoat was dragged halfway over her head and she was thrown sideways into the snow.

Auntie Florrie had recovered.

Harry dragged himself from beneath the dazed Colonel. At his side Gestapo Lil was struggling with her coat. Instantly he jumped on top of her, caught an arm up her back and pressed her head down into the snowdrift.

"Stay there!" Auntie Florrie stood above Colonel Priestly with the heavy torch. "Don't get up! I warn you!"

Colonel Priestly ignored the little old lady with her yellow curls.

WALLOP! THUD!

"I told you! Now stay there – or else!"

Hands over his head he lay face down in the middle of the track.

"What do we do now?" called Harry.

Gestapo Lil struggled. He pulled her arm a few centimetres higher.

"Well, we can't stay like this all night, dear." Auntie Florrie thought. "I know. You," she addressed Colonel Priestly. "Take off that string holding up your trousers."

"But they'll – "

"Never mind that. Just take it off!"

With numb fingers Colonel Priestly tugged at the knot and pulled the cord from his waist. Sulkily he passed it up.

"Hands," said Auntie Florrie briefly.

He hesitated.

BOP!

"Hands, I said!"

Reluctantly he put them behind. Swiftly Auntie Florrie caught his wrists in a noose and pulled it tight. Torch at the ready, she wrapped the ends round and through and fastened them with a knot.

"Good!" She stood back. "Now, you can get up if you like."

Harry pulled the belt from Gestapo Lil's raincoat. With Auntie Florrie to help him, it was an easy job to tie her hands also.

A minute later all four stood in the middle of the track. The cold had intensified. Their breath smoked.

Harry was hot with his exertions. Colonel Priestly and Gestapo Lil were freezing.

"Well, we don't want you to die on us," said Auntie Florrie. "Back into the car with you."

"There's a tartan rug in the boot."

"All right. If you're good we'll get it in a minute. Maybe switch on the heater. Now in you go."

Stumbling and defeated, Colonel Priestly and his fiancée crossed the verge. Clutching the seat of his pyjamas, the fat man slid headfirst over the snowy wing and in through the windscreen of the Rolls-Royce. He was followed by Gestapo Lil. They landed upside down in a heap.

"Uggh! Get off me!" Colonel Priestly gave her a shove with his shoulder. "Get off! You're soaking!"

"And whose fault is that!" she snapped back. "Stop pushing!" She gave him a kick.

At last, very uncomfortably, they got settled in their seats.

"You look terrible!" said Colonel Priestly.

"Thank you very much." She shivered. "At least I'm not wearing yellow pyjamas halfway to my knees! Porky!"

They glared at one another.

Out in the moonlight Harry explored his black eye with his fingertips. It felt very puffy.

"Well, dear, wasn't that *exciting*! Great fun!" Auntie Florrie smiled happily and balanced her torch on the Rolls-Royce. "Quite like the old days. Bridget will be *furious* she missed it."

Harry laughed.

She unzipped a leather pocket. "Fancy a choc?"

"Yeah."

"A bit squashed, I'm afraid."

"That's OK."

Leaning against the car he unpicked the wrapper. "I wonder how long we'll have to wait."

Auntie Florrie shrugged. "No hurry, dear. Anyway, there'll be a car along soon – or a snowplough. One of us can wait at the road end."

"We could phone from the Rolls." He indicated the stubby gold aerial.

"What a splendid idea!" She laughed. "But let's leave it a bit. I like it here. It's so – " She broke off, listening.

Then Harry heard it.

Miles away, faint as a gnat, the siren of a police car wailed across the sleeping countryside.

"Oh, dear! Here they come." Auntie Florrie sighed. "Too soon as always. Story of my life."

"But this time it's different."

"Yes, dear, I know. But all the questions." Absently she brushed the snow from her curls and felt for a lipstick. "Always so many questions!"

Harry pulled his jersey comfortable, tucked in his scarf and looked around.

Somewhere a farm dog barked across the fields.

He thought of Tangle and Mrs Good and his high room at Lagg Hall.

Beyond the wintry hedge a faint glow announced the dawn. It was New Year's Day.